PROMISES OF SEDUCTION

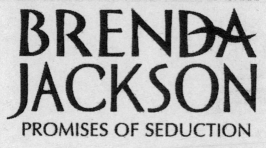

BRENDA JACKSON

PROMISES OF SEDUCTION

A Westmoreland Novel

ARABESQUE®

Recycling programs
for this product may
not exist in your area.

PROMISES OF SEDUCTION

ISBN-13: 978-0-373-53470-8

Copyright © 2012 by Harlequin Books S.A.

The publisher acknowledges the copyright holders
of the individual works as follows:

THE DURANGO AFFAIR
Copyright © 2006 by Brenda Streater Jackson

IAN'S ULTIMATE GAMBLE
Copyright © 2006 by Brenda Streater Jackson

CONTENTS

THE WESTMORELAND FAMILY

Scott and Delane Westmoreland

John (Evelyn)   **James (Sarah)**   **Corey (Abbie)**
                                                        Madison

②   ③   ④   ⑤   ⑦   ①

Dare (Shelly)   **Thorn (Tara)**   **Stone (Madison)**   **Storm (Jayla)**   **Chase (Jessica)**   **Delaney (Jamal)**
A.J., Allison   Trace   Rock   Shanna, Johanna   Carlton Scott   Ari, Arielle

⑥   ⑪   ⑧   ⑨   ⑭   ⑮

Jared (Dana)   **Spencer (Chardonnay)**   **Durango (Savannah)**   **Ian (Brooke)**   **Quade (Cheyenne)**   **Reggie (Olivia)**
Jaren   Russell   Sarah   Pierce, Price   Venus, Athena, Troy   Ruark

⑫   ⑬   ⑩

Clint (Alyssa)   **Cole (Patrina)**   **Casey (McKinnon)**
Cain   Emilie, Emery   Corey Martin

① Delaney's Desert Sheikh
② A Little Dare
③ Thorn's Challenge
④ Stone Cold Surrender
⑤ Riding the Storm
⑥ Jared's Counterfeit Fiancée
⑦ The Chase is On
⑧ The Durango Affair
⑨ Ian's Ultimate Gamble
⑩ Seduction, Westmoreland Style
⑪ Spencer's Forbidden Passion
⑫ Taming Clint Westmoreland
⑬ Cole's Red-Hot Pursuit
⑭ Quade's Babies
⑮ Tall, Dark…Westmoreland!

THE DENVER WESTMORELAND FAMILY TREE

Raphel and Gemma Westmoreland

Stern Westmoreland (Paula Bailey)

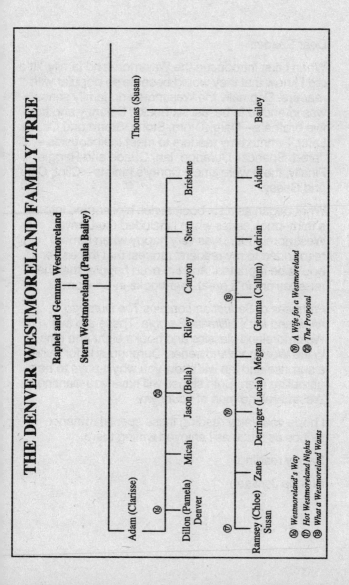

Thomas (Susan)

Adam (Clarisse) ⑯

Dillon (Pamela) Denver

Zane

Micah

Derringer (Lucia) ⑲

Jason (Bella) ⑳

Riley

Caryon

Stern

Brisbane

Ramsey (Chloe) Susan ⑰

Megan

Gemma (Callum) ⑱

Adrian

Aidan

Bailey

⑯ *Westmoreland's Way*
⑰ *Hot Westmoreland Nights*
⑱ *What a Westmoreland Wants*
⑲ *A Wife for a Westmoreland*
⑳ *The Proposal*

Dear Reader,

When I first introduced the Westmoreland family, little did I know that they would become so popular with readers. Originally the Westmoreland family series was intended to be just six books, Delaney and her five brothers—Dare, Thorn, Stone, Storm and Chase. Later, I wanted my readers to meet their cousins— Jared, Spencer, Durango, Ian, Quade and Reggie. Finally, there were Uncle Corey's triplets—Clint, Cole and Casey.

What began as a six-book series blossomed into a thirty-book series when I included the Denver Westmorelands. I was very happy when Kimani responded to my readers' request that the earlier books be reprinted. And I'm even happier that the reissues are in a great, two-books-in-one format.

Promises of Seduction contains *The Durango Affair* and *Ian's Ultimate Gamble*. These are two Westmoreland classics and books eight and nine in the Westmoreland series. Durango is in for quite a surprise and Ian will show you why it pays to be a gambling man. Both stories will have you wanting a Westmoreland man of your own.

I hope you enjoy reading these special romance stories as much as I enjoyed writing them.

Happy reading!

Brenda Jackson

THE DURANGO AFFAIR

Ponder the path of thy feet,
and let all thy ways be established.
—*Proverbs* 4:26

To the love of my life, Gerald Jackson, Sr.

Happy New Year to everyone!
May this year be the best ever!

Chapter 1

Durango Westmoreland stood at the window and focused his gaze on the mountains as a dark frown marred his handsome face. He had awakened that morning with an ache in his right knee, which could only mean one thing. A snowstorm was coming. The forecasters were reporting that it wouldn't hit Bozeman and would veer north toward Havre. But he knew differently. His knee didn't lie.

There was nothing scientific about his prediction. Still, even with a clear blue Montana sky, he knew he was right. A man didn't live in the mountains unless he was in sync with his environment. The mountains could hold you prisoner in the valley whenever a snowstorm hit, and their snowslides struck fear in the hearts of unsuspecting skiers.

These were the mountains that he loved and considered home even on the worst days.

Durango's thoughts shifted to another place he considered home: the city where he was born, Atlanta. He often missed the closeness of the family he had left behind there, and although he would be the first to admit that he liked his privacy—and his space—it was times like this when he missed his family most.

He did have an uncle who lived nearby, although definitely not a skip and a hop by any means. Corey Westmoreland's breathtaking ranch was high in the mountains on a peak that everyone referred to as Corey's Mountain. However, now that Corey had gotten married, he didn't visit as often. So Durango had become somewhat of a recluse who was satisfied with enjoying the memories of his occasional visits home.

One such visit was still vividly clear in his mind. It was the time he'd returned to Atlanta for his cousin Chase's wedding and had met Savannah Claiborne, the sister of the bride.

From the moment their eyes had connected there had been a startling attraction. He couldn't recall the last time he'd been so taken with a woman. In no time at all she had turned his world upside down. She had actually charmed her way past his defenses and his common sense.

Later that evening, after seeing the bride and groom off, everyone, still in a festive mood, had remained in the hotel's ballroom and continued to party, intent on celebrating the night away.

Both he and Savannah were more than a little tipsy when he had walked her to her hotel room at midnight.

And at the time, accepting her offer of a nightcap had seemed like the right thing to do. But once alone, one thing led to another and they had ended up making love.

That night his total concentration had been on her. Even now the memories of their one night together were tucked away and reserved for times like this when loneliness clutched at him, and made him think about things that a devout bachelor had no business thinking about— like a woman in his life who would always be within arm's reach.

"Damn."

He shook such foolish thoughts away and blamed his uncle's recent marriage for such crazy notions. Durango quickly reminded himself that he had tried love once and it had earned him a scar on his heart. That wound was a constant reminder of the pain he had suffered. Now he much preferred the easy life with just him and his mountains. He kept women at arm's length, except for when he sought out their company to satisfy his physical needs. Emotional need was as foreign a concept to him as sunbathing in the snow-covered Rockies. He had risked his heart once and refused to do so ever again.

But still, thoughts of Savannah Claiborne clung to him, did things to him. And no matter how many times he told himself she was just another woman, some small thing would trigger memories of that night, and along with the memories came the startling realization that she wasn't just another woman. She was in a class all by herself. At those times he could almost feel her lying beside him, beneath him, while he touched her, stroked her and coaxed her to take him deeper while he satisfied the pulsing ache within him.

Needing to get a grip, he forced his breathing back to normal and compelled his body to relax. He turned around and headed for the phone, deciding to call the rangers' station. They were down one park ranger due to Lonnie Berman being in the hospital for knee surgery, and if they needed an extra hand, Durango had no problem going in.

As he dialed the phone he felt his control sliding back into place. That was good. That was the way he wanted it and that was the way he intended to keep it.

Savannah Claiborne stood in front of the solid oak door, not believing that she had finally arrived in Montana and that in a few moments she would come face-to-face with Durango Westmoreland again. When she had made the decision to come and meet with him instead of making a phone call, she hadn't thought that delivering the news would be difficult.

Now that she was here she was discovering that it was.

She shook her head at her own stupidity, asking herself for the one hundredth time how such a thing could have happened to her. She wasn't a teenager who hadn't known about safe sex. She was a twenty-seven-year-old woman who knew the score about birth control. Too bad she had been too busy celebrating her sister's nuptials to remember to take her Pill, which had left her unprotected and was the main reason she would be having a baby in seven months.

And to make a sad song even sadder, she knew very

little about her baby's daddy other than that he was a park ranger and that, in her opinion, he was an expert at making love…and, evidently, at making babies, whether he had intended to make this one or not.

She also knew from the conversations she'd had with her sister that Durango was a confirmed bachelor and intended to stay that way. She had no plans to change that status but was merely here to deliver the news. What he did with it was his business. Her goal was to return to Philly and become a single parent. Getting pregnant might not have been in her immediate plans, but she definitely wanted this baby.

She paused after lifting her hand to knock on the door and released a deep breath. She was actually nervous about seeing Durango again. The last time she had seen him was when he had walked out of her hotel room two months ago after spending the night with her.

A one-night stand was definitely not her style. She had never been one to indulge in a casual affair. But that night she had gotten a little tipsy and emotional after seeing just how happy her sister was. It really was pathetic. She could never handle alcohol and she knew it. And yet she had fallen into the partying spirit and had imbibed a little anyway.

Since that night, Durango had haunted her dreams and had been the cause of many sleepless nights…and now it appeared he was partly to blame for interrupting her mornings, as well. Recently she had begun to experience bouts of morning sickness.

The only other person who knew about her pregnancy was her sister, Jessica. Jess had agreed with her

that Durango had a right to know about the pregnancy
and that Savannah should tell him in person.

Breathing in deeply, she inhaled and knocked on the
door. His SUV was parked out front, which meant he
was home.

Savannah swallowed against the thickness in her
throat when she heard the sound of the doorknob turning. Then the door opened. She literally stopped breathing when she looked into Durango's face, beyond his
toe-curling handsome features to see the surprise that
lit his eyes.

Standing tall in the doorway, wearing a pair of jeans
and a Western-style shirt that covered his broad shoulders and muscular chest, he looked just as gorgeous as
before—bigger than life and sexier than sin. Her gaze
studied all the features that had first captured her attention: the close-cropped curly black hair, his chestnut
coloring, well-defined mouth and intense dark eyes.

"Savannah? This is a surprise. What are you doing
here?"

Savannah's stomach tightened once again; she knew
what she was experiencing was probably the same
effect Durango had on countless other women. She took
a deep breath and tried not to think about that. "I need
to talk to you, Durango. May I come in?" she said in a
quick rush.

He quirked an eyebrow and stared at her. Then he
took a step back and said, "Sure. Come on in."

Durango was certain he didn't possess a sixth sense;
however, he found it pretty damn eerie that the woman
he had been thinking about just hours earlier had mate-

rialized on his doorstep at the worst possible time to be in Montana. Although January was the coldest month in the mountains, February wasn't much better. Whatever she wanted to talk to him about had to be mighty important to bring her all the way to his neck of the woods in the winter.

He studied her for a moment, watched as she removed her overcoat, knitted hat and gloves. "Would you care for something to drink? I just made a pot of hot chocolate," he said, still at a loss as to why she was there and finding it hard to believe that she really was.

"Yes, thanks. It would certainly warm me up some."

He nodded. Now that she had removed all the heavy outer garments and stood before him in a pair of designer slacks and a cashmere pullover sweater, he couldn't stop his gaze from wandering over her body. It was as perfect as he remembered. Her breasts were still full and firm, her waist was small and her hips were nicely curvy. His gaze then moved to her caramel-colored face. It was as beautiful as before, even more so, he thought. And those eyes…

He inhaled deeply. Those hazel eyes had been his downfall. He had been a goner from the moment he had first stared into them at the rehearsal dinner. And the night when they had made love and he had held her gaze when she had reached a climax, looking into those eyes had sent him over the edge. He had experienced an orgasm that had been out of this world. Even now he couldn't help but swallow hard at the memory.

But then all it took was a look at her sleek designer attire for Durango to remember that Savannah was a city girl. She had the words *dignified* and *refined* stamped all over her, although he could clearly remember when she'd tossed gentility out the window and displayed a streak of wildness that one night.

Suddenly the memory of all they had done that night made every ounce of blood in his body race to his groin. Jeez. He had to get a grip. What happened to that control he had gotten hold of earlier? He was behaving like a horny teenager instead of a thirty-five-year-old man.

"Make yourself comfortable," he managed to say after clearing his throat. "I'll be back in a second."

He walked off, wondering why he was handling her with kid gloves. Usually when a woman showed up at his house unannounced he told them in a nice or not-so-nice way, depending on his mood, to haul ass and not come back unless he issued an invitation. The only excuse he could come up with was that since she was Chase's sister-in-law, he was making her an exception to his rule. And yet he had an unsettling feeling that there was something different about her, something he couldn't put his finger on.

When he returned with the hot chocolate he intended to learn the real reason for Savannah's surprise visit.

Savannah watched Durango leave the room. What she was about to do wouldn't be easy, but she was determined to do the right thing. He deserved to know. Who knows? He might end up being a better father to his child than her father had been to her, Jessica and their brother, Rico.

She smiled when she thought of her brother. Although he wouldn't like the thought of her being a single parent, he would look forward to being an uncle. And if Durango didn't want to play a part in his child's life, Rico would readily step in as a father figure.

Savannah sighed and glanced around, taking a real good look at her surroundings through the eyes of the photographer she was, and noticing just how massive Durango's home was, the spaciousness spread over two levels. The downstairs interior walls were washed stone, a massive brick fireplace was to her right and a huge built-in bookcase adorned one single wall. The book-case was completely lined with books. She couldn't help but smile, thinking that she certainly couldn't imagine Durango spending his free time reading.

In the center of the room were a comfy-looking sofa and love seat that were separated by a coffee table. There were also a couple of rocking chairs sitting in front of huge windows that provided a beautiful view of the mountains. Wooden stairs led up to what appeared to be a loft with additional rooms. All the furnishings looked comfortable yet stylish.

"Here we go."

She turned when Durango reentered the room carrying a tray with two cups of steaming hot chocolate. Even doing something so domesticated, he oozed a masculine sensuality that was playing havoc with her body. Her hormone level was definitely at an all-time high today. Even her breasts felt more sensitive than usual.

"Thanks," she said, crossing the room to where he stood.

Durango set the tray down on the table. Savannah was standing next to him, so close he could smell her perfume. It was the same scent she had worn that night. He had liked it then and he liked it even more now. He handed her a cup, deciding that he had played the role of Mr. Nice Guy long enough. He needed to know what the hell she was doing here and why she needed to talk to him.

He glanced at her; their gazes met. The eyes staring back at him were anything but calm. "What's this about, Savannah?" he asked smoothly, deciding to cut to the chase. She had no reason to show up on his doorstep in the dead of winter to talk to him, two months after they had last seen each other, slept together, made love…unless…

His eyebrows furrowed at the same moment as he felt a jolt in the pit of his stomach. For a moment he couldn't breathe. He hoped to hell he was all wrong, but he had a feeling that he wasn't. He wasn't born yesterday and was experienced enough to know that one-night stands only showed up again if they were interested in a repeat performance—or if they had unwanted news to drop into your lap.

His heart began to pound when he saw the determined expression on her face. All of a sudden, the thought that she had tracked him to his mountain refuge to bear her unwanted news made him furious. "Let's have it, Savannah. What's the reason for your visit?"

Savannah slowly placed her cup back down on the tray, tilted her head and met Durango's accusing stare. There was razor-sharp intelligence in the dark depths of his gaze and she knew he had figured things out. So there was no reason to beat around the bush.

She momentarily looked away, inhaled deeply and

then met his gaze once more. He had no reason to be angry. She was the one enduring bouts of morning sickness, and she definitely wasn't there to make any demands on him.

Lifting her chin, she met his glare with one of her own and said, "I'm pregnant."

Chapter 2

Durango inhaled sharply when he experienced what felt like a swift, hard kick in the gut. She didn't say the baby was his but he knew damn well that was what she was insinuating. He made love. He didn't make babies. However, with the memories of that night constantly on his mind, anything was possible. But still, he remembered what she had told him that morning before he'd left. And with that thought, he summoned up a tight smile. "That's not possible."

Savannah lifted an eyebrow. "If you want me to believe that you're sterile, forget it," she said through gritted teeth.

He leaned back against the table, casually crossing his arms over his chest. "No, I'm not sterile. But if I remember correctly, the morning after you told me not to worry about anything because you were on birth control."

Unconsciously mirroring his stance, Savannah also crossed her arms over her chest. "I was. However, I forgot to take the Pill. Usually missing one pill wouldn't hurt, but in this case...I seem to be the exception and not the norm."

"You forgot to take the Pill?" Durango's heart continued to pound and he shook his head in disbelief. The one time she should have taken the Pill she had forgotten? How much sense did that make? Unless...

"Were you trying to get pregnant?" he asked in a quiet voice.

He watched her jaw drop in shock, and saw the stunned look in her eyes before anger thinned her lips. It was anger he felt, even with the distance that separated them. "How dare you ask me that!"

"Dammit, were you?" he asked angrily, ignoring her reaction to his question. He'd heard of women who slept with men just for that purpose, either to become a single parent or to snare a husband. And the thought that she had used him, set him up, raised his anger to the boiling point.

"No, I was not trying to get pregnant, but the fact of the matter is that I did. You fathered my child whether you want to believe it or not. Trust me, if I had been trying to get pregnant, you would not have been the choice for my baby's daddy," she said, snarling the words.

Durango's jaw tightened. *What the hell did she mean by that? And why wouldn't he have been the choice for her baby's daddy?* He shook his head, not believing he was asking himself that question. It wasn't like he wanted to be a father to any woman's baby.

"I think it's best that I leave."

Her words snapped him out of his reverie. His glare deepened. "Do you honestly think you can show up here and drop a bomb like that and then leave?"

She glared right back. "I don't see why not. The only reason I came here to tell you in person was because I thought you deserved to know and now you do. I've accomplished my goal. I didn't come here to ask you for anything. I'm capable of caring for my child without any help from you."

"So you plan to keep it?"

Fury raced through Savannah. "Yes, I plan to keep it, and if you're suggesting that I don't then you can—"

"No, dammit, that's not what I'm suggesting. I would never propose such a thing to any woman carrying my child. *If* the baby is mine, I take full responsibility."

Her stomach twisted, seeing the doubt in his eyes. "And that's the problem, isn't it, Durango?" she asked, shaking her head sadly. "You don't believe that the child I'm carrying is yours, do you?"

Durango studied her silently for a moment, remembering everything about the night of passion that they'd shared. He knew there was a very strong possibility, a high likelihood, that she had gotten pregnant if she hadn't been using birth control, but he was still too stunned to admit anything. "I believe there might be a chance," he told her.

That wasn't good enough for Savannah. Whether he knew it or not, he was questioning her character. Did he think she would get pregnant by one guy and try pinning it on another?

Without saying another word she walked back over to where she had placed her coat, hat and gloves and began putting them on. "There is more than a chance. It doesn't matter whether you want to believe it or not, there is something wonderful growing inside me that you put there. Not knowing your child will be your loss. Have a nice life."

"Where the hell do you think you're going?" he asked in a growl of both anger and frustration.

"Back to the airport to catch the next flight out of here," she said, moving toward the door. "I've done what I came here to do."

"One moment, Savannah," he grated through clenched teeth when she reached the door and opened it.

She turned around and lifted her chin. "What?"

"If your claim is true then we need to talk."

"My claim *is* true, Durango, and considering your attitude, we have nothing more to say."

Before he could draw in his next breath she walked out and closed the door behind her.

Durango stood at the window and watched Savannah get in a rental car and pull away. He was still reeling from the shock of her announcement and waited a tense moment to make sure she was out of sight before moving away from the window.

He glanced across the room to the clock on the wall and saw it was just past noon. He wished he could turn back time to erase what had just happened in this very living room. Savannah Claiborne had come all the way from Philadelphia to tell him that he was going to be a father, and he had all but told her to go to hell.

No doubt Chase would have his ass when he heard how shabbily he had treated his sister-in-law. Crossing the room, he dropped down into a leather recliner. It was so hard to believe. He was going to be a father. No way. The mere thought sent him into a state of panic. It seemed that babies were sprouting up everywhere in the Westmoreland family. Storm and Jayla had had twins a few months back; Dare and Shelly had announced over the holidays that they were expecting a baby sometime this summer; and when he had talked to Thorn last week, he had mentioned that Delaney and Jamal were also having another child.

Durango was happy for everyone. But babies were things other people had—not him. It wasn't that he'd never wanted a child; he'd just never given thought to having one anytime soon. He enjoyed the carefree life of a bachelor too much. He was a man who loved his solitude, a man who took pride in being a loner.

However, the one thing a Westmoreland did was take responsibility for his actions, no matter what they were. His parents had taught him, relentlessly drilled it into him and his five brothers, that you could distinguish the men from the boys by how well they faced whatever challenges were put before them.

Another thing he had been taught was that a Westmoreland knew when to admit he was wrong. If Savannah Claiborne was pregnant—and he had no reason to believe that she wasn't—then the baby was his.

Admitting that he was going to be a daddy was the first step.

He inwardly cringed at what he knew should be his second step—take whatever action was needed to take care of his responsibility. He checked his watch as he stood up. He wasn't sure what time her plane would depart, but if he left now there was a chance he might be able to stop her.

The woman was having his baby and if she thought she could pop up and drop the news on him without any further discussion then she needed to think again. She was going to have to deal with him even if the very thought of getting involved with a city girl made his skin crawl.

It didn't take much for him to remember Tricia Carrington, the woman he had fallen in love with four years earlier. She had come to Yellowstone on a two-week vacation from New York with some of her high-society girlfriends. During those two weeks they had an affair, and he had fallen head over heels in love with her. His uncle Corey had seen through Tricia, had picked up on the manipulator and insincere person that she was and had warned him. But at the time, he had fallen too much in love with her to heed his uncle's warnings.

Durango hadn't known that he'd been the subject of a wager between Tricia and her friends. She had bet her friends that she could come to Yellowstone and do a park ranger before marrying the wealthy man her parents had picked out for her. After confessing his undying love, she had laughed in his face and told him she had no intentions of marrying him, because he was merely a poor country bum who got dirt under his fingernails for a living. She was too refined for such a dead-end union and fully intended to return to New York to marry a wealthy man with connections. Her words had cut him to the core, and he had sworn that he would never give his heart to a woman again, especially to a stuck-up city girl.

And Savannah was definitely a city girl.

He had known it the moment he'd seen her. She had looked high-class, polished and refined. It had been noticeable in the way she'd been dressed, the way she had moved gracefully around the room. She was confident and looked as if she could be married to a member of the president's cabinet. She was exactly the type of woman that he had tried to avoid during the last four years.

However, he refused to let her being a city girl deter from what he needed to do. Now that the initial shock had worn off and he had accepted that he had unintentionally aided in increasing the Westmoreland line, he would take full responsibility and take charge of the situation.

Savannah had not been surprised by the way Durango had handled the news of her pregnancy. However, the one thing she had not expected and could not accept was his questioning if he was her baby's father.

"Do you want to return your rental car?"

The question from the woman standing behind the counter snatched Savannah's attention back to the present, making her focus on the business at hand. "Yes, please." She glanced at her watch, hoping that it wouldn't be difficult to get a return flight to Philadelphia. And once there, in the peaceful quiet of her condo, she would make decisions that would definitely change her life.

One thing was for certain—she would have to cut back her schedule at work. As a freelance photographer she could be called to go any place at any time. She realized she would miss the adventure of traveling both in this country and abroad.

But now she would need to settle down. After all, she had prenatal care and visits to the doctor to consider. She would talk to her boss about assigning her special projects. She appreciated the fact that over the years she had built a pretty hefty savings account and could afford to take time off both before and after her baby was born. She planned to take six months of family leave time when the baby came.

The one thing she didn't want to do was depend on anyone. Her mom would be overjoyed at the news of becoming a grandmother, but since Jennifer Claiborne had finally found real happiness with a man by the name of Brad Richman, and their relationship seemed to be turning serious—if their planned trip to Paris this week was any indication—the last thing Savannah wanted was for her mother to devote her time to her. Her sister, Jessica, was still enjoying the bliss of being a newlywed, and her brother, Rico, would be busy now that he had started work as a private investigator.

As Savannah stepped aside for the next customer be served, she placed her hand on her stomach, knowing whatever changes she made in her life would be worth it. She was having a baby and no matter how Durango Westmoreland felt, she was very happy about it.

Durango stood next to the water fountain and took in the woman standing across the semicrowded airport.

Damn, she was beautiful…and she was carrying a baby in her shapely body.

His baby.

He shook his head. What the hell was he supposed to do with a baby? It was too late to ask the question now, since the deed was already done. He sighed when he saw her head over toward the ticket counter, knowing what he had to do. He quickly crossed the room to block her path.

"We need to talk, Savannah."

Durango's words startled Savannah to the point that she almost dropped her carry-on bag. She narrowed her gaze at him. "What are you doing here? We don't have anything to talk about. I think we said everything, so if you will excuse me—"

"Look, I'm sorry."

She blinked as she stared at him. "What did you say?"

"I said I'm sorry for acting like an ass earlier. My only excuse is that your news came as a shock."

Savannah's eye's shot fire at him. "And…?"

"And I believe that your baby is mine."

She crossed her arms over her chest and glared at him, refusing to let go of her emotions and start crying. Since becoming pregnant she had turned into a weepy mess. "And what has made you a believer all of a sudden?"

"Because of everything that happened between us that night and the fact that you said I'm the father. I have no reason not to believe you." A slow smile played on his lips. "So that settles it."

If he believed that settled anything then he had another thought coming. "Nothing is settled, Durango.

Fine, you've acknowledged that I'm having your baby. That means you'll be one of the first people on my list to get an announcement card with pictures when it's born."

She turned to walk away and he blocked her path again. "Like I said, Savannah, we need to talk. I won't let you deny me the right to be a part of my child's life."

Savannah raised her eyes to the ceiling. An hour ago he had been humming a different tune. "If I had planned to do that, I wouldn't be here." After a deep, calming breath, she added, "I came because I felt you should know and to give you a choice. I didn't come to ask you for anything."

She suddenly felt her face flush from the way he was looking at her. Was her hair standing on end? Were her clothes wrinkled? The flight hadn't been kind to her and she'd almost gotten sick from all the turbulence they had encountered while flying over the mountains. Her hair was a tangled mess and her makeup had worn off hours ago. By the time the plane had landed and she had gotten a rental car to drive out to his ranch, she had been so shaken up she hadn't cared enough about her appearance to even put on lipstick.

"Whether you ask for anything or not, I have certain responsibilities toward my child and I want to talk about them," Durango said. "You've done what you came here to do and now that my head is back on straight, we need to sit down and discuss things like two mature adults."

Savannah lifted an eyebrow and gave him a speculative look. What did they have to talk about? She'd already told him she wouldn't be making any demands on him. She swallowed thickly when a thought suddenly

popped into her head. What if he planned to make demands on her regarding their child? Just last week there
was an article in the Philadelphia newspaper about a
man who had sued his girlfriend for joint custody of
their newborn child.

Maybe talking wasn't such a bad idea. It would be
better if they got a few things straight in the beginning so there wouldn't be any misunderstanding later.
"Okay, let's talk."

When they reached an empty table in the airport
coffee shop, Durango pulled out a chair for Savannah
to sit down on and she did so, on shaky legs. Her gaze
drifted over his handsome face and latched on to his full
lips. She couldn't help remembering those lips and some
of the wicked—as well as satisfying—things they had
once done to her.

She glanced away when his eyes met hers, finding it
strange that the two of them were sitting down to talk.
This was the first time they had shared a table. They
had once shared a bed, yes, but never a table. Even
the night of the rehearsal dinner he had sat at a different table with his brothers and cousins. But that hadn't
stopped her from scrutinizing and appreciating every
inch of him.

"Would you like something to drink, Savannah?"

"No, I don't want anything."

"So how have you been?" Durango asked after he
had finished ordering.

She raised her eyebrows, wondering why he hadn't
asked her that when he'd first seen her earlier that day.

He had picked a hell of a time to try to be nice, but she would go along with him to see what he had to say.

She managed to be polite and responded, "I've been fine, and what about you?"

"Things are going okay, but this is usually the hardest time of year for rangers."

"And why is that?"

"Besides the icy cold weather conditions, we have to supervise hunters who won't abide by the rules and who want to hunt during the off season. And even worse are those who can't accept the restrictions that no hunting is allowed in Yellowstone's backcountry."

Savannah nodded. She could imagine that would certainly make his job difficult. Jessica had said he was a backcountry ranger. They were the ones who patrolled and maintained trails in the park, monitored wildlife and enforced rules and safety regulations within the areas of Yellowstone. She shuddered at the thought of him coming face-to-face with a real live bear, or some other wild animal.

"You okay, Savannah?"

He had leaned in after seeing her tremble. Surprise held her still at just how close he was to her. "Yes, I'm fine. I just had a thought of you coming into contact with a bear."

He pulled back, smiled and chuckled. "Hey, that has happened plenty of times. But I've been fortunate to never tangle with one."

She nodded and glanced around, wondering when he would forgo the small talk and get down to what was really on his mind.

"What do you need, Savannah?" he finally asked after a few moments of uncomfortable silence.

She met his gaze as emotions swirled within her. "I told you, Durango, that I don't want or need anything from you. The only reason I'm here is because I felt you should know. I've heard a lot of horror stories of kids growing up not knowing who fathered them or men not knowing they fathered a child. I felt it would not have been fair to you or my child for that to happen."

He raised an eyebrow. "Your child? You do mean *our* child, don't you?"

Savannah bit her lip. No, she meant *her child*. She had begun thinking of this baby as hers ever since she'd taken the at-home pregnancy test. She'd begun thinking of herself as a single mom even before her doctor had confirmed her condition. She had accepted Durango's role in the creation of her child, but that was as far as it went.

"Understand this, Savannah. I want to be a part in *our* child's life."

She felt a thickness in her throat and felt slightly alarmed. "What kind of a part?"

"Whatever part that belongs to me as its father."

"But you live here in Montana and I live in Philadelphia. We're miles apart."

He nodded and studied her for a moment then said, "Then I guess it will be up to us to close the distance."

Savannah sighed. "I don't see how that is possible."

Durango leaned back in his chair. "I do. There's only one thing that we can do in this situation."

Savannah raised an eyebrow. "What?"

Durango met her gaze, smiled confidently and said, "Get married."

Chapter 3

Savannah blinked, thinking she had heard Durango wrong. After she was certain she hadn't, she couldn't help but chuckle. When she glanced over at him she saw that his expression wasn't one of amusement. "You are joking, aren't you?"

"No, I'm not."

"Well, that's too bad, because marriage is definitely not an option."

He crossed his arms over his chest. "And why not? Don't you think I'm good enough for you?"

Savannah glared at him, wondering where that had come from. "It's not a matter of whether or not you're good enough for me, and I have no idea why you would believe I'd think otherwise. The main reason I won't marry you is that we don't know each other."

He leaned in closer, clearly agitated. "Maybe not.

But that didn't stop us from sleeping together that night, did it?"

Savannah's eyes narrowed. "Only because we'd had too much to drink. I don't make a habit out of indulging in one-night stands."

"But you did."

"Yes, everyone is entitled to at least one mistake. Besides, we just can't get married. People don't get married these days because of a baby."

His lips twitched in annoyance. "If you're a Westmoreland you do. I don't relish the idea of getting married any more than you, but the men in my family take our responsibilities seriously." In Durango's mind, it didn't matter that he wasn't the marrying kind; the situation dictated such action. Westmorelands didn't have children out of wedlock and he was a Westmoreland.

He thought about his cousin Dare, who'd found out about his son A.J. only after Shelly had returned to their hometown when the boy was ten years old. Dare had married Shelly. His uncle Corey, who hadn't known he'd fathered triplets over thirty years ago, was an exception to the rule. Corey Westmoreland could not have married the mother of his children because he hadn't known they existed. Durango's situation was different. He knew about Savannah's pregnancy. Knowing about it and not doing something about it was completely unacceptable.

He had knocked her up and had to do what he knew was the right thing. Given the implications of their situation, getting married—even for only a short period of time—was the best course of action. He and Savannah were adults. Surely they could handle the intimacies of a brief marriage without wanting more. It wouldn't be as if he was giving up being a bachelor forever.

"Well, consider yourself off the hook," Savannah said, reclaiming his attention. "The only person who knows you're my baby's father is Jessica, although I'm sure she's shared the news with Chase by now. If we ask them not to say anything to anyone I'm sure they won't."

"But *I'll* know, Savannah, and there's no way I'm going to walk away and not claim my child."

For a quick second she felt a softening around her heart and couldn't help appreciating him for declaring her child as his. But she would not marry him just because she was pregnant.

She gave him a brittle smile as she rose to her feet, clinging to her carry-on bag and placing her camera pack on her shoulders. The sooner she left Montana and returned to Philadelphia, the better. "Thanks for the offer of marriage, Durango. It was sweet and I truly appreciate it, but I'm not marrying you or anyone just because I'm pregnant."

Durango stood, too. "Now, look, Savannah—"

"No, you look," she said, eyes narrowing, her back straight and stiff. "That's what happened with my parents. My mother got pregnant with my brother. Although my father did what some considered the decent thing and married her, he was never happy and ended up being unfaithful to her. It was a marriage based on duty rather than love. He met another woman and lived a double life with her and the child they had together."

She inhaled deeply before continuing. "Dad was a traveling salesman and my mother didn't know that he had another family, which included Jessica, on the West Coast. His actions were unforgivable and the people who suffered most, besides his children, were the two women who loved him and believed in him. In the end one of them, Jessica's mother, committed suicide. And I watched the hurt and pain my mother went through when she found out the truth about him. So no matter what you say, I would never let a man use pregnancy as a reason to marry. I'm glad we had this little chat and I'll keep in touch."

Chin tilted, she turned and quickly walked away.

"I'm sorry, ma'am, due to the snowstorm headed our way, all flights out have been canceled until further notice."

Savannah stared at the man behind the counter. "All of them?"

"All of them. We have our hands full trying to find a place for everyone to stay so they won't have to bunk here for the night. It seems that all the hotels in the area are full."

The last thing she wanted to do was sleep sitting up in a hard chair.

"You're coming with me, Savannah."

She turned around upon hearing the firm voice behind her. "I'm not going anywhere with you."

Durango took a step forward. "Yes, you are. You heard what the man said. All flights out have been canceled."

"Is this man bothering you, miss? Do you want me to call security?"

Savannah smoothed the hair back from her face.

This was just great. All she had to do was look at Durango's angry expression to see he did not appreciate the man's question. To avoid an unpleasant situation, she glanced over her shoulder at the ticket agent and smiled. "No, he isn't bothering me, but thanks for asking. Excuse me for a moment."

She then took Durango's arm and walked away from the counter. She was feeling frustrated and exhausted. "I think we need to get something straight."

Durango rubbed his neck, trying to work away the tension he felt building there. "What?"

She leaned over and got all into his face. "Nobody, and I mean nobody, bosses me around, Durango Westmoreland."

Durango stared at her for a long moment then forced back the thought that she was a cute spitfire. Okay, he would be the first to admit that for a moment he had been rather bossy, which was unlike him. He'd never bothered bossing a female around before. He then thought about his cousin Delaney, and remembered how overprotective the Westmoreland men had been before she'd gotten married, and figured she didn't count. But this particular woman was carrying his baby and he'd be damned if she would spend the night at the airport when he had a guest room back at his ranch that she could use. He decided to use another approach. It was well-known within his family that he could switch from being an ass to an angel in the blink of an eye.

He reached out and took her hand. "I do apologize if I came off rather bossy just now, Savannah. I was merely thinking of your and the baby's welfare. I'm sure sleeping here in one of those chairs wouldn't be comfortable. I have a perfectly good guest room at the ranch and you're welcome to use it. I'm sure you're tired. Will you come to the ranch with me?"

His words, spoken in a soft plea, as well as his ensuing smile, only made Savannah's blood boil even more. She recognized the words for what they were—smooth-talking crap. Her father had been a master at using such bull whenever he needed to unruffle her mother's feathers. And she was close to telling Durango in an unladylike way to go to hell.

And yet, spending the night here at the airport wouldn't be the smartest thing to do. She would love to go someplace, soak in a tub then crawl into a bed. Alone.

She met his gaze, studied his features to see if perhaps there was some ulterior motive for getting her back to the ranch. She knew from her sister's wedding that Durango Westmoreland was full of suave sophistication and he was an expert at seduction. And although the damage had been done, the last thing she wanted was to lose her head and sleep with him again.

She pulled her hand from his. "You really have an extra guest room?"

He grinned and her breath caught at his sexy dimples. Those dimples had been another one of her downfalls that night. "Yes, and like I said, you're welcome to use it."

Savannah toyed with the strap on her camera pack as she considered his invitation. She then met his gaze again. "Okay, I'll go with you if you promise not to bring up the subject of marriage again. That subject is closed."

She saw a flash of defiance in his eyes and then just as quickly it was gone. After a brief span of tense silence he finally said, "Okay, Savannah, I'll abide by your wishes."

Satisfied, Savannah nodded. "All right, then. I'll go with you."

"Good." He took the carry-on bag from her hand. "Come on, I'm parked right out front."

As Durango led her out of the terminal, he decided that what Savannah didn't know was that before she left to return home to Philadelphia, he and she would be man and wife.

"Here we are," Durango said, leading Savannah into a guest room a half hour later. "I have a couple of other rooms but I think you'll like this one the best."

Savannah nodded as she glanced around. The room was beautifully decorated with a king-size cherry-oak sleigh bed, with matching armoire, nightstands, mirror and dresser. Numerous paintings adorned the walls and several silk flower arrangements added a beautiful touch. It was basically a minisuite with a sitting area and large connecting bath.

"My mom fixed things up in here. She says the other guest rooms looked too manly for her."

Savannah turned and looked into Durango's eyes. Their gazes locked for the space of ten, maybe twelve heartbeats. "I like it and thank you. It's beautiful," she said, moments later breaking eye contact and glancing around the beautifully appointed room once again, attempting to get her emotions under control.

Out of the corner of her eyes she saw him move

closer into the room. She turned slightly and watched as he walked over to the window and pulled back the curtains. His concentration was on the view outside, but heaven help her, her concentration was on him. And what a view he was. How a man so tall, long-legged and muscular could move with such fluid grace was beyond her. But he managed to do so rather nicely.

She had noticed that about him from the first. There was something inherently masculine about Durango Westmoreland and the single night they had made love, she had discovered that what you saw was what you got. He definitely could deliver. That night he had tilted her universe in such a way that she knew it would never be the same again. Even now, a warmth moved slowly through all parts of her body just thinking about all the things they had done that night. No second, minute or hour had been wasted.

Durango suddenly turned and his gaze rested on her, longer than she deemed necessary, before he said, "It looks simply beautiful out of this window. Nothing but mountains all around. And this time of year when the snow falls, I think it's the most gorgeous sight that you'd ever want to see." He then turned back around and looked out the window again.

Mildly interested and deciding not to pretend otherwise, Savannah crossed the room to stand beside him and her breath caught. He was absolutely right. The panoramic view outside the window was beautiful. She hoped she had the chance to capture a lot of it on film before she left. "Have you lived here long?" curiosity pushed her to ask.

He met her gaze and smiled. "Almost five years

now. After I finished college and got a job with the park ranger service, I lived with my uncle Corey on his mountain for a couple of years, until I saved enough money to buy this land. It was originally part of a homestead, but after the elderly couple who owned it passed on, their offspring split up the property and put individual parcels up for sale. My ranch sits on over a hundred acres."

"Wow! That's a lot of land."

He smiled. "Yes, but most of it is mountains, which is one of the things that drew me to it. And a good portion of it is a natural hot springs. The first thing I did after building the ranch house was to erect my own private hot tub out back. If the weather wasn't so bad, I'd let you try it out. A good soak in it would definitely guarantee you a good night's sleep."

Savannah couldn't help but smile at the thought of that. "A good night's sleep sounds wonderful. The flight out here was awful."

Durango chuckled. "Unfortunately it usually is." He then checked his watch. "How about I put dinner on the table? Earlier I prepared smothered chicken in gravy, and made cabbage and mashed potatoes. You're welcome to join me after you settle in."

Savannah felt her stomach growl at the mention of food. Dinner was her favorite mealtime since she could never keep any breakfast down for too long. The only thing she had risked eating that day had been saltines. "Thanks, and I'd like that. Do you need any help?"

"No, I have everything under control." He turned to leave the room then stopped before walking out the door. "You're a city girl, but your name isn't."

Savannah arched a brow. She remembered what Jessica had shared with her once regarding Durango's aversion to city women. "It's my mom's favorite Southern city and she thought the name suited me."

He nodded, thinking the name suited her very feminine and genteel charm, as well.

A short while later Savannah followed the aroma of food as she walked down the stairs to the kitchen. She stopped and glanced around, getting a good look at the butcher-block kitchen counters and the shiny stainless-steel appliances. The kitchen was a cook's dream. From one side of the ceiling hung an assortment of copper pots. Unlike most men, Durango evidently enjoyed spending time in the kitchen.

He must have heard her sigh of admiration because he then turned, looked at her and smiled. "All settled in?"

Forcing her nervousness away, she nodded. "Yes. I didn't bring much since I hadn't planned on staying."

"You might as well get comfortable. I wouldn't be surprised if you're stuck here for a couple of days."

Savannah frowned. "Why would you think that?"

Durango leaned back against the counter and gestured toward the window. "Take a look outside."

Savannah quickly walked over to the window. There was a full-scale blizzard outside. She could barely see anything. She turned around. "What happened?"

Durango chuckled. "Welcome to Montana. Didn't you know this was the worst time of year to come visit?"

No, she hadn't known. The only thing that had been

on her mind, once she'd made her decision, was to get to him and tell him about the baby as soon as she could.

She glanced back out the window. "And you think this will last a couple of days?"

"More than likely. The only thing we can do is to make the most of it."

Savannah turned and met his gaze, taking in what he'd just said. It was simply a play on words, she presumed. She hoped. Being cooped up in the house with Durango for a couple of days and *making the most of it* wasn't what she'd planned on happening. It didn't take much to recall just how quickly she had succumbed to his sexiness. All it had taken was a little eye contact and she'd been a goner.

"Come on, Savannah. Let's eat."

Savannah regarded him for a moment before crossing the room to the table where he'd placed the food. "Aren't you concerned about losing power?"

Durango shook his head. "Nope. I have my own generator. It's capable of supplying all the energy I need to keep this place running awhile. Then there are the fireplaces. I had one built for every bedroom as well as the living room. No matter how cold or nasty the weather gets outside, you can believe we'll stay warm and cozy inside."

Staying warm and cozy was another thing she was afraid of, Savannah thought, taking a seat at the table. There was no doubt in her mind that she and Durango could supply enough sensuous heat to actually torch the place.

"Everything looks delicious. I didn't know you could cook," she said, helping herself to some of the food he had prepared, and trying not to lick her lips in the process. She was so hungry.

Durango smiled as he watched her dig in, glad she had a good appetite. A lot of the women he'd dated acted as if it was a sin to eat more than a thimbleful of food. "I'm a bachelor who believes in knowing how to fend for myself. On top of that I'm Sarah Westmoreland's son. She taught me Survival 101 well."

Savannah tasted the mashed potatoes and thought they were delicious. "Mmm, these are good."

"Thanks."

After a few moments of silence Durango said, "I noticed you aren't showing yet."

Savannah met his eyes. She had felt the heat of his gaze on her, checking out her body, when she'd crossed the room to stand at the window. "I'm only two months, Durango. The baby is probably smaller than a peanut now. Most women don't start showing until their fourth month."

He nodded. "How has the pregnancy been for you so far?"

She shrugged. "The usual, I guess. What I'm battling now more than anything is the morning sickness. Usually I don't dare eat anything but saltines before two o'clock every day, which is why I'm so hungry now."

Durango's eyes widened. "You're sick every day?"

He looked so darn surprised at the thought of such a thing that she couldn't help but chuckle. "Yes, just about. But according to the doctor, it will only last for another month or so."

She tilted her head and looked at him. "Haven't you ever been around a pregnant woman?"

"No, not for any length of time. When I went home for Easter last year, Jayla was pregnant and boy, was she huge. Of course, she was having twins." He grinned. "Twins run in my family and there's even a set of triplets."

Savannah raised her eyes heavenward. "Thanks for telling me."

Catching her off guard, Durango reached across the table and captured a lock of her hair in his hand, gently twining the soft, silky strands in his fingers. "I think triplets would be nice, and all with beautiful hazel eyes like yours."

Savannah swallowed tightly as her grip on sanity weakened. The way he was looking at her wasn't helping matters. She sensed his intense reaction to her was just as potent as hers to him. It was just as strong as it had been that night, and at that moment the desire to have his hands on her again, touching her breasts, her thighs, the area between her legs, was strong and unexpected. If he were to try anything right now, anything at all, it would take all her willpower to resist him.

"I want to be around and see how your body changes with my baby growing inside you, Savannah," he whispered huskily.

His words flowed over Savannah, caressing her in places she didn't want to be touched, and making a slow ache seep through her bones. "I don't know how that will be possible, Durango," she whispered softly.

"It would be possible if we got married."

She frowned and pulled back from him, breaking their contact. "You agreed not to bring that up again."

A smile touched the corners of his lips. "I know,

but I want to make you an offer that I hope you can't refuse."

She lifted her eyebrows. "What kind of offer?"

"That we marry and set a limit on the amount of time we'll stay together. We could remain married during the entire length of your pregnancy and for a short while afterward—say six to nine months. After that, we could file for a divorce."

She was stunned by his proposal. "What would doing something like that accomplish?" she asked, feeling the weight of his gaze on her and wishing she could ignore it.

"First, it would satisfy my need and desire to be with you during your pregnancy. Second, it would eliminate the stigma of my child being born illegitimate, which is something that is unacceptable to me. And third, because you believe I'll end up doing to you what your father did to your mother, at least this way you'll know up front that the marriage will be short-term and you won't lose any sleepless nights."

Savannah's frown deepened. "I never said I thought you would do me the way my father did my mother."

"Not in so many words, but it's clear you believe if I married you just for the baby that things wouldn't work out between us. And in a way I have to agree. You're probably right. Our marriage would be based on a sense of obligation on my part. There has to be more to hold a marriage together than just a baby. And to be quite honest with you, I'm not looking for a long-term marriage. But a short-term union, for our baby's sake, would be acceptable to me. I believe it would be acceptable to you, as well, because we'd know what to expect and not to expect from the relationship."

It seemed like a million questions were flashing in Savannah's mind, but she knew the main one that she needed to ask. "Are you saying you'd want a marriage in name only? A marriage of convenience?"

"Yes."

She swallowed and continued to meet his gaze. "And that means we won't be sharing a bed?"

He studied her for a moment and knew what she was getting at. His desire for her was as natural as it could get, and he didn't see it lessening any. If he wanted her this much now, he could just imagine how things would be once they were living together as man and wife under the same roof. Yes, he would definitely want to sleep with her.

Leaning back in his chair, he said, "No, not exactly. I have other ideas on the matter."

She could just imagine those ideas. "Then keep whatever ideas you have to yourself. *If,* and I said *if,* I go along with what you're proposing, we will *not* share a bed."

"Are you saying that you didn't enjoy sleeping with me?"

Savannah huffed an agitated sigh. Who had slept that night? Neither of them had until the wee hours of the morning. From what she remembered—and she was remembering it quite well—it was round-the-clock sex. And she had to admit, it was the best she'd ever had. The year she'd spent with Thomas couldn't even compare. "That's not the point."

"Then what *is* the point?" Durango countered.

"The point is," Savannah said, narrowing her eyes at him, "regardless of the fact that I did sleep with you that night, I usually don't jump into any man's bed unless I'm serious about him." She decided not to tell him that she'd only been serious with two other guys in her entire love-life history.

He leaned forward. "Trust me, Savannah, once we're married, we'll be as serious as any couple can get, even if we plan for our marriage to last a short while. Frankly I see no reason why we shouldn't sleep together. We're adults with basic needs who know what we want, and I think we need to start being honest with ourselves. We're attracted to each other, and have been from the first, which is why we're in this predicament. Things got as hot as it gets.

"And," he continued with an impatient wave of his hand to stop her from saying whatever it was that she was about to say, "we might not have been in our right minds that night, since we might have overindulged in the champagne, but we did enjoy making love. So why pretend otherwise?"

Savannah scowled. She wasn't pretending; she just didn't want a repeat performance, regardless of how enjoyable it had been. "You're missing the point."

"No, I think that you are. You're pregnant and I want to be a part of this pregnancy. It's important that I be there with you during the time you're carrying our baby, to bond with him or her while he or she's still in your womb and for some months after that."

"And just how long are you talking about?"

"Whatever period of time we agree on, but I prefer

nothing less than six months. I'd even go into another
year if I had to."

She frowned. "I wouldn't want you to do me any
favors."

"It's not about doing you any favors, Savannah. I
intend to always be a part of my child's life regardless
of whether you and I are together. But I think six months
afterward should be sufficient, unless you want longer."

When hell freezes over. For a few moments Savannah didn't say anything. What could she say when he
was right? They had been attracted to each other from
the start.

But what happened that night was in the past and
she refused to willingly tumble back into bed with him
again, and he had another thought coming if he assumed that she would. Evidently he was used to getting what he wanted, but in this case he wouldn't be so
lucky.

She then thought about the other thing he'd said,
about wanting to connect to their child while it was
still in her womb. She remembered reading in one of
her baby books how such a thing was possible and important to the baby's well-being. Some couples even
played music and read books to their child while it was
still growing inside the mother. Never in her wildest
dreams would she have thought that Durango would
know, much less care, about such things.

She pushed her plate back, glad she had eaten everything since it would probably be the last meal she'd
be able to consume until this time tomorrow. "I need
to think about what you're suggesting, Durango."

At the lift of his brow she decided to clarify. "I'm

talking about the marriage of convenience *without* you having any bedroom rights. If your offer hinges on the opposite then there's nothing for me to think about. I won't be sleeping with you, marriage or no marriage." She then thought of something.

"And where would we live if I went along with what you're proposing?" she asked.

He shrugged broad shoulders. "I prefer here, but if you want I can move to Philly."

Savannah knew that Durango was a man of the mountains. Here he was in his element and she couldn't imagine him living in Philadelphia of all places. "What about your job?"

"I'll take a leave."

She lifted an eyebrow. "You'd be willing to do that?"

"For our child, yes."

She searched his face and saw the sincerity in his words, and they overwhelmed her as well as frightened her. He was letting her know up front that although he didn't want a long-term commitment, he was willing to engage in a short-term one for the sake of her child.

Their child.

She stood. "Like I said, I need to think about this, Durango."

"And I want you to think about it and think about it good. If you're dead set against us sharing a bed then that's fine. My offer of marriage still stands."

He stood and came around the table to stand in front of her. "There are bath towels, a robe and whatever else you might need in the private bath adjoining your room. If you need anything else let me know. Otherwise, I'll see you in the morning."

"I'll help you with the dishes and—"

"No, leave them," he said quickly, releasing a frustrated breath. There was only so much temptation that he could handle and at that moment he wanted nothing more than to kiss her, taste her. But he knew that now was not the time. She needed a chance to think about his offer.

"I'll take care of the dishes later after checking out a few things around my property," he added.

"You sure?"

"Yes."

"All right."

Durango watched as Savannah quickly walked off. He couldn't help but shake his head. Nothing had changed. The attraction between them was still as hot as it got.

Chapter 4

The next morning Savannah awoke more confused than ever. She had barely gotten any sleep thinking about Durango's proposal. In a way it could make their mistake even bigger. On the other hand, he seemed sincere in wanting to help her through her pregnancy, and she wouldn't deny him the chance to bond with his child, especially when very few men would care to do so.

Deciding she didn't want to think about Durango's proposal any longer, she sat up in bed and glanced out the window. The weather was worse than it had been the day before, which meant she couldn't leave today unless the conditions miraculously cleared up.

At least the fireplace was blazing, providing warmth to the room. She settled back in bed, and remembered opening her eyes some point during the night and seeing Durango in front of the fireplace, squatting on his heels and leaning forward, trying to get the fire going. At the time she had been too tired and sleepy to acknowledge his presence.

With the moon's glow streaming through the window, she had lain there and watched him. A different kind of heat had engulfed her as she watched him working to bring warmth to the room. His shirt had stretched tight to accommodate broad shoulders and the hands that had held the wrought-iron poker had been strong and capable...just as they'd been the night he had used them on her. And later, when he had pushed himself to his feet, she had admired his physique—especially his backside—through heavy-lidded eyes, thinking that he had the best-looking butt to ever grace a pair of jeans.

She was startled when there was a knock on her door. Knowing it could only be Durango, she swallowed hard and said, "Come in."

He walked in, bringing enough heat into the room to make the fireplace unnecessary, and his smile made Savannah's insides curl, making her feel even hotter there. How would she ever be able to remain immune to his lethal charm?

"Good morning, Savannah. I hope you rested well."

"Good morning, Durango, and I did. Thanks. I see the weather hasn't improved," she said, sitting up in bed and tucking the covers modestly around her chest. Because she hadn't figured this would be an extended trip, besides her camera pack, which she was rarely without, she'd only brought a book to read on the plane, her makeup and one change of clothing. She'd been forced to sleep in an oversize Atlanta Braves T-shirt that she had found in one of the dresser drawers.

"No, the weather has gotten worse and I need to leave for a while and—"

"You're going out in that?" she asked.

His eyebrows raised a half inch and the smile on his face deepened. "This is nothing compared to a storm that blew through last month. I'm a member of the Search and Rescue Squad so I'm used to going out and working in these conditions. I just got a call from the station. A couple of hikers are missing so we have to go out and find them. There're a number of isolated cabins around these parts and I'm hoping they sought shelter in one of them."

She nodded and moved her gaze from his to glance out the window again. She couldn't imagine anyone being caught out in the weather and hoped the hikers were safe.

"Will you be all right until I get back?" he asked.

She met his gaze again. "I'll be fine." She watched as he turned to leave and quickly said, "Be careful."

Pausing to glance back at her, he said, "I will." He smiled again and added, "I don't intend for you to give birth to our child without me."

Savannah had hoped this morning would be different, but as soon as her feet touched the floor she began experiencing her usual bout of morning sickness and quickly rushed to the bathroom.

A short while later, after brushing her teeth, rinsing out her mouth and soaking her body in a hot tub of water, she wrapped herself in a thick white velour robe that was hanging in the closet and padded barefoot to the kitchen, hoping Durango kept saltine crackers on hand.

A sigh of gratitude escaped her lips when she found a box in his pantry and opened the pack and began consuming a few to settle her stomach. She walked over to the window and glanced out at the abundance of twirling snowflakes. If it kept snowing at this rate there was no telling when she would get a flight out.

Durango stomped the snow off his shoes before stepping inside his home. The thought of Savannah being there when he returned was what had gotten him through the blinding cold while the search party had looked for the hikers. Luckily they had found them in fairly good condition in an old, abandoned cabin.

Quietly closing the door behind him, he slid out of his coat and glanced across the room. Savannah was curled up on the sofa, asleep. Her dark, curly hair framed her face, making her even more beautiful. She looked so peaceful, as if she didn't have a care in the world, and he could have stood there indefinitely and watched her sleep.

When she stirred slightly it hit him that even now something was taking place inside her body. His seed had taken root and was forming, shaping and growing into another human being. For a brief moment a smile touched his lips as he envisioned a little girl with her mother's black curly locks, caramel-colored skin and beautiful hazel eyes.

Girls born into the Westmoreland family had been a rarity. For almost thirty years his cousin Delaney had been the only one, having the unenviable task of trying to handle a dozen very protective Westmorelands—her father, five brothers and six male cousins. Then, just eighteen months ago, it was discovered that his uncle Corey had fathered triplets that included a girl—Casey. Mercifully, this discovery had taken some of the attention off Delaney.

Now Storm and Jayla had daughters and he heard that Dare and Shelly, as well as Delaney and Jamal, who had sons already, were hoping for girls this time around. Just the thought of a future generation of female Westmorelands made him shudder. But still, he liked the idea of having a daughter to pamper, a daughter who was a miniature version of Savannah.

He had to admit there were a number of things about the woman asleep on his couch that stirred feelings inside him. One was the fact that she hadn't used her pregnancy to force his hand. He could name a number of women who definitely would have shown up demanding that they marry by the end of the day. Savannah, on the other hand, hadn't been thrilled by the suggestion and even now hadn't agreed to go along with him on it. For some reason Durango liked the thought of having her tied to him legally, even for a short while.

He gazed down at her. She was wearing the oversize T-shirt and jogging pants that he had left out for her. Both were his and fit rather large on her. Even so, he couldn't help but notice the curve of her breasts under the cotton shirt. They seemed larger than he'd remembered. It was going to be interesting, as well as fascinating, to watch her body go through the changes it would undergo during the coming months. And more than anything, he wanted to be around to see it.

He shook his head, thinking that if anyone had told him last week he would be feeling this way about a pregnant woman, he would not have believed them. He knew he would have a hard time convincing his best friend, McKinnon Quinn, that he'd not only accepted Savannah's pregnancy but was looking forward to the day she gave birth. He and McKinnon were known to be the die-hard bachelors around these parts and had always made it a point to steer clear of any type of binding relationship.

When Savannah made a soft, nearly soundless sigh in her sleep and shifted her body, making the T-shirt rise a little to uncover her stomach, Durango stifled a groan and was tempted to go over and kiss the part of her body where his child was nestled. He closed his eyes as his imagination took over when he knew he wouldn't want to stop at just her stomach. Even now her seductive scent filled the room and tantalized his senses. He felt tired, exhausted, yet at the same time he felt his body stirring when he remembered the heated passion the two of them had once shared. A passion he was looking forward to them sharing again one day.

Savannah awoke with a start, immediately aware that she was no longer alone. The smell of food cooking was a dead giveaway.

Her memory returned in a rush and she recalled her bout with morning sickness and how she had decided to lie on the sofa when a moment of dizziness had assailed her. She must have fallen asleep. She couldn't help wondering when Durango had returned. Why hadn't he awakened her? Had they found the missing hikers?

"Did you eat anything?"

The sound of Durango's deep voice nearly made her jump. She met his gaze and instantly, her body was filled with a deep, throbbing heat. He had removed the pullover sweater he'd been wearing over his jeans earlier and was dressed in a casual shirt that was open at the throat, giving him a downright sexy appeal, not that he needed it.

There was something about him that just turned her on. It would be hard to be married to him—even on a short-term basis—without there ever being a chance of them sharing a bed. But she was determined to do just that.

Knowing she hadn't answered him, she said, "No, but thanks for leaving breakfast warming for me in the oven. My stomach wasn't cooperating and I wouldn't have been able to keep anything down. I found some saltines in your pantry and decided to munch on those."

Durango nodded, recalling her mentioning the previous day that she'd been unable to eat most mornings. "Have you seen a doctor?"

"Yes, although I'm going to have to find another one soon. Dr. Wilson is the same doctor who delivered me and Rico and he's retiring next month."

"Isn't he concerned with you being sick every day? Are you and the baby getting all the nutrients you need?"

Savannah shrugged as she sat up. "Healthwise Dr. Wilson says that both the baby and I are fine."

He leaned back against the wall. "When you go to the doctor again I'd like to be there."

"In Philadelphia?"

"Wherever you decide to go doesn't matter. And since your doctor is retiring, just so you'll know, there's a good obstetrician here in Bozeman and she's female."

She tipped her head back and looked at him and wished she could stop her pulse from racing at the sight of his lean, hard body. "Really? That's good to know."

He smiled. "I thought it would be."

He came into the room and sat in the chair across from her, stretching his long legs out and crossing them at a booted ankle. "Have you thought about what I proposed last night?"

"Yes, I thought about it."

"And?" he asked gently, knowing she was a woman who couldn't be rushed.

"And I need more time to make up my mind," she said, fixing her gaze on his boots.

"I wish I could tell you to take all the time you need, but time isn't on our side, Savannah. If we do decide to get married there needs to be a wedding."

Her head snapped up. "A wedding?"

He smiled at her surprised expression. "Yes. I don't anticipate one as elaborate as Chase's, but as you know, we Westmorelands are a large family with plenty of friends and acquaintances and—"

"It's not as if it would be a real marriage, Durango, so why bother?"

"Because my parents, specifically my mother, who won't know why we're getting married, would expect it."

"Well, personally I can't see the need for a lot of hoopla over something that won't last. If I decide to accept your proposal, I prefer that we go off somewhere like Vegas and not tell anyone about it until it's over.

They will eventually know the real reason we got married in a few months anyway."

Durango nodded, knowing she was right. His family, who knew how he felt about marriage, would know it wasn't the real thing no matter what he told them. "What about your mother?"

"She's leaving tomorrow for Paris and won't be back for a couple of weeks. If I do decide to marry you, she'll be okay with my decision and it won't bother me that she won't be at the ceremony since she knows I don't believe in happily-ever-after."

Durango rubbed the back of his neck with an irritated frown. It wasn't that he didn't believe in fairy-tale romances, but after Tricia he figured it would be more fantasy than reality for him. "Fine. If you agree, we can elope and then if our parents want to do something in the way of a reception later, that will be fine. All right?"

She sighed. "All right."

"So when will you let me know your decision?"

"Before I leave here. Do you think the weather will have improved by tomorrow?"

"I'm not sure. Usually these types of snowstorms can last for a week."

"A week? I didn't bring enough clothes with me."

He thought now was not a good time to tell her he wouldn't mind if she walked around naked. "The last time Delaney was here she left a few of her things behind. The two of you are around the same size so you should be able to fit into them if you want to try."

"You don't think she'd mind?"

"No."

"All right then, if you're sure it's okay."

He stood. "Do you think your stomach has settled enough for dinner? I cooked a pot of beef stew."

"Yes, I think it will be able to handle it. Would you like some help in the kitchen?"

"If you're up to it you can set the table."

She stood. "I'm up to it. Did you find the hikers?"

"Yes, we found them and they're fine. Luckily one was a former Boy Scout and knew exactly what to do."

She smiled, relieved, as she followed him into the kitchen. "I'm glad."

Savannah was amazed at the size of her appetite and flushed with embarrassment when she noted that Durango had stopped to watch her, with amusement dancing in his eyes, as she devoured one bowl of stew and was working on her second.

She licked her lips. "I was hungry."

"Apparently."

When she pushed the empty bowl aside, he chuckled and said, "Hey, you were on a roll. Don't stop on my account."

Her brows came together in a frown. "I've had enough, thank you."

"You're welcome. I've got to keep the ballerina on her toes."

"What ballerina?"

"Our daughter."

Savannah raised a glass of milk to her lips, took a sip and then asked, "You think I'm having a girl?"

"Yes."

She tipped her head, curious. "Why?"

He leaned forward to wipe the milk from around her lips with his napkin, wondering when was the last time he had given so much time and attention to a woman. "Because that's what I want and I'm arrogant enough to think I'll get whatever I want."

Savannah didn't doubt that—not that she thought he got anything and everything he wanted, but that he was arrogant enough to think so. "Why would you want a girl?"

"Why wouldn't I want one?" he asked. There was no way he would tell her the reason he wanted a little girl was that he wanted a daughter who looked just like her. He couldn't explain the reason behind it and at the moment he didn't want to dwell on the significance of it.

"There are more men in your family, and considering that, I'd think for you a son would be easier to manage," she said.

He chuckled, amused. "I think we managed my cousin Delaney just fine. With five brothers and six older male cousins we were able to put the fear of God into any guy who showed interest in her. I see no problem with us getting the same point across with the next generation of Westmoreland females."

His smile deepened. "Besides, don't you know that girls are the apples of their fathers' eyes?"

"Not in all cases," she said, thinking of the relationship she and Jessica never had with their father.

"But let me set the record straight," Durango said, breaking into her reverie. "I would love either a boy or girl, but having a daughter would be extra, extra special."

Savannah smiled, thinking his words pleased her, probably because she was hoping for a girl, as well. In some ways it surprised her that a man who was such a confirmed bachelor would want children or be interested in fatherhood at all.

At that moment an adorable image floated into her mind of Durango and a little girl who looked just like him sitting on his lap while he read her a story.

"So what do you think?" Durango asked.

Savannah glanced up after going through the items of clothing that Durango had placed on the bed. "I think they'll work. I don't wear jeans often so the change will be nice, and the sweaters look comfy. They will be good for this weather."

"So what do you plan to do tonight?"

The low-pitch murmur of his voice had her lifting her head and meeting his gaze. She wished there was some way she didn't get turned on whenever she looked into their dark depths. "I thought I'd try and finish a book that I brought with me."

"Oh, and what type book is it?"

She shrugged. "One of those baby books that tells you what to expect during pregnancy and at childbirth."

"Sounds interesting."

"It is." She tried ignoring the sensations that were moving around in her stomach. Having Durango in her bedroom wasn't a good idea and the sooner she got him out, the better, but there was something that she needed to find out first.

"There's something I'd like to ask you, Durango. It's

something I need to know before I can make a decision about marrying you."

He lifted an eyebrow. "And what is it you need to know?"

She moved away from the bed and sank down on the love seat. She would have preferred having any conversation with him someplace else other than here, in the coziness of the bedroom with a fireplace burning with its yellow glow illuminating Durango's handsome features even more. At least she wasn't standing next to the bed any longer.

Knowing he was waiting for her to speak, she met his gaze and asked, "I want to know what you have against *city women*."

Chapter 5

Some questions weren't meant to be asked.

Savannah quickly reached that conclusion when she saw Durango's jaw clench, his hands tighten into a fist by his side and an angry glare darken his eyes. Another thing that was a dead giveaway was the sudden chill in the air, not to mention the force of his stare, which caused her to draw a quick breath.

Her question, which had evidently caught him off guard, required every bit of his self-control and she began feeling uneasy. Still, she needed to know the reason for his aversion since it was something that obviously quite a few people knew, at least those who were close to him.

She watched his lips move and knew he was muttering something under his breath. That only increased her curiosity, her need to know. "Durango?"

When he finally spoke his voice was low with an edginess that hinted she had waded into forbidden waters. "I'd rather not talk about it."

Savannah knew she should probably let the matter drop, but she couldn't let the question die because a part of her really wanted to know.

Evidently he saw that determined look in her features and he said, "It doesn't concern you, Savannah. You're having my baby. I've asked you to marry me so there's no need for us to start spilling our guts about every little thing that happened in our pasts. I'll respect your right to privacy and I hope that you will respect mine."

Savannah couldn't help wondering about what he didn't want to tell her. What pain was he still hiding in his heart? God knew she had plenty of skeletons she'd kept hidden in her mental closet. Secrets she'd only shared with Jessica. His request for privacy was a reasonable one. She shouldn't be digging into his past, but she needed assurance that whatever his problem was, she wouldn't be affected by it, and until she had that certainty, she wouldn't back off.

"All that's well and good, Durango, but if I am to marry you, even if it's only for a short while, I need to know I won't be mistreated because of someone else's transgressions."

"You won't."

The words had been spoken so quickly that Savannah hadn't had a chance to blink. She heard both regret and anger in his voice.

"This is only about you and me, Savannah, and no

one else. Don't let anything that happened before sway your decision now."

Savannah's gaze wandered over his muscular form. He was leaning with a shoulder pressed up against a bedpost, his booted feet crossed at the ankles and his arms folded over his chest. He was watching her with as much intensity as she was watching him.

Seconds ticked by and with the passing of time something heated and all-consuming was passing between them. And she knew if it continued that she couldn't be responsible for her actions...and neither could he.

Even now heat was spiking inside her just looking at him standing there, saying nothing. She continued to feel an overpowering need. Desire was inching its way up her spine and then she remembered his taste and how she couldn't get enough of him the last time.

He continued to hold her gaze and he was having a hypnotic effect on her. And then he moved toward her, with his slow, graceful stride. Crossing the room, he reached out and gently tugged her up off the sofa.

She knew at that moment what he wanted, what he needed. They were the same things she desired. Lowering his face, bending to cup the back of her head with his hand, he kissed her. The moment their lips touched, her hands automatically slipped inside the back pockets of his jeans. It was that or remain free and be tempted to squeeze his butt like Mr. Whipple used to squeeze the Charmin.

And when their lips locked and he inserted his tongue inside her mouth, the contact was so intimate, heated and passionate that she knew there was nothing she could do but stand there and enjoy it.

And she did.

They were consenting adults and a little kiss never hurt anyone, she convinced herself when her tongue joined with his. But this was no little kiss, she discovered moments later. The tongue stroking hers was strong and capable, arousing her to a pitch higher than he'd done that night in her hotel room.

It was the usual Durango kiss—long, hot, sexy. The kind of kiss that made your toes curl, your breasts feel full and your stomach tingle. She closed her eyes to feel more deeply the sensations that crowded her mind and the electrical charges that were burning all over her body. She breathed in his scent, reveling in the slow, methodical way he was making love to her mouth.

He reluctantly broke off the kiss. She slowly opened her eyes, met the deep intensity of his gaze, expelled a deep breath, then dragged in an unsteady one, feeling satisfied. And even now she saw his gaze was still locked on to her lips.

"I enjoy kissing you," he said softly, throatily, as if that explained everything, especially every tantalizing stroke of his tongue.

She watched those dark, intense eyes that were focused on her mouth get even darker. "Um, I can tell."

She had to admit that nothing about her visit to his home had turned out like she'd planned. She had come to tell him her news and leave. It was too bad she hadn't stuck to her plans. But then, if she had, she wouldn't be standing here discovering once again what true passion was like. Before meeting him, she hadn't had a clue.

"I think I'd better go. I'll see you in the morning," he whispered low against her moist lips.

And before she could blink or catch her next breath, he was gone.

The moment the door closed behind Durango, Savannah could feel her stomach muscles tightening. She swayed slightly when the floor beneath her feet felt shaky. Talk about a kiss!

Muttering darkly—probably some of those same words Durango had said earlier, but hadn't wanted her to hear—she crossed the room and dropped down on the bed. His kiss was one of the reasons she was in this predicament. She had invited him into her room for the two of them to indulge in some more champagne. She hadn't gotten to completely filling his glass before he had taken both the bottle and glass from her hand and had filled her mouth with his instead. He hadn't kissed her silly—he had kissed her crazy. The taste of him had been hot, delicious and incredibly pleasurable. She had lusted for him, after him, with him and by the time they had made it to the bed, they had stripped naked.

They were extremely attracted to each other. Deep down inside she knew that Durango didn't like their explosive chemistry any more than she did. She had seen the way his eyes had flashed when he had lifted his mouth from hers, as well as the way his jaw muscles had tightened. Also, there was the way he always looked after kissing her senseless, like he needed divine intervention to help him deal with her and the sexual response they stirred up in each other.

"And to think that he's proposing marriage," she mumbled in a low voice that rattled with frustration. "So okay, it will only be for a short while, as he's quick to remind me every chance he gets," she said, shifting to her back and folding her arms over her chest. "What will I get out of this arrangement?"

More kisses, her mind immediately responded. *And if you stop being so dang stubborn, you'd also get a temporary bed partner. What do you have to lose? You'll be entering into a relationship with your eyes open and no expectations. You'll know up front that love has nothing to do with it. Besides, you'll be giving your child a chance to develop a relationship with a father who cares.*

Because of her experience with her father, that meant everything to Savannah. She believed that even when their marriage ended, Durango would remain a major part of his child's life.

Savannah also needed to think about the other reasons why marrying Durango was a good idea.

Pulling her body up, she shifted to her side. First was the issue of having a temporary bed partner if she decided to go that route. She'd dated but had never been into casual sex so she hadn't been involved with anyone since Thomas Crawford. She had dated Thomas exclusively for a year and things between them had been going well until he'd gotten jealous about an assignment she'd gotten that he had wanted. He'd even tried convincing her to turn the job down so he could have it—talk about someone being selfish and self-centered.

It had been over a year, close to two since she'd broken up with Thomas or slept with anyone. The night she had shared a bed with Durango hadn't just been a night of want for her; it had been a night of need, a strictly hormonal affair in which she really hadn't acted like herself.

She tipped her head to the side and moved on to the other reason for marrying Durango. *Expectations.* Their expectations would be set and neither of them would be wearing blinders. She knew their marriage would not be the real thing. He didn't love her and she didn't love him. Having reasonable expectations would definitely make things easier emotionally when the time came for them to split.

The more she thought about it, the more she knew that accepting his offer of marriage was the best thing. Her child would be getting the kind of father that she never had—a father her baby would be able to depend on.

And then there were all the other Westmorelands who would be her child's extended family. She had seen firsthand at Chase and Jessica's wedding just what a close-knit group they were. Being part of a large family was another thing she'd missed growing up, but it was something her child could have.

Her brain began spinning with all the positives, but she forced herself to think about the negatives, as well. At the moment she could only imagine one. *The possibility of her falling in love with him.*

She couldn't even envision such a thing happening, but she knew there was that possibility. Durango would not be a hard man to love. A woman could definitely lose her heart to him if she wasn't careful. He was so strong and assertive and yet, he was also a giving and a caring person. She noticed his sensitivity in the ways that he saw to her needs: making sure he'd left breakfast for her; coming into her room in the dead of night to make sure she was warm enough; inquiring about her and their baby's health.

But still, there was no way she could ever fall in love. She doubted that she could give him or any man a part of her soul or a piece of her heart.

She knew that no matter how much she enjoyed the time she would spend with Durango during her pregnancy, she could not lose her heart to him. Ever.

Several hours had passed since Durango and Savannah had shared that heated kiss, and the residual effects were so strong that he couldn't think straight enough to balance his accounting records. Instead of concentrating on debits and credits he was way too focused on the incredible sensations he was still feeling, the jolts of electricity that were still flowing through his body.

He had kissed women, plenty of times, but none had left a mark on him like Savannah Claiborne had. There was something about her taste, a succulent blend of sweetness, innocence and lusciousness, all rolled into one tangy, overpowering flavor that sent all kinds of crazy, out-of-control feelings slithering all through his body. She made his temperature rise, clogged his senses and made his pulse to race.

"Dammit."

He slapped the accounting ledger shut and turned away from the computer screen. The last thing he needed was to make a bookeeping miscalculation in the horse-breeding business he co-owned with his good friend McKinnon Quinn.

He leaned back in his chair and his thoughts returned to Savannah. He just hoped her decision would be the one he wanted. He simply refused to consider any other possibility.

Chapter 6

"What the hell! Savannah? Are you all right?"

Savannah heard the footsteps behind her. She also heard the concern as well as the panic in Durango's voice, but she was too weak to lift her head and turn around. She didn't want him to see her like this. How humiliating was it to be on your knees on the floor of a bathroom, holding your head over a commode?

"Savannah, what's wrong?"

The moment she could, she expelled a breath and said the two words she hoped would explain everything. It appeared that he hadn't gotten the picture yet. "Morning sickness."

"Morning sickness? Is this what morning sickness is all about?"

Savannah suppressed a groan. What had he thought it was about? She was about to give him a snappy answer when her stomach clenched in warning. It was just as well since at that moment her body quickly reminded her of her condition and without any control, she closed her eyes, lowered her head and continued to throw up yesterday's dinner.

"What can I do?"

It was on the tip of her tongue to tell him what he could do was go away. She didn't need an audience. "Nothing," she managed to say moments later. "Please, just leave me alone."

"Not even if your life depended on it, sweetheart," he said softly. Crouching down on the floor beside her, he wrapped his arms gently around her and whispered, "We're in this thing together, remember? Let me help you."

Before she could tell him that she didn't need his help and there wasn't anything he could do, he proved her wrong when she felt another spasm of nausea. He took a damp washcloth and began tenderly wiping her face and mouth.

Then he held her while her stomach began settling down. She was so touched by this generous display of caring, she leaned against his supporting body, while his huge hand gently stroked her belly into calmness. And as if it had a will of its own, her head fell inside the curve of his shoulder. No man had ever shown her so much tenderness. Okay, she confessed silently, Rico had always been there for her when she needed him, but since he was her brother he didn't count.

"That's right, baby, just relax for a moment. Everything is going to be fine. I'm going to take care of you," he murmured softly, brushing his lips against her temple and placing a kiss on her forehead.

Then she heard the toilet flushing at the same time as she was scooped up in Durango's strong arms. And after closing the toilet lid, he sat down on it with her cradled in his arms as he continued to gently stroke her stomach. A short while later, as if she weighed nothing, he stood and sat her on the countertop next to the sink.

"Do you think a soda will help settle your stomach?" he asked, staring into her eyes.

With the intensity of his gaze, her breath nearly got clogged in her throat but she managed to say, "Yes."

"Will you be okay while I go and get you one?"

"Yes, I'll be fine."

He nodded. "I'll be right back."

As soon as he left, Savannah inhaled a deep breath. As usual, her bout with nausea was going away just as quickly as it had come. Deciding to take advantage of the time Durango was gone, she gently lowered her body off the counter and immediately began brushing her teeth. She had just finished rinsing out her mouth when Durango returned.

"Here you go."

She took the cold can of ginger ale he offered and after quickly pulling the tab, she took a sip, immediately feeling better. After finishing the rest she lowered the can from her mouth, licked her lips and said, "Thanks, I needed that."

She quickly began studying the can. Durango was staring at her and she felt embarrassed. She knew she looked a mess. One of the things she had learned at the all-girl school her grandparents had sent her to was that a lady never showed signs of weakness in front of a man. She'd also been taught that a man was not supposed to see a woman at her worst. Unfortunately some things couldn't be helped. Besides, it wasn't as if she had invited him to join her in the bathroom this morning. Why had he come, anyway?

As if reading her mind, he said, "I know you said you usually don't eat anything in the morning, but I was about to have breakfast and wanted to check to make sure you didn't want to join me."

"I would not have been able to eat anything."

"Yeah, I can see why. And you go through this every morning?" he asked. Once again she heard the deep concern in his voice.

"Yes, but it's not always this bad. I guess eating all that stew at dinner last night wasn't such a good idea."

"Evidently. What did your doctor say about it?"

She sighed deeply. "There's not a lot he could say, Durango. During the early months of pregnancy, morning sickness happens."

"That's not good enough."

She held up both hands to stop him. She knew he was about to urge her to see a local doctor. "Look, not now, okay? More than anything I need to get myself together. Just give me a few minutes."

"And you're sure you're okay?"

"I'm sure."

"Is there anything else I can get you?"

She shifted uneasily, not used to this amount of attention. "No, thanks. I don't need anything."

He nodded. "Okay then, I'll leave you alone to get dressed."

He turned to leave then slowly turned back around and surprised her when his mouth brushed over hers. "Sorry my kid is causing you so much trouble," he said after the light caress.

And before she could gather her wits and say anything, he had walked out of the bathroom, leaving her alone.

Durango paced the living room, glad he hadn't gone out. He winced at the thought of how things would have been for Savannah if she'd been alone. Then it struck him that she *had* gone through it alone before. She lived by herself and there had to have been times when she'd been sick and no one had been there with her. When she'd first mentioned this morning sickness thing, he'd thought she just experienced a queasy stomach in the morning and preferred not eating until later. He had no idea she spent part of each morning practically retching her guts out.

He paused and rubbed his hand down his face. It was easy to see he wasn't used to being around a pregnant woman. There hadn't been any babies in his family until Delaney had given birth a few years ago, and then she'd spent most of the time during her pregnancy in her husband's homeland in the Middle East.

Although he had only been around Jayla a few times while she was pregnant, the only thing he'd been aware of was that she was huge. Because she had been carrying twins she always looked as if she was about to deliver at any moment. He didn't recall Storm ever mentioning anything about Jayla being sick and throwing up every morning. It seemed that he needed to be the one reading a baby book.

Shoving his hands into the pockets of his jeans, he began pacing again. Okay, so maybe he was getting freaked out and carried away. Savannah had claimed what she was going through was normal, but even so, that didn't mean he had to like it.

He turned when he heard the sound of her entering the room. As he studied her he found it hard to believe she was the same woman who just moments ago had looked as if she were on the brink of death. Talk about a stunning transformation. She had changed into a pair of jeans and a top and both looked great on her. Immediately the thought came to his mind that she looked good in anything she put on her body, whether it was an expensive gown, slacks and a top, jeans or an oversize T-shirt.

She had added a touch of makeup to her features, but mainly her natural beauty was shining through, and it was shining so brightly that it made the room glow...which wasn't hard to do considering the weather outside. The storm was still at its worst, although the recent weather reports indicated things would start clearing up at some point that day.

"You okay?" he asked, quickly crossing the room to her.

She smiled faintly up at him. "Yes, I'm fine and I want to apologize for—"

"Don't. There's nothing to apologize for. I'm glad I was here."

She hated to admit it, but she was glad he'd been there, too. Although she had gone through the same ordeal alone countless times, it had felt good to have a shoulder to lean on. And it had been extremely nice knowing that that particular shoulder belonged to the man who had a vested interest in her condition.

She also didn't want to admit that she was fully aware of how handsome he looked this morning. Though to be honest, he always looked good in jeans and the western shirts he liked to wear. Deciding she needed to think about other things, she walked over to the window and glanced out. She noticed the weather was still stormy. "Will you have to go out today?"

He moved to stand beside her and glanced out the window, as well. "Maybe later. The weather reports indicate it will begin clearing up soon."

"It will?" she asked, surprised, turning to face him. "Yes."

She smiled brightly. "That means there's a possibility I'll be able to leave today."

"Yes, there is that possibility," he said. "I know you can't eat a heavy breakfast but is there something I can get for you that might agree with your stomach?"

"Um, a couple of saltines and a cup of herbal tea might work."

"Then saltines and herbal tea it is," he said, turning and walking toward the kitchen.

"And Durango?"

He turned back to her. "Yes?"

With her heart pounding she said, "I've made a decision about your proposal. I think we should talk about it."

He nodded. "All right. We can sit and talk at the kitchen table if you'd like."

"Okay," she said, and followed him into the kitchen.

* * *

"So, what have you decided?"

Savannah lifted her head from studying the saltines on the plate in front of her. She had thought things through most of the night but his actions that morning had only solidified her decision.

She set down her cup of tea and met his gaze. "I'm going to take you up on your offer and marry you."

She watched as he sat back in the chair and looked at her with something akin to relief. "But I'd like to explain the reasons for my decision and why I still won't sleep with you," she added.

"All right."

She paused after taking another sip of her tea, and then said, "I think I told you I didn't want to get married just because I was pregnant."

He nodded. "Because of that ordeal with your father, right?"

"Yes."

"How did your parents meet?"

"In college. When Mom showed up at her parents' house with my father over spring break in her senior year of college and announced that she planned to marry him after she graduated and that she was pregnant, my grandparents hit the roof. You see, my maternal grandparents never approved of interracial romances, so they weren't too happy about my parents' relationship."

"I can imagine they weren't."

"Those were certainly not the future plans that Roger and Melissa Billingslea had for their daughter. But nothing would change my mother's mind. She thought

Jeff Claiborne was the best thing since raisin bread and when they couldn't convince her that he wasn't, my grandparents threatened to disown my mother."

"Did that work?"

"No. Mom and Dad were married a few months later. According to Mom things were great at first, but then he lost his job with this big corporation and had to take a job as a traveling salesman. That's when things started going downhill. Dad began changing. However, it took almost fifteen years for her to find out that he'd been living a double life and that he had a mistress as well as another daughter living out West."

Durango took a sip of coffee. Chase had pretty much told him the story one night over a can of beer.

"It wasn't easy for me and Rico growing up," she said, reclaiming his attention. "Some people view children of mixed marriages as if they are from another planet. But with Mom's help we got past all of that, and eventually my grandparents came around. And it didn't take long for them to try to take over our lives. My grandmother even paid for me to go to an all-girls high school. But when it came time for college, I decided to attend one of my own choosing and selected Tennessee State. I'm glad I did."

Durango took another sip of his coffee. He appreciated her sharing that bit of history with him but felt compelled to ask, "So what does any of that has to do with my asking you to marry me…or why you won't sleep with me once we're married?"

Savannah leaned back in her own chair. "More than anything I want my child to be a part of a large, loving family. I also want my child to know that its father is a part of its life because he wants to be, and not because he was forced to be."

A part of Durango reached out to her, feeling her pain caused by a father who hadn't cared. He was not that kind of man and he was glad she knew it. "I will be a good father to our child, Savannah."

She smiled wryly. "I believe that you will, Durango. Now the issue is whether I believe you will be good to me, as well."

He lifted his brow. "You think I'll mistreat you?"

She shook her head. "No, that's not it. I think you are a man who likes women but I don't want to be just another available body to you, Durango. Not to you or to any man."

Durango placed his teacup down, thinking that if she expected an apology from him for all the women he'd enjoyed before meeting her, she could forget it. Like he'd told her before, what was in the past should stay in the past, unless...

His stomach tightened at the thought that she might assume he would mess around on her. He met her gaze. "Are you worried about me being unfaithful during the time we're married?"

She met his gaze. "That has never crossed my mind. Should it have?"

"No."

He was glad it hadn't crossed her mind because even if she did deny him bedroom rights, he would never give her a reason to question his fidelity. He shook his head. If nothing else, since that night they'd spent together, Savannah had shown him that there was definitely a difference between women. Some were only made to bed and some were meant to wed. Savannah, whether she knew it or not, was one of the marrying kind.

She deserved more than a short-term marriage. She deserved a husband who would love and pamper her, for better or for worse and for the rest of her life. A smart man would be good to her and treat her right. Someone who would treat her like a woman of her caliber should be treated. And more importantly, he should be a man who could introduce her to the pleasures men and women shared, pleasures she was denying herself.

He would never forget that night when she had gotten an orgasm. She had acted as if it had been her first one and she hadn't expected the magnitude of the explosion that had ripped through her body. And now he was glad he had shared that with her. But he wanted to share other things with her, as well. And she was wrong if she thought them sleeping together would just be for his benefit. Somehow he had to convince her it would be for her benefit, as well. She needed to understand that a woman has needs just like a man. If nothing else, he needed to prove that to her.

But now was not the time to make waves. He was fairly certain there would be opportunities for what he had in mind before and after their wedding, and he planned to take advantage of both.

"I think of you as more than an available body, Savannah," he said truthfully. "And I'm sorry that you see things that way. In my book, there's nothing wrong with men and women who like and respect each other satisfying their needs, needs they might not be able to control...especially when they're alone together."

He sighed. She was listening to everything he said yet he could tell his discussion of needs was foreign to her. She might have experienced wanting and desire in her lifetime, but she hadn't had to tackle the full-fledged need that sent some women out to shop for certain types of sex toys.

He studied her, watched how her fingertips softly stroked the side of her cup. Her light touch made him wish that she would stroke him the same way. He realized that although she had no idea what the gesture was doing to him, he was excruciatingly aware of her. She looked beautiful just sitting there, absorbing his words yet not fully understanding what he meant.

But eventually she would understand.

"However, if you prefer that we don't share a bed during our marriage, then I will abide by your wishes." Even as he said those words, in his heart he intended that in time her wishes would become the same as his.

She smiled, appearing at ease with what he had said. "So I guess the only other thing we need to agree on is when the marriage will take place and where we'll live afterward."

He nodded. "Like I told you, I'm flexible as far as living arrangements. But I think we should get married right away, considering you're already two months along."

Savannah did agree with the need to move forward with their marriage but she didn't want him to have to take a leave of absence from his job because of her. It would be easier for her to move to Montana. She could do freelance work anywhere. He could only work as a ranger here.

"I think I'd rather live out here, if you don't mind."

That surprised him. A city girl in the mountains? "What about your job? I thought as a freelance photographer you traveled a lot, all over the country."

"Yes, but being pregnant will slow down my travels a bit. Besides, I think I'll be able to work something out with my boss, if my moving out here won't be a problem with you."

Durango shook his head, still bemused but pleased. "No, it won't be and I think you'll be able to adjust to the weather."

"I think so, too."

A feeling of happiness—one he wasn't ready to analyze—coiled through him as he thought of getting married to the mother of his child. "So, when can we marry?"

Savannah shrugged. "I'll let you make all the arrangements. Just tell me when and where you want me to show up."

"And then afterward you'll move in here with me?"

"Yes, and we'll remain married until the baby is at least six months old, which is probably the time I'll be going back to work. Is that time period okay with you?"

"Yes, that's okay. And you still prefer a small wedding?"

"Yes, the smaller the better. Like I said, I don't have a problem eloping to Vegas. A lot of hoopla isn't necessary," she said.

Durango smiled at her. "All right. Considering everything, omitting the hoopla is the least I can do."

* * *

Later that day, while Savannah was taking a nap, Durango had a chance to sit down, unwind and think about her decision to marry him.

She understood, as he did, that short-term was short-term. They weren't talking about "until death do us part" or any nonsense like that. They were talking about him being there during the months of her pregnancy, the delivery and the crucial bonding period with his son or daughter.

Hearing about his marriage would be a shocker to everyone since the family all knew he'd never intended to ever settle down. But the one thing he did know was that his mother would be elated. She had initiated a campaign to marry her sons off. Jared had been the first to go down in defeat, and ever since she'd been eyeing him with hope in her eyes. It didn't bother him that Sarah Westmoreland would enjoy the taste of victory, at least for a short while.

No matter how brief it would be, Durango wanted to make his marriage to Savannah special. He thought of a place they could elope to rather than Vegas. His brother Ian had recently sold his riverboat and was now the proud owner of a casino resort on Lake Tahoe. Durango hadn't had a chance to check things out for himself, but he'd heard from his brothers and cousins that Ian's place was pretty nice. Perhaps Lake Tahoe would be a classier destination for his and Savannah's quickie wedding.

A smile touched the corners of his lips. His elopement with Savannah was one that she wouldn't forget.

* * *

Now that her decision had been made, Savannah had to tell someone about it. She would tell the one person with whom she shared all her secrets, her sister, Jessica.

She reached for her cell phone off the nightstand and quickly punched in her sister's number in Atlanta. Jessica answered on the second ring.

"Hello."

"Jess, it's me, Savannah."

"Savannah, how did things go in Montana? What did Durango say when you told him? What are you going to do now that he knows?"

Savannah smiled. She'd known Jessica would be full of questions. "I'm still in Montana. I can't fly out due to a severe snowstorm."

"Where are you staying?"

"With Durango. He offered me a place to stay and I accepted."

"That was nice of him."

"Yes, it was. Besides, we had a lot to talk about. And as for your second question, I think I shocked him when I told him I was pregnant. At first he was in denial but then he came to his senses, and…"

"And?"

"And he asked me to marry him."

"Oh, and what was your answer?"

Savannah knew Jessica's point in asking that question. Jessica knew better than anyone how she felt about marrying as the result of an unexpected pregnancy. Her parents had been a prime example that a marriage based on responsibility rather than love didn't work out. "At first I told him no, and—"

"At first?" Jessica cut in abruptly and asked, "Does that mean you eventually told him yes?"

A slight smile touched Savannah's lips. "Yes, I've decided to marry him, but it's going to be to my baby's advantage and it's only going to be on a temporary basis."

"I don't understand. What's going to be on a temporary basis?"

"Our marriage."

There was a pause and then Jessica said, "Let me get this straight. You and Durango have agreed to marry in name only for just a short while?"

Savannah sighed. "Yes, we've agreed to marry and stay married until our child is at least six months old. That's about the time I'll be ready to return to work full-time."

"And what about you and Durango during this marriage of convenience?"

"What about us?"

"Will the two of you share a bed?"

"No. Our marriage will only be temporary."

"But the two of you will live together? Under the same roof? In the same house? Breathe the same air?"

Savannah frowned, wondering what Jessica was getting at. "Yes. Is there a problem with that?"

"Savannah, the man is a Westmoreland."

Savannah rolled her eyes upward. "And? Am I missing some point here?"

"Think about it, sis. You've slept with him before."

"Yes, and I wasn't fully in my right mind when I did so."

"And you think you won't want him when you're sober?"

"Honestly, Jess, of course I'll want him! Durango is a sexy man. I might not be as sexually active as some women, but I'm not dead, either. A woman would have to be dead or comatose not to notice Durango. I'll admit that I'm attracted to him but that's as far as things are going to go. I can control my urges. I don't have to be intimate with a man, no matter how sexy he is."

"But we're not talking about any man, Savannah, we're talking about a Westmoreland. Trust me, I know the difference. Once you become involved with one, it won't be easy to deny yourself or to walk away later."

"For crying out loud, no matter what you might think, Jessica, he's just a man," Savannah said, intent on making Jessica understand.

"If he was just a man you wouldn't be in the situation you're in now. Okay, you did overindulge in champagne that night, but you can't convince me that you weren't hot for him already. You asked me about him just moments before the wedding, remember? You *were* interested. I even saw the heat in your eyes. Durango had gotten inside your head before you'd taken your first sip of champagne. That should tell you something."

Savannah expelled a breath. "It does tell me something. It tells me that I'm attracted to him. I've already admitted that. But what you don't realize is that now I'm immune to him."

"And what about falling in love?"

"Falling in love? Lord, Jessica, you know I'm immune to that, as well, doubly so thanks to our poor excuse for a father. Besides, if I even thought about falling in love with Durango, which I won't, all it will take is for me to remember that the only thing connecting us is the baby. The only reason I'm even considering marrying him is to give my child the things I never had, exposure to a warm and loving large family, which I believe the Westmorelands are, and to give Durango a chance to bond with our child. He really wants that and I feel good that he does. Our father didn't care. He was too busy playing two women to give us the time of day."

"At some point you have to let all that go, Savannah," Jessica said softly. "You can't let what Jeff Claiborne did or didn't do dictate your life or your future."

Savannah swallowed a lump in her throat. Some things were easier to get past than others. Her father's callousness towards his three kids as well as two good women was one of them. "I can't, Jess, and I honestly don't understand how you can. You lost your mother because of him."

"Yes, but I never thought all men were like him, and neither should you."

When Savannah didn't say anything for a long time, Jessica said, "Savannah?"

"Yes," Savannah answered and then sighed.

"Be careful."

"Be careful of what?"

"Of being surprised by the magnitude of a Westmoreland's charm and appeal. When they decide to lay it on thick, watch out. Whether you want to believe it or not, it's easy to fall in love with a Westmoreland man. Trust me, I know. I never intended to fall in love with Chase, remember? He was supposed to be the enemy.

And now I can't imagine living my life without him. I love him so much."

"And I'm happy for you, Jess. But you and I are different people. I never believed in happy endings—you did. Just accept my decision and know that for me it's the right one. When I walk away, that will be it. No love lost because there isn't any. Durango doesn't love me and I don't love him, but we're willing to come together in a relationship for our child."

There was a lengthy pause and Savannah wasn't sure she had convinced her sister she had nothing to worry about, but she hoped that she had.

"So, when will the wedding take place?"

"I told Durango that considering the circumstances, I don't want a lot of fuss. So we're eloping to Vegas or someplace and then we'll tell everyone afterward. In a few months, when I begin looking like a blimp, they'll figure out why we married, anyway."

"And you're okay with that?"

"Sure, I'm okay with it. And for the time being, be happy for me, Jess."

"I am happy for you. Have you told Jennifer and Rico yet?"

"No, not yet. I'm not telling either of them until after the marriage takes place. I don't want anyone to try to talk me out of it. You're the only one I've told. I don't know if Durango will tell anyone in his family."

"And when is the trip to Vegas?"

"I don't know, but I'm sure it will be soon. Probably in the next couple of weeks. Durango wants us to get married right away. But he's warned me that once his family hears about our marriage that his mother will probably want to do a huge reception. I'm okay with that."

"And knowing Jennifer, she'll want to do one, as well."

"And I'll be fine with that, too. It will be simpler if they combine their efforts and host one party together. Mom met Mrs. Westmoreland at your wedding and they hit it off so I can see them getting together and planning a nice celebration."

"Yes, I can see them doing that. I'm getting excited just thinking about it."

Savannah smiled. "Get as excited as you want, as long as you remember the marriage won't last. I'll come out of this the same way I'm going into it."

"And what way is that?"

"With realistic expectations."

Chapter 7

As soon as Savannah walked out of the bedroom and saw Durango, their gazes met. The instant attraction that was always there between them began sizzling toward a slow burn.

She would love to photograph him, appreciating the image captured through the lens of her camera. She would tuck away the developed pictures and pull them out whenever her wild fantasies kicked into gear.

"How was your nap?"

His question snapped her out of her thoughts. Because she'd gone to sleep right after talking with Jessica, she had closed her eyes with Durango on her mind. She had thought about him, dreamed about him, relived the night they had made love....

"Savannah?"

She quickly realized she hadn't answered him. "The

nap was good. How about if I make dinner tonight? While hunting for saltines the other day I came across all the ingredients I'd need to make spaghetti."

He lifted a concerned eyebrow. "Will that agree with your stomach?"

She chuckled as she dropped down on the sofa, trying to ignore just how sexy he looked with his shoulder leaning against a doorway that separated the living room from the dining area. He was standing with his thumbs hooked in the front pocket of his jeans, and the chambray shirt he was wearing was stretched across his muscular chest.

"In the afternoon everything agrees with my stomach, Durango. It's the mornings that I have to worry about. So how does spaghetti sound?" she asked, hoping her voice didn't contain the sizzle that she felt.

He lifted one shoulder in a shrug. "Great, if you're up to it. That will give me a chance to take a shower. And I need to talk to you about a few things."

Savannah's dark brow lifted, which helped to downplay the fluttering she felt in her stomach. "Talk to me about what?"

"While you were resting I took the liberty of making a few calls and checking on some things. You did say you were leaving all the arrangements to me and would be fine with everything as long as I left out the hoopla."

"Yes, I did."

"Well, I've made wedding plans and want to discuss them with you, to make sure they meet with your approval."

She blinked in surprise. While she'd been napping,

he'd evidently been busy. "Wedding plans? Then we definitely need to talk after your shower."

"All right, I'll be back in a minute." Before turning to leave, he asked, "Are you sure you don't need my help with dinner?"

"No, I can handle things."

"Yes, I'm sure you can," he countered, smiling.

And when he walked out of the room she had a feeling that he'd been hinting at more than just her spaghetti.

"Everything tastes good, Savannah."

"Thank you." She tried looking at anything and everything other than the man sitting across the table from her. Doing so was simply too tempting. After glancing out the window and seeing it was still snowing, she scanned the room and took in the beauty of his kitchen and again mentally admired the setup of everything, including the pots that...

"Are you okay?"

His question forced her to do something she hadn't wanted to do. Look directly at him. The moment she did so she felt fiery tingles move down her spine. "Yes, I'm okay. Why do you ask?"

"No particular reason."

Sitting this close to him she could actually smell his scent, one that was all man. But that didn't compare to how he'd looked when he had entered the kitchen after his shower wearing jeans that hung low on his hips and a shirt he hadn't bothered to button.

"Are you ready to talk about the plans I've made?"

His question pulled her mind back from territory where it had no business going. "Sure."

He stood and began gathering the dishes off the table. "Instead of going to Vegas I thought it would be nice if we went to Lake Tahoe instead."

She raised an eyebrow. "Lake Tahoe?"

"Yes, my brother Ian recently bought a casino resort there. I heard it's truly spectacular and I would like to take you there."

"Lake Tahoe," she said again, savoring the idea. She had visited the area a few years ago and had thought it was beautiful. She smiled across the table at Durango. "All right. That sounds like a winner to me, so when do you want to do it?"

"Day after tomorrow."

"What!"

He chuckled at her startled expression. "I think Friday would be a perfect day for us to leave for Lake Tahoe. Starting today the weather will begin improving and tomorrow you can—"

"Hold up. Time out. Cut." She caught her breath for a moment and then said, "Durango, there's no way I can marry you on Friday. I have to go back home and take care of a few things. I have to plan for the wedding. I have to—"

"We're eloping, remember? And besides, I thought you didn't want a lot of hoopla."

He had her there. "I don't, but I hadn't thought about getting married *this* soon."

"The sooner the better, don't you think? You're a couple of months already. Jayla began really showing by the fourth month. I remember when I went home for my father's birthday during Easter and she was huge, almost as big as a house."

Savannah raised her eyes to the ceiling, hoping he had the good sense not to mention such a thing to Jayla. Even pregnant women were sensitive when it came to their weight. "She was carrying twins, Durango, for heaven's sake."

"And how do you know you aren't? Multiple births run in my family. My father is the twin brother of Chase's father and both of them had twins. Then Uncle Corey had triplets, so anything is possible."

That wasn't what Savannah wanted to hear. She much preferred having one healthy baby, but of course she would gladly accept whatever she got. "I couldn't possibly get ready for Lake Tahoe by Friday. I didn't bring any clothes here with me and I would need to purchase some things."

"There're several stores in Bozeman that will have everything you need. Tomorrow can be a shopping day."

Savannah felt hurried and decided to let him know it. "I feel like you're rushing me," she said briskly.

A smile touched his lips. "In a way I am. Now that we've decided to do this, why wait? I want us to marry as soon as possible."

She couldn't help wondering why. Did he think she would change her mind or something? She was carrying his baby, and until she'd shown up and announced that fact, he hadn't been interested in marriage. She had thought she would have at least a couple of weeks, maybe even a month before they actually eloped. She'd assumed she would leave tomorrow to return to Philadelphia and they would make plans for the wedding over the phone. This was definitely not what she had expected.

"Savannah, why are you hesitating? We should move forward and get things over with."

Get things over with? Well, he certainly didn't have to make it sound like marrying her was something being forced upon him. No one had asked him to do it. Getting married was his idea and not hers. She was about to tell him just that when he did something she hadn't expected. He tugged her hand and pulled her out of her chair, wrapping his arms around her and pulling her against him.

Startled, her head came up the moment her body pressed against his. Very little space separated them. A smile touched the corners of his mouth for a few seconds before he said softly, "You're trying to be difficult, aren't you?"

She swallowed. It wasn't easy to gaze into the dark eyes holding hers captive. "Not intentionally."

"Then why the cold feet? I've already checked the airlines and there are plenty of flights available, and I've talked to my brother Ian."

At her frown he said, "And yes, I told him we decided to get married, but I didn't tell him why. He said that he would love to have us as his guests for the weekend. He's making all the necessary arrangements."

He studied her features for a moment then asked, "Are you having second thoughts about eloping, Savannah? Do you prefer having a small wedding here so that we could invite our families?"

"No," she said quickly. "I still prefer keeping things

simple. I guess I'm hesitating because it never dawned on me that I might be returning to Philadelphia a married woman."

"Then I guess you aren't prepared to return to Philadelphia with a husband in tow, either."

His words were a shocker. "You're going back with me?"

"Yes. You'll have to introduce me to your family sometime."

Her head was reeling from the thought of him returning to Philadelphia with her. "You've already met my family at Chase and Jessica's wedding."

"Yes, but I met them as Chase's cousin, not as your husband. Besides, we'll be newlyweds and it will seem strange for us not to be together."

"Yes, but—"

"And I want to take you home to Atlanta, as well, to meet my family. Not as Jessica's sister but as my wife. Although everyone will probably reach their own conclusions as to why we eloped and got married, it's really none of their business. We'll tell them that we met at the wedding, fell madly in love and decided to get married."

Savannah couldn't help but smile at Durango's ridiculous statement. There was no way anyone would believe such a thing, and from the mischievous grin touching his lips, he knew that, as well.

"Let's keep them guessing," Durango said, chuckling. "Our decision doesn't concern anyone but us."

Savannah couldn't help but agree with that, especially after her conversation with Jessica. Everything he was saying made sense. Now that they had decided to marry, why prolong things? "Fine, if you think we can pull it off, then Friday is fine."

"Good. And there's something else you'll need to do tomorrow."

"What?"

"Visit the doctor in town. I've already made you an appointment for tomorrow morning."

Savannah pulled back slightly and frowned. "Why? Don't you believe I'm pregnant? Or do you want to have it verified before going through with the marriage ceremony?"

"No, that's not it," he said tightly. "I just want the doctor to check you out to make sure you're okay. You gave me a scare this morning and I just want to make sure you and the baby are fine."

Savannah met his gaze and saw the sincerity in his eyes and knew he had spoken the truth. "Okay," she finally said. "I'll go to the doctor for a checkup if it will make you happy."

"It will," he said. "And thank you."

Savannah drew in a deep breath. She needed space from Durango and took a step back. "I'll get started on the dishes and—"

"No, you did the cooking so it's only fair that I clean up the kitchen."

"Durango, I can manage to—"

"Savannah, that's the way it's going to be. Just relax. You'll have more than enough to do over the next couple of days, and it seems the weather is going to cooperate."

She glanced out the window and saw it had stopped snowing. This was the break in the weather she'd been waiting for. But now, instead of packing to return home to Philly, she'd be preparing for a wedding.

"If you're sure that you can handle the dishes by yourself, then I need to call and talk with my boss. I had told him I would be back in the office on Monday."

"Okay." When she turned to leave he said, "And Savannah?"

She turned back around. "Yes?"

"I planned for us to stay in the same suite but it has two bedrooms. Will that be a problem?"

She swallowed deeply as her gaze held his. "No, that won't be a problem as long as there will be two bedrooms."

The smile that suddenly touched his lips made her stomach flutter and made heat flow all over her. "Then we're all set. I'll call the airlines and book us a flight."

They were eloping to Lake Tahoe.

Durango's announcement of last night was the main reason for Savannah's sleepless night. And the magnitude of it must have shocked her system because she had awakened the next morning without any feelings of nausea.

However, it seemed that Durango intended to be prepared because when she opened her eyes, she found him sitting in the chair beside her bed with a plate of saltines and a cup of tea all ready for her.

"Good morning."

The sensuous sound of his voice so early in the morning sent shivers all through her, and the concerned smile that touched his lips wasn't helping matters, either.

"Good morning," she said, pulling herself up in bed. Although she appreciated his kindness and thoughtfulness, she would have much preferred if he had given her a minute or two to freshen up. She would have liked to comb her hair and wash the sleep from her eyes.

"Are you feeling okay this morning?"

"Yes, thanks for asking. For some reason I'm not feeling nauseated." She decided not to tell him her suspicions as to the reason why.

"I'm glad to hear that." He then nodded his head toward the fireplace. "I tried keeping it warm in here during the night."

Her gaze followed his to the roaring fireplace. "Thank you." Because she hadn't been able to sleep, she had been aware of each and every time he had come into her room and checked the heat.

"This is going to be a busy day for us since we'll be flying out first thing the next morning."

Savannah's gaze returned to his. "I imagine that it will be."

"After the doctor's visit, I'll take you to the mall. I figure you'll probably want to shop alone, so I'll use that time to pay McKinnon a visit and then come back later for you. You do remember my best friend McKinnon, don't you?"

"Yes, I remember him." She definitely remembered McKinnon Quinn, just like she was sure a number of other women would. With his beautiful golden-brown complexion and thick ponytail, she had admired his handsome features that reflected his mixed-race ancestry. She had actually blinked twice when she'd first seen him because the man had been simply gorgeous. But even with McKinnon's striking good looks, it had been Durango who had caught her eye and held it.

"I guess I'll leave you alone so you can get dressed now," Durango said, standing and placing the tea and saltines on the nightstand.

It took fierce concentration to keep Savannah's mind on their conversation and not on Durango as he got out of the chair. He was dressed in a pair of jeans, a pullover sweater and a pair of black leather boots. She didn't care how many times she saw him dressed that way, but each time his appearance grabbed her attention. "Thanks for the crackers and tea," she said.

Durango smiled. "Don't mention it."

Savannah's breath caught in her throat from that one smile, and when he turned his head to glance out the window, she grabbed the opportunity to study him some more. His eyes were focused on the mountains as if weighing a problem of some kind, and she wondered if perhaps he thought the good weather wouldn't last. When he turned his head he caught her staring at him and for a brief breath of a moment she felt the sizzle that always seemed to hang in the air between them.

"I'd better be going. There's a couple of things I need to check on outside before we leave," he said and, as if tearing his gaze from hers, he glanced over at the fireplace. "That thing keeps this room pretty hot, doesn't it?"

She followed his gaze. It was on the tip of her tongue to say that at the moment she thought it was him, and not the fireplace, that made the room pretty hot. Instead she said, "Yes, it does."

Savannah had to admit, however, that she did enjoy

sleeping in a room with a fireplace. She had gotten used to the smell of burning firewood, the sound of kindling crackling as it caught fire, and more than anything, she liked the comforting warmth the fire provided.

"Do you think you'll be able to eat any food this morning?" Durango asked, interrupting her thoughts.

She frowned, deciding not to chance it. "I'd better not try it. Those saltines and tea will do just fine. Thanks."

Moments after Durango had left the room, Savannah sat on the edge of her bed thinking about all the things she had to do to get ready for tomorrow. Just thinking about everything made her feel exhausted. But she was determined to get through the day and in a way, she was looking forward to her visit to the doctor.

A quiver raced through her stomach at the thought that Durango would be there, too, sharing the experience with her.

Chapter 8

"So how's the baby?" Durango asked the doctor nervously.

Lying flat on her back on the examination table, Savannah shifted her gaze to Durango, who was standing beside her. She heard the deep concern in his voice and saw how his eyebrows came together in a tense expression.

She then switched her gaze to Dr. Patrina Foreman. Dr. Foreman was a lot younger than Savannah had expected. She was a very attractive woman and she appeared to be about twenty-eight. Within minutes of talking to her, Savannah was convinced that even though she might be young, she was definitely competent. Dr. Foreman had explained that her mother, grandmother and great-grandmother had been midwives, but that she had decided to complete medical school to offer her patients the best of both worlds. She could practice modern medicine as well as provide the kind of care and personal attention that midwives gave.

Dr. Foreman lifted her gaze from applying the gel to Savannah's stomach and smiled before saying, "Listen to this for a moment and then tell me what you think."

And then they heard it, the soft thumping sound of their child's heartbeat, for the first time. Hearing the steady little drumbeat did something to Savannah, touched her in a way she hadn't expected and made her realize that she really and truly was going to have a baby.

Tears, something else she hadn't expected, welled up in her eyes and she glanced up at Durango and knew he was just as moved by the sound as she was. He reached out and firmly touched her shoulder, and at that moment she knew that no matter how they did or didn't feel about each other, her pregnancy was real and they were listening to valid proof of just how real it was. There was no doubt that hearing the sound was a life-altering experience for both of them.

"You hadn't heard it before?" Durango asked softly.

"No. This is my first time."

"There's nothing like parents hearing the fetal heartbeat for the first time," Dr. Foreman said quietly. "There's always something special and exciting about it. The baby's heartbeat is strong and sounds healthy to me."

Durango chuckled. "Yes, it does, doesn't it? This is all rather new to me and I was kind of worried."

"And you have every right to be concerned, but it seems mother and baby are doing just fine," Dr. Foreman replied, removing the instrument from Savannah's stomach. "Make sure that you continue to take your prenatal vitamins, Savannah."

"And what about all that vomiting she's been doing?" Durango asked, wanting to know.

Dr. Foreman glanced at him. "Morning sickness is caused by the sudden increase in hormones during pregnancy and is very common early in the pregnancy, but it's usually gone by the fourth month." She smiled at Savannah and said, "So, hopefully you won't have to suffer too much longer."

"I prefer she didn't suffer at all. And what about the baby? Will it be hurt by it?" Durango asked, in a tone that said he really needed Dr. Foreman's assurance.

"It shouldn't, but of course it can become a problem if Savannah can't keep any foods or fluids down or if she begins to lose weight. Otherwise, morning sickness is a positive sign that the pregnancy is progressing."

Dr. Foreman then opened a drawer and pulled out a package and handed it to Savannah. "This might help. It's the same type of acupressure wristbands that doctors give out on cruise ships to prevent seasickness. A lot of my patients swear that wearing it helps to reduce the morning sickness."

For the next ten to fifteen minutes, Dr. Foreman answered all of Savannah and Durango's questions. Then she congratulated them when Durango mentioned they were getting married.

"I really like her," Savannah told Durango when they left the doctor's office. "And I hadn't expected her to be so young."

Durango smiled as he ushered Savannah out the

building to where he had parked his truck. "Yes, Trina is young but I've heard that she is one of the best. She was born and raised around these parts and her husband Perry was the sheriff. He was killed a few years ago in the line of duty while trying to arrest an escaped convict."

"Oh, how awful."

Durango nodded. "Yes, it was. Perry was a good person and everyone liked and respected him. He and Trina had been childhood sweethearts."

Durango opened the door to his truck and assisted Savannah in settling in and buckling her seat belt. "Was it a coincidence or did you deliberately buy this particular SUV?" she asked, grinning. It was ironic that his name was Durango and that was also the model of the vehicle that he drove.

He chuckled as he snapped her seat belt in place. "Not a coincidence. I thought I'd milk it for all it's worth since Dodge decided to name a vehicle after me," he said arrogantly, giving her that smile that made her stomach spin. "Besides, we're both known to give smooth and unforgettable rides," he added softly while gazing into her eyes.

For a moment Savannah couldn't speak since she of all people knew about the smoothness, as well as the intensity, of Durango's ride. The very thought was generating earth-shattering memories of the time he had pleasured her in bed.

She watched as he walked around the front of the truck to get into the driver's seat. "You're taking me to the mall now?" she asked, trying to get her heartbeat back on track. If she was having trouble keeping her thoughts off him now, she didn't want to think how things would be once they were married.

"Yes, I'm taking you to the Gallatin Valley Mall," Durango said, pulling out of the parking lot and returning her attention. "You should be able to find everything you need there. Do you want me to stay and shop with you?"

"No, I'll be fine," she quickly said, knowing she needed her space for a while. "If there's one thing a woman knows how to do on her own it's shop."

Stealing a glance at him she couldn't help wondering how he really felt about marrying her and suddenly needed to know that he was still okay with their plans.

"Durango?"

"Yes?"

The truck had come to a stop at a traffic light and she knew his gaze was on her but she refused to look at him. Instead she looked straight ahead. "Are you sure getting married is what you really want to do?" she asked as calmly as she could.

"Yes, I'm sure," he said in a voice so low and husky, Savannah couldn't help but turn to meet his gaze. Then in a way she wished she hadn't when she saw the deep, dark intensity in his eyes. He then smiled and that smile touched her, and she couldn't help but return it.

"If I wasn't before, Savannah, I am now, especially after listening to our baby's heartbeat. God, that was an awesome experience. And according to Trina, it has all the vital organs it will need already. It's not just a cluster of cells but a real human being. A being that we created and I want to connect to it more so than ever."

Savannah sighed in relief. The last thing she wanted was for him to ever regret marrying her. She was satisfied that he wouldn't.

Bozeman, one of the most diverse small towns in the Rocky Mountains, was known for its hospitality and was proud of its numerous ski resorts. It was a city that attracted not only tourists, but also families wanting to plant their roots in a place that offered a good quality of life.

Durango drove straight to the mall and parked the truck. He even took the time to walk Savannah inside, saying there were a couple of things he needed to purchase for himself. He gave her his cell phone number in case she finished shopping early so she could reach him.

Once they parted ways, Savannah became a woman on a mission as she went from store to store. Within a few hours she had purchased everything she needed and had indulged herself by getting a few things she really hadn't needed, like a few sexy nightgowns she had purchased from Victoria's Secret. It wasn't as if Durango would ever see her in any of them, but still, she couldn't help herself. She liked buying sexy things.

A few hours later Savannah had made all of her purchases, and contacted Durango on his cell phone. He told her he had just pulled into the parking lot and would meet her at the food court in the center of the mall. He suggested that they grab dinner at a really good restaurant there.

She had been in the food court for only a few minutes when she glanced across the way and saw him. Her pulse quickened. There was no way she could discount the fact that he was a devastatingly handsome man, and she wasn't the only female who noticed. As he crossed the mall in long, confident strides, several heads turned to watch him, and for a moment Savannah felt both pride and a tinge of jealousy.

She quickly dismissed the latter emotion. He wasn't hers and she wasn't his. But still, as he continued to walk toward her, closing the distance separating them, she saw the look in his eyes, deciphered the way he was looking at her with that steady dark gaze of his. It was the same way he had looked at her the night of Chase and Jessica's wedding.

And as if it was the most natural thing to do, when he reached her he leaned down and kissed her. Surprised, she returned the brief, but thorough kiss while her heart thumped ominously in her chest.

"Did you get a lot accomplished today?" he asked softly against her moist lips.

Not able to speak at first, she nodded. Then she said breathlessly, "Yes, I think I have everything I'm going to need. And I think I found an appropriate dress for tomorrow."

Durango chuckled as he took her hand in his and led her toward the restaurant where they would dine. "I'm sure it's more than appropriate. I bet it's perfect and I can't wait to see you in it."

Later that night while packing, Savannah had to admit that it had been a simply wonderful day. First the visit to the doctor and then her shopping trip to the mall and last, having dinner with Durango at that restaurant. The food had been delicious and Durango's company had been excellent. Over a candlelight dinner he had told her about his partnership with McKinnon's horse farm and how well it was doing.

Closing her luggage, Savannah smiled when she recalled the message Jessica had left on Durango's answering machine, telling them to expect her and Chase at Lake Tahoe tomorrow. A part of Savannah had been both elated and relieved that elopement or not, a stubborn Jessica would not let her get married without her sister being there. Durango also seemed pleased that his cousin was coming, as well.

She looked up when she heard the knock on her bedroom door. "Come in."

Durango entered, dressed in a pair of jogging pants and a T-shirt with a towel wrapped around his neck. "I was about to get into the hot tub and was wondering if you would like to join me."

"But it's cold outside."

He smiled ruefully. "Yes, but once you get into the tub you'll forget how cold it is. It's the best thing to stimulate sore, aching muscles. Try it. I guarantee that you'll like it."

Savannah thought of all the walking she had done earlier that day at the mall and decided a soak in the hot tub sounded good. But still...

"Is it large enough for the both of us to fit comfortably?" The thought of being crammed into a hot tub with Durango was too much to think about.

"Yes, it can hold five to six people without any problems."

She nodded. Good. He could stay on his side of the tub and she could stay on hers. "All right, then let me change into a swimming suit." She had bought one that day at the mall and had to dig it out from the suitcase.

After Durango left Savannah changed her clothes, thankful that the swimming suit she had purchased was a one-piece and wasn't overly provocative. The attraction between her and Durango was bad enough without adding fuel to an already hot fire.

"For a moment I thought I was going to have to come back inside to get you."

She chuckled and quickly padded on bare feet across the deck to the hot tub. "Sorry. My mom called right when I was about to come outside."

His eyebrows lifted. "Did you tell her about our plans for tomorrow?"

"Yes," Savannah said as she quickly dispensed with her robe and eased inside the tub, deliberately sinking as far down as she could and letting the "ahh" sound ease from her lips. Once she was settled in a comfortable position she said, "I didn't give her a lot of details and told her we would have a long discussion when she returns from Paris. But she is very astute in reading between the lines, so I'm sure she has a pretty good idea why we're having a quick wedding."

Durango studied her eyes since her face was the only part of her he could see. Water covered her entire body, from her shoulders to her toes. She was almost completely submerged.

"Did your mom know we'd been involved?" he asked, wishing he had X-ray vision to see her body through the water. He had caught a glimpse of her curves when she removed her robe. Although she had tried to be quick about it and not draw attention to herself, she had failed miserably. Her swimsuit was sexy, and the cut was a snug fit that showed off her shapely thighs and bottom.

"If she does it's not because I've told her anything," Savannah said, cutting into his thoughts. "However, she did mention when we met for lunch last month that she couldn't help noticing that we were having a hard time keeping our eyes off each other at the wedding." She decided not to add that her mother had also noticed when the two of them had left the reception together.

"Hey, this feels nice," she said, liking how the hot water seemed to penetrate her tired muscles. "And you were right. I don't feel how cold the temperature is."

"I'm glad. And by the way, you can stop hiding under the water. I promise not to jump your bones if you do," he said slowly, grinning.

She met his gaze and smiled sheepishly. "I didn't think you would. I was merely making sure I wouldn't freeze to death."

"And now that you know that you won't?"

She took a deep breath and eased more of her body out of the water. When the warm, bubbly, swirling water receded to her waist like it did his, she felt a sizzling sensation flow down her spine and settle in the pit of her stomach. He was staring at her. Her bathing suit was decent, but it was fashioned in a style that revealed the fullness of her breasts.

"I like your swimming suit. At least what I've seen of it so far," he said. His voice was low and sexy.

"Thanks." She then glanced around. "So what made you decide to put this hot tub in?"

He gave her an intense look, knowing she was trying to change the subject. "It was an easy decision since I was taking advantage of one of the natural hot springs located on my property."

"Oh, there are others?"

He grinned, knowing he had told her that already. "Yes, but don't expect me to show them to you tonight," he said, leaning back against the wall of the tub and deliberately stretching out one of his legs. He made it seem like an accident, an innocent mistake when his thigh touched her thigh. She gasped and slowly eased back to give him more space.

"Going someplace?" he asked with a totally innocent look on his face.

"No, I'm just trying to give you more room."

"I don't need more room."

"Could have fooled me," she muttered under her breath.

"You say something?"

She glanced over at him. "No, just thinking out loud."

Before she could blink he had pushed away from the wall and had glided over to her, putting his face inches from hers. "Now what did you say, Savannah?"

Savannah pulled in a sharp intake of breath. Not only was Durango's face near hers, but she could feel the heat from his entire body. He was within touching distance. He was making the already hot water that much hotter.

"Did I ever tell you how much I like kissing you, Savannah?" he asked.

A shudder of desire ran through her, first starting

at her toes and easing its way to the top of her head. "I don't recall if you have or not," she said silkily, watching his lips inch even closer.

"Well, let me go on record and say that I do. You have a unique taste," he said in a deep, husky tone.

"I do?"

"Yes. It's so tantalizingly sweet that I can feast on it for hours."

Another shudder ran through her. "No man has ever told me that before."

He smiled. "Then maybe you haven't kissed the right man."

"Maybe."

"And although you haven't given me bedroom rights after we're married, you haven't denied me kissing privileges, have you?" he asked in a sensual tone.

"Ahh, no." *But maybe I should,* she quickly thought.

"Good, because I'm going to enjoy kissing you whenever I can."

She held her breath when he leaned forward, wrapped his arms around her waist and took the tip of his tongue and began slowly, sensuously, passionately tracing the outline of her mouth.

She moaned deep and slowly emitted his name from her lips just moments before he slipped his tongue inside her mouth. She returned his kiss as their tongues mingled and stroked each other. The signals they exchanged were intimately familiar, and all it took was the shift of their legs to bring their bodies together, making her feel the very essence of his heat. She knew exactly what that huge, hot, engorged body part pressed against her midsection meant.

Savannah wanted to pull back, stop playing with fire and avoid the temptation, but she couldn't. Her legs felt weak, her thighs were quivering and her mouth was definitely being branded the Durango way. And when he reached and touched the tip of her breasts through the soft, clingy latex of her swimsuit, she almost lost her bearing. She would have done so if his hands weren't still around her waist, holding her close.

He pulled back slightly and whispered hotly against her moist lips, "I also like touching you. You feel hot all over."

It was on the tip of her tongue to say that thanks to him she *was* hot all over, but at that moment he leaned forward and took her tongue into his mouth again, ending further conversation. Her heartbeat kicked up a notch when his hand moved from her waist and slid lower and when he shifted their bodies so he could sufficiently caress the area between her legs, through her swimsuit, she almost cried out at the sensations he elicited.

"I know this part of you is off-limits," he said in a deep, throaty voice that sent even more heat running through her. "But I can tell it wants me. It wants how I can make it feel, Savannah. It's hot for me, the same way I'm hot for you. For two months I've laid in my bed at night and thought about us, how we were that night, how good we were together and how good we could be again."

While he was talking, drumming up memories, his thumb continued to caress her, driving her mad, insane with desire and her head fell forward to his chest, her breathing became choppy and her mind was overtaken by passion.

"It's going to be hard for us to share space being such passionate people and not want to do something about it, don't you think?" he asked hotly against her ear.

"Yes, I'm sure it will be," she agreed, easing the words from between her lips.

"But I'm honor bound to abide by your wishes and I will…unless you change your mind and allow me to do otherwise. And then there won't be any stopping me, Savannah."

Savannah didn't know what to say. And when she thought of what would happen if she ever changed her mind, she thought while she was conscious of the movement of his fingers on her body, a needy ache flamed to life between her legs. And when a shudder passed through her again, igniting every cell in her body, sending sensations rushing through her, she called out his name. With just the use of his fingers he had pushed her over the edge, giving her the big "O" without penetrating her.

Durango gently pulled on her hair to bring her face back to his and he kissed her, literally drank his name from her lips, as his hungry and demanding mouth devoured her, giving her a taste of what she would miss, and giving him a thorough taste of her.

Savannah pulled her mouth away from his when breathing became a necessity. The first thing she noticed was that sometime during their kiss she had wrapped her legs around him. She didn't remember doing it but Durango *had* been kissing her senseless and the only thing she did remember was the magnitude of that kiss, the explosiveness of it.

She inhaled deeply. Jessica was right. This wasn't a regular man. This was a Westmoreland and they didn't do anything halfway. Her pregnancy proved it. What other man could make a woman scream his name in ecstasy while still wearing clothes?

She looked up at him to say something and he leaned forward and kissed her again. This kiss was slow, lingering and just as hot as the kisses that he'd lavished on her before.

When he pulled back, his dark eyes held her with deep intensity. His voice was strained when he said, "I meant what I said, Savannah. I want to make love to you again, but unless you give me the word, kissing is as far as it will go between us."

She nodded and closed her eyes, knowing he would respect the boundaries she had set. But she also knew that he intended to use his kisses to break down her defenses. When she felt him easing away, she opened her eyes and watched him get out of the hot tub. His wet swimming trunks clung to his body like a second layer of skin, and the evidence of his desire for her was apparent.

He was silent as he toweled off, watching her watch him. He smiled knowingly. "Tomorrow is our wedding day and regardless of the reason that brought us to this point, Savannah, I intend to make it a special day for you. For the both of us."

Moments later when the patio door closed behind him, Savannah sank deeper into the water, already feeling the loss of Durango's heat. Whether she wanted to or not, a part of her couldn't help but look forward to tomorrow, the day when—even though it would be temporary—she would become Mrs. Durango Westmoreland.

Chapter 9

The following day when they pulled up to the entrance of the Rolling Cascade Casino and Resort, Savannah was at a loss for words. As a photographer she had traveled to many picturesque sites, but she thought nothing could have prepared her for the drive from Reno to Ian Westmoreland's exclusive resort on Lake Tahoe.

She and Durango had flown into Reno and had rented a car for the trip to Lake Tahoe. They decided to take what he described as the scenic route; the panoramic view was spectacular and more than once she had asked Durango to stop the car so she could take pictures of the snowcapped mountains, the enormous boulders and the clusters of shrubs and pine trees that grew close to the lake.

Just minutes from Stateline, Nevada, the Rolling Cascade looked different from the other sprawling casinos they had passed. Ian's resort was a beautifully designed building that overlooked Lake Tahoe and was surrounded by a number of shops, clothing stores and restaurants.

Durango explained that the Cascade had been vacant for almost a year after the previous owner had been using the casino as a front for an illegal operation. When it had gone up for sale, Ian and his investors were ready to bring their casino business on land. Hurricane Katrina had made it impossible to continue his riverboat casino along the Mississippi from New Orleans to Memphis.

Ian had remodeled the casino to be a small self-contained resort. Open for just six months, the resort had already shown amazing profits and was giving plenty of stiff competition to the likes of the Las Vegas–style casinos situated nearby.

"This place is simply beautiful," Savannah said when Durango brought the car to a stop. Within seconds, the resort's staff were there to greet them and to assist with their luggage.

Durango smiled as he placed a muscled arm around her shoulders as they walked inside the building. Inside the Cascade was just as impressive as the outside. Durango stopped and glanced around, letting out a low whistle. Moments later he said, "Ian really did it up this time. I think he's found his calling."

"I think so, too, brother."

Both Durango and Savannah turned to find a smiling Ian standing directly behind them. He gave Durango an affectionate bear hug and leaned over and brushed a kiss on Savannah's cheek. "I'm glad you like what you see," Ian said and smiled.

"We do," Savannah replied, returning his smile and thinking that all the Westmoreland brothers and cousins resembled each other. They were all tall, dark and handsome; however, Ian's neatly trimmed short beard added a rakish look to his face. "And I appreciate you having us here," she added.

Ian grinned. "No reason to thank me. It's about time Durango came down from the mountains and went someplace other than Atlanta. Besides, it's not every day that a Westmoreland gets married. Come on and let me get the both of you checked in. I have the wedding chapel reserved for five o'clock. That will give you time to rest and relax a bit before the ceremony."

"Have Chase and Jessica arrived yet?" Durango asked as he and Savannah followed Ian over to the check-in desk.

"Yes, they got in a few hours ago and last time I checked they were getting ready to take a stroll around the shops."

A huge smile then touched Ian's lips. "And I have a surprise for you, Durango."

"What?"

"I got a call from McKinnon. That appointment he had scheduled for today got canceled and he was able to get a flight out and will be arriving just in time for the wedding."

Durango smiled, pleased that his best friend would make the wedding after all.

Less than ten minutes later Durango and Savannah were stepping inside what Ian had described as the owner's suite, which to Savannah's way of thinking looked more like an exclusive condo with its three bedrooms, two full baths, gigantic fireplace, kitchen and beautiful balcony that overlooked Lake Tahoe.

Savannah gave an inward sigh of relief at seeing the three bedrooms, although one of them she assumed due to its size was intended to be a master suite. She didn't want a repeat of the temptation she had faced the previous night in the hot tub with Durango, and was grateful for the spaciousness of the place.

"I'll let you choose whichever bedroom you prefer," Durango said, closing the door behind him.

She turned around and smiled sheepishly. "Because of all the stuff I brought along with me, I'll take the biggest of the three bedrooms, if you don't mind."

He chuckled. "No, I don't mind." He glanced at his watch. "We have a few hours to kill. Do you want to take a walk around the lake?"

"I'd love to, and it was nice of Ian to let us use this suite, wasn't it?"

Durango grinned. "Yes, he can be a nice enough guy when he wants to be. But there are times when he's a pain in the ass."

Savannah knew he was kidding. Anyone who hung around the Westmorelands for any length of time could tell they were a close-knit group. "Give me a few minutes to freshen up, okay?"

"Sure."

When she reached her bedroom, Durango called out to her.

"Ian mentioned there's a private hot tub on the twelfth floor if we wanted to try it out," he said.

Images of the two of them in the hot tub last night and the heated kiss they had shared floated into Savannah's mind. Just the thoughts made a tingly feeling settle in the pit of her stomach. "I think I'll pass on that."

"You sure?" he asked, grinning, making her remember in blatant details their hot-tub antics of the night before.

"I'm positive."

"If I didn't know the score I'd think you and Durango were excited about getting married."

Savannah glanced at her sister as she slipped into her wedding dress. She and Durango had run into Chase and Jessica while touring the grounds around the lake. Jessica had suggested that Savannah get dressed for the ceremony in the suite she and Durango shared. Durango would dress in Chase and Jessica's room. That way the bride and groom wouldn't see each other in their wedding attire before they were married.

"You're imagining things. Durango and I came to an agreement to do what's in the best interest of our child. That's the only reason we're getting married."

Jessica Claiborne Westmoreland laughed, reached out and hugged her sister and said, "Hey, whatever, I still think the two of you look good together."

Savannah looked at Jessica in mild exasperation. "And I told you not to get any ideas, Jess."

"If you don't want me to get any ideas, then how about explaining these?" she said, gesturing to all the sexy nighties Savannah had unpacked earlier. "If these aren't for Durango's enjoyment then who are they for?" she asked, picking up one of the negligees.

"For me. You know how much I like wearing sexy things to bed," Savannah said, reaching out and taking the teddy from Jessica and tossing it back on the bed. "Since Durango and I won't be sharing a bed, what I sleep in is no business of his."

Jessica tipped her head, regarded Savannah thoughtfully and said, "You still haven't gotten it yet, have you?"

"Gotten what?"

"The fact that a Westmoreland man isn't anyone to play with. How long do you think the two of you will be able to fight this intense attraction? Even today he was looking at you when he thought you weren't looking and you were looking at him when you thought he wasn't looking. The two of you were doing the same thing at my wedding."

"And your point?"

"The point is that you know what happened as soon as the two of you were alone and behind closed doors."

"We indulged in too much champagne that night, Jess. That won't happen this time because I don't plan to consume any alcohol while I'm pregnant."

"There's another way a woman can get tipsy, Savannah. There is such a thing as being overtaken by sexual chemistry and losing your head," she said, letting her gaze stray to the nighties once again.

"I don't plan to lose my head."

"What about your heart?"

"That, either. Now tell me how I look."

Jessica glanced up and fell silent. She had seen the

short, white lace dress on the hanger and thought it looked okay, but on Savannah the dress looked like it had been made just for her, and just for this special occasion. Savannah looked so beautiful it almost brought tears to Jessica's eyes.

"Well, what do you think?" Savannah asked when Jessica didn't say anything.

"I think that you look simply beautiful and I'm sorry that Jennifer isn't here to see you," Jessica said, almost choking with emotion.

"Hey, knock it off, Jess. This wedding is no big deal. The only reason we're getting married is because I'm pregnant...remember?"

Jessica reached out to pick up another skimpy piece of lingerie only to have Savannah shoo her hand away. She chuckled and then asked, "So when are you going to let Rico know you're a married woman?"

Savannah closed her luggage with a firm click. "Durango and I will be calling and telling everybody the news when we get back. We had hoped to take off for Philly and Atlanta next week to drop the bomb in person, but because one of the park rangers is out on medical leave, it will be another month before Durango can take time off from work. Maybe that's just as well since it will give everyone a chance to get used to the idea."

"I can't wait to see the Westmorelands' reaction when they hear the news. Durango is the last person anyone would have thought would marry."

"Yes, but let me remind you again that the only reason he's doing so now is because I'm pregnant, and don't you forget it."

Jessica laughed. "After seeing all those sexy things, the big question is whether after this weekend you'll forget it."

Durango turned around the moment he felt Savannah's presence in the wedding chapel. Immediately his breath caught at the sight of how strikingly beautiful she looked in her dress. It was perfect. Normally you can't improve on perfection, but in Savannah's case she had by adding a string of pearls around her neck. The way her hair shimmered like a silk curtain around her face made her hazel eyes that much more striking. She was a vision straight out of any man's fantasy.

"Your bride is a beautiful woman, Rango. I'm not sure that's a good sign."

Durango arched an eyebrow and turned his gaze from Savannah to the man standing by his side, who'd leaned closer to whisper in his ear. McKinnon Quinn was the only person to whom he had told the real reason he was getting married, although he was sure Chase knew, as well. "Somehow I'll deal with it, McKinnon."

McKinnon chuckled. "I'm glad it's you who'll be doing the dealing and not me. A woman that beautiful might cause me to have a few weak moments."

Durango hoped like hell that he would be a stronger man than McKinnon when and if those moments occurred. He glanced over at Chase and Ian, wondering if they had the same thoughts as McKinnon since they had shifted their gazes from Savannah to stare at him.

A few moments later Durango was standing beside Savannah as they faced the older man who was employed by the Cascade to perform wedding ceremonies. Durango had no problem saying *I do* to any of the things the man asked him since he planned to adhere to his marriage vows for the brief time the marriage lasted.

Although he had been fully aware of each and every question he'd been asked, he'd also been fully aware of the woman standing beside him. The subtle scent of her perfume was teasing his senses. She could arouse feelings in him that were better left alone. And today of all days, the flesh under his suit was burning with memories of the time they had spent in the hot tub together.

"I now pronounce you man and wife. You may kiss your bride."

The officiate's words intruded on Durango's thoughts, giving him a mental start at the realization that the ceremony was over. He was now a married man and it was time to seal his vows with the traditional kiss. He turned to Savannah and saw her tense although she gave him a small smile.

At that moment he wanted to assure her that everything was going to be all right and they had done the right thing for their child. He reached out and touched her, gently ran the backs of his knuckles down her cheek while looking deeply into her eyes. And within seconds he felt her relax.

When a sigh of contentment eased from her lips he leaned forward. He'd intended the kiss to be brief and light. But the moment his mouth touched hers, a strong sense of desire overtook him and he kissed her with a force that surprised even him.

His common sense told him that now was not the time for such a strong display of passion, but slipping his tongue into her mouth, wrapping his arms around her small waist and hungrily mating his mouth with hers seemed as natural as breathing. And the feel of her palms gliding over his shoulders wasn't helping one iota.

It was only when McKinnon touched his shoulder and jokingly said aloud, "I see these two are off to a good start," that Durango pulled back.

"I'd rather the two of you not mention anything to the family about my marriage just yet," Durango said to Ian and Chase a few minutes after the ceremony had ended and he could speak with them privately. "I want to be the one to tell them."

Both men nodded. Then Ian said, "Mom isn't going to be happy about not being here at your wedding."

"Yes, but this is the way Savannah and I wanted to do things."

"When are you going to tell everyone?" Chase inquired. It wasn't easy keeping secrets in the Westmoreland family.

"I'm going to call the folks when we get back. Once I tell Mom, the news will spread like wildfire. But it will be another month before we'll be able to travel home. One of the rangers is out on medical leave and we're shorthanded."

"When you do come home expect Aunt Sarah to have one hell of a wedding reception planned," Chase said, grinning. "She might be upset at first about your elopement, but she'll be ecstatic that another one of her sons has gotten married."

Durango nodded, knowing that was the truth. "I don't

have a problem with her planning a reception," he said, thinking his mother was going to be surprised when she did see Savannah because she'd be showing a little by then. Then Sarah Westmoreland would be happy for two reasons. Another one of her sons would have married and she would have her first grandchild on the way.

"Your bride is on her way over here to claim you for more pictures," Ian said, grinning since he had been the one to hire a photographer for the occasion. He wanted to have lots of pictures for his mother once she found out about the quickie wedding. Although Durango hadn't told him why he and Savannah had eloped, Ian thought he knew his brother well enough to know there was only one reason why a confirmed bachelor like Durango would have gotten married. Time would tell if his assumption was true.

"Savannah is a beautiful woman," Ian said, pretty sure his brother already knew it.

"She is, isn't she?" Durango agreed as he watched Savannah cross the room.

"You're a lucky man," Ian decided to add for good measure.

Durango continued to watch as Savannah came closer and at that moment he couldn't help but think the very same.

An hour or so later Savannah stepped out of the shower. She glanced around the bathroom and noticed that the spa-style bathtub was large enough to accommodate at least four people.

She couldn't help but wonder what Durango was doing. After sharing dinner with Ian, Chase and Jessica after the wedding ceremony, they had returned to their suite, said goodnight and gone to separate bedrooms.

A part of her was disappointed that he hadn't kissed her goodnight. But she knew the reason why he hadn't. One kiss would lead to another, then another and eventually to something neither of them could handle. Durango was intent on keeping his word to keep his distance and she appreciated him for doing so.

He had looked so darn good at the ceremony that for one tantalizing moment she had wished that their wedding was real. But she knew that wasn't possible. In about a year or so, he would be going his way and she would be going hers. After all, they were sharing an in-name-only marriage.

But still...

Would having Durango for a temporary lover be so bad? It was amazing how you could develop an all-consuming craving for something you were perfectly fine doing without only months before. Before her one night with Durango she'd dated, but had never been into casual sex. She hadn't been involved with anyone since she'd broken up with Thomas Crawford and she hadn't felt as if she was missing out. But all of that changed the night she and Durango had conceived their baby. From that night on she had been acutely aware of her body and its needs.

And then there were the memories that wouldn't go away. Durango and their night together had definitely left her with some lasting, vivid ones and a particularly special little moment, she thought, affectionately rubbing her tummy.

She glanced over at the bed and looked at the gown

she intended to sleep in tonight. Alone. If she decided to share an intimate relationship with Durango, she had to remember that it would be with no strings attached. He didn't love her and she didn't love him. Remembering that would definitely make things easier emotionally when the time came for them to part ways.

She crossed the room and picked up the low-cut, short, barely there, flesh-tone nightgown and thought about the kiss they had shared after the man had pronounced them man and wife. She could still feel the heat from his lips on hers and just thinking about that kiss and the one they had shared last night in the hot tub sent shudders racing through her body. There was something about Durango Westmoreland that just heated her blood. Jessica had been right. Westmorelands weren't ordinary men.

Durango had been right, as well. There was no way they could entertain the thought of being married—even on a short-term basis—without there ever being a chance of them sharing a bed. She could see that now. Some marriages could truly be in *name* only, but she realized now that theirs would have to be in *bed* and *name* only. And she could handle that because once the marriage ended, she would begin living a solitary life. She would be concentrating on raising her child. She wouldn't have time to become involved with a man. To be perfectly honest, it wouldn't matter to her if she never had another lover. Her affair with Durango would be enough to sustain her.

She knew that he meant what he said about abiding by her decision until she indicated she wanted things to be different between them. Well, now she had decided. She wanted things to be different.

Savannah saw Durango the moment she stepped out of the bedroom. He was standing on the balcony, gazing out at the lake. His chest was bare and he was wearing a pair of black silk pajama bottoms. His broad muscled chest and shoulders seemed to catch the reflection of the fading sunlight, which gave his dark skin an even richer glow. She wished she had time to get her camera and capture him on film so she could always have the breathtaking image at her fingertips.

As she continued to watch him her heartbeat quickened and the heat he had deliberately turned up earlier with his kiss was inching its way into a flame as she felt her body respond to his mere presence. And then, as if he'd sensed her, he turned slowly, capturing her eyes with his.

They stood there for a moment, separated by a few feet while sexual tension flowed between them the same way it had that night in Atlanta, and Savannah could feel herself slowly melting under the heat of Durango's intense stare.

And then he moved, slowly closing the distance separating them, as his bare feet quietly touched the carpeted floor. She wondered if he knew the effect he was having on her, or if he knew just how beautiful he looked.

Usually one didn't think of a man as beautiful, but in this case she had to disagree. Durango Westmoreland was handsome, good-looking and devastating. But he was also beautiful in a manly sort of way. It was there in the shape of his face, the intensity of his dark eyes, the structure of his high cheekbones and the fullness of his lips. The closer he got to her, the more her body responded and she braced herself for the full impact when he came to a stop in front of her. He glanced down at her negligee and then met her gaze. She saw the questions in his eyes and felt the heat in them, as well.

"I've changed my mind about a couple of things," she said softly, thinking how good he smelled.

"Have you?"

She met his gaze levelly. "Yes."

"And what have you changed your mind about?" he asked in a voice that Savannah thought sounded way too sexy.

"About my wedding night."

His eyebrows lifted. "*Your* wedding night?"

"Yes, I've decided that I want one."

He studied her. His gaze dark and heated. "Do you?"

"Yes." She was fully aware that he knew what she meant, but because he hadn't wanted to risk a misunderstanding, he had to be absolutely sure.

"Okay, I can handle that. Is there anything else that you want?"

She bit her lip a few times before saying, "I want for us to share a bed during the time we're married. I think we're mature enough to handle it, don't you?"

For a minute he seemed to absorb her words in silence before allowing a smile to touch his lips. "Sure, I don't see any problem in that. Do you mind telling me what made you change your mind?"

"I think it would be hard for us to share a house

without sharing a bed. We're too attracted to each other and…"

He arched an eyebrow when she didn't finish. "And what?"

A smile touched the corners of her lips. "And I don't handle temptation very well, especially the Durango Westmoreland kind."

He reached out and placed his hand on her waist and leaned forward slightly. "Can I let you in on a little secret?" he whispered against her lips.

"Sure."

"I don't handle temptation well, either. Especially the Savannah Claiborne kind, so I guess on some things we see eye to eye. That's a good sign."

"Is it?" She couldn't help but look at his mouth since it was so close to hers.

"Mmm, let me show you just how good it is."

And then he captured her lips and the moment he did so a wave of desire swept across her to settle in the pit of her stomach. He wrapped her tight into his arms and the intensity of the kiss made her bones melt. Moments later he reluctantly released her mouth.

"There is something I want to do, Savannah, and it's something I had intended to do at Chase and Jessica's wedding reception but never got around to doing," he said as his lips gently kissed the corners of her mouth and slowly moved to the side of her ear.

"What?" she asked softly, barely able to get the question out.

"Dance with you," he murmured in a low, sexy voice. He took a step back and held his hand out to her.

It was then that she heard the music, a melodic,

soulful ballad by Anita Baker. The slow-tempo, jazzy sound of a saxophone in the background began flowing through her, touching all her senses, revving every nerve in her body and turning the heat up a notch more. Anticipation surged through her veins when she placed her hand in his.

Her pulse quickened when he pulled her closer into his arms, and she came into contact with his bare chest.

"Enjoy the dance," he said, his voice a sensuous whisper against her ear. He pulled her even closer and she knew the exact moment he dropped a kiss on the top of her head. Their bodies meshed together perfectly as they moved to the slow beat, making them fully conscious of the flimsy clothing they were wearing. She could feel the heat deepening between them, and the way her negligee clung to her, shifting, parting with every movement of her body against his, she was certain he was aware of it, which only made her more aware of him. Especially the thick hardness of him that was pressed against her stomach.

Sighing deeply, she buried her face into his bare shoulder, absorbing his strength, his scent, the hard masculine feel of him. And as if by instinct, she gently licked his skin with her tongue. She knew he felt it when his arms tightened around her waist.

"If you lick me I get to lick you back," he murmured gently. "And in a place of my own choosing," he said in a low, sexy voice.

Savannah lifted her head and their eyes met, and held. Deep down she anticipated and hungered for his next move, knowing it would be another kiss. And when he stopped moving and slowly lowered his head to hers, an urgent need took hold of her senses once again.

A mixture of need, greed and unadulterated longing flowed through her veins the moment their lips touched. His mouth fastened tightly on hers and she instinctively absorbed everything there was about him. His tongue was unbelievably skillful when it came to giving her pleasure. It was like a magnet, clinging to whatever was in its path, drawing in her own tongue, taking hold of it, dominating it, eliciting surrender, giving off heat.

She heard herself whimper, while shiver after sensuous shiver coursed through her body. She was helpless to do anything but return the kiss with equal intensity while his body strained against hers.

And then she felt herself being lifted effortlessly into his arms and at that moment she knew that this was just the beginning.

Durango broke off the kiss the moment he placed Savannah on the huge bed in the bedroom she had chosen. Then he stood back and gazed down at her. Her negligee was feminine and enticing. Seeing her in it nearly sucked the very breath from his lungs.

Coming back to the bed he placed a knee on the pillow-top mattress and reached out and touched her breasts through the flimsy material. She made a low, sensuous sound the moment his hand came in contact with her and his fingers moved slowly, tracing a path around her nipples, feeling them harden beneath his fingertips.

His hand then slid down to her stomach. The flesh was exposed from the design of her lingerie, and he touched her bare skin, made circles around her navel, massaging it, caressing it, feeling the way her muscles tightened beneath his hand. Knowing his self-control was slipping, in one smooth sweep he removed the negligee completely, leaving her totally naked.

For the second time that night he actually felt the air he was breathing being drawn out of his lungs. No woman, he quickly decided, should have a body this beautiful, this tempting, this seductive.

A slow, throbbing ache began inching its way through every part of him and as he stared at Savannah he felt an intense desire to possess her. Wanting to be sure she was ready for him, he reached out and touched the area between her legs, dipped his finger inside of her, stroked her, and saw she was indeed ready for him. She made a low moaning sound and he ceased what he was doing just long enough to remove his pajama bottoms.

"Durango."

His name was a whispered purr from her lips and he knew he was going to make love to her and not just have sex with her. The impact of that almost sent his mind spinning, but he refused to dwell on it now. He was too engrossed in how Savannah was making him feel and how his body was responding to the very essence of her. He was experiencing emotions he had not felt since the last time he had been with her. Nothing and he meant nothing would stop him from sharing this night with the woman who was now his wife.

Easing back on the bed with her, he kissed her, discovering again the sweetness that always awaited him in her mouth. And then he covered her body with his, lifted her hips and broke off the kiss to look deep into her eyes. He slowly entered her. The impact of their joining was so profound his body momentarily went still as their gazes locked.

"I know this might sound arrogant," he said in a low, husky tone. "But I think this," he said, pushing deeper into her body, "was made just for me."

Savannah smiled, adjusting her body to the intimate fit of his. "If you really believe that then who am I to argue? You definitely won't hear a peep out of me."

A sexy, amused chuckle rumbled from his lips. "Let's just see about that because I like the noises you make," he said, remembering the sounds she had made the last time they had been together.

He began moving at a slow pace, needing to feel himself thrusting deep inside her, needing to arouse even further that feminine hunger within her that he longed to release. He wanted to stir it up in a way she had never felt before and then give her what they both needed. He wanted her hungry for him, starving for him, desperate for him.

Durango refused to let her hold back anything with him, especially his need to become one with her. His desire became even more feverish with the rhythmic movements of Savannah's hips.

He wanted it all and more than anything he needed to hear her express her satisfaction. And with that goal in mind, he continued to move against her, sliding back and forth, stroking in and out between her legs, letting her feel the workings of his solid shaft inside her as his hand lifted her hips for better access, more intense pleasure. Several times his body nearly shuddered with the force of his own release but he found the strength to hold back, keep himself in check.

But the moment Savannah cried out in ecstasy, and he felt her body tighten around his, using every feminine muscle she possessed to aggressively claim what she wanted, he gave in and succumbed to his powerful release that pushed him over the edge.

And when he leaned down and captured her mouth, clung to it, devoured it like a starving man, he tightened his arms and legs around her, tilted her body at an angle that would increase their pleasure. Durango knew at that moment if he lived to be a hundred years old, he would only find this degree of pleasure here, in Savannah's arms.

He was forced to admit that only with this woman would he find complete sexual satisfaction. Only with her.

Chapter 10

Durango shook his head as he raised his eyes to the ceiling. He and Savannah had returned to his ranch that morning and he had decided to wait until late afternoon to make the call to his family.

"Yes, Mom, I'm telling you the truth. I got married on Friday, and yes, I married Jessica's sister, Savannah."

He gazed across the room at Savannah, who was walking out of the bathroom. She had just showered and was wearing a beautiful blue silk bathrobe. A towel was wrapped around her head because she'd also washed her hair.

"Mom, Savannah and I eloped and got married in Lake Tahoe. Ian knew about it but I swore him to secrecy, so he was right not to tell you."

He nodded moments later. "Yes, it's okay for you and Savannah's mom to get together and plan a reception, but I'll have to get back to you and let you know when we can come to Atlanta. It won't be for another three to four weeks."

After a few moments of nodding, he said, "Savannah and I met at Chase's wedding, fell in love and decided to get married quietly. Without any hoopla," he tacked on, borrowing Savannah's words.

He turned and watched as she removed the towel from her head, and he saw how the mass of dark, curly hair tumbled around her shoulders. He watched as she lifted her arms and began drying her hair. Doing so stretched her silk robe, showing off her generous curves. There was something about watching her dry her hair that was a total turn-on. He hoped it had nothing to do with the fact that this was his bedroom and she looked so damn good in it. Even her clothes that were hanging next to his in the closet looked right.

He frowned, not liking the thought of that. And then he cleared his throat, trying to concentrate on what his mother was saying. "Yes, Mom, you can tell the rest of the family, and yes, Savannah is here. Would you like to speak with her?" he asked, eager to get off the phone.

He could last only so long under his mother's intense inquisition. Just like Ian had said, their mother had been angry at first, but the news that another of her sons had married had smoothed her ruffled feathers. And it amused him that already she had her sights on the next one of her sons who she felt was ready for matrimony. He chuckled, thinking Ian, Spencer, Quade and Reggie had better watch out.

"Okay, Mom, and I love you, too. Give Dad my best. Now here's Savannah."

"Be prepared," he whispered, before handing her the phone.

He then watched and listened while Savannah began talking to his mother. She first apologized, and accepted all the blame for their decision to elope. Then told Sarah Westmoreland in an excited voice that she would love for her to plan a reception, and agreed with the older woman that it would be a wonderful idea to get her mother involved, too.

Durango was about to walk out of the room when Savannah promised to send his mother digital pictures taken at the wedding. Sending pictures was a nice touch that was sure to win Savannah brownie points with his mom.

When Durango returned twenty minutes later after taking a shower, Savannah was still on the phone with his mother. He gave Savannah an apologetic smile as he sat on the bed beside her. After another ten minutes he'd had enough and surprised Savannah by taking the phone out of her hand.

"Mom, I think you've talked to my wife long enough. It's our bedtime. We're newlyweds, remember?"

"Durango!"

He placed a finger to his lips, prompting Savannah to silence. "Thanks, Mom, for understanding. And yes, I'll make sure Savannah sends those photos to you tonight before she…ahh, goes to sleep. Good night, Mom." He chuckled as he quickly hung up the phone.

Savannah glared at him. "Durango Westmoreland, how could you embarrass me that way by insinuating that we—"

He kissed her mouth shut and then tugged her backward on the bed, removing her robe in the process. "I didn't imply anything that isn't true," he said, after releasing her lips.

He kissed her again, then pulled back and said, "Mmm, this is how I like you—naked and submissive." He knew his words would definitely get a rise out of her.

She pushed against his chest. "And just who do you think is submissive? I want you to know that…"

He kissed her again, thinking how dull his life had been before she came into it. Then just as quickly he decided that kind of thinking sounded like he was getting attached—and he didn't do attachments. But then again, he had to be honest enough and admit that for a man who'd always liked his privacy, he was thoroughly enjoying having Savannah around…even if she would only be there on a temporary basis.

When he finally released her mouth, she looked at him as desire darkened her eyes and said softly, "You aren't playing fair."

He met her gaze with an intensity he felt all the way to his toes and said hoarsely, "Sweetheart, I'm not playing at all."

Durango then stripped off his robe and stretched his naked body out beside her, pulling her into his arms and kissing her again. When he finally broke off the kiss he smiled down at her. "So, did you enjoy our trip to Lake Tahoe?"

She reached up and ran her fingers through the hairs on his chest, thinking about all the things they had done together, especially the time they had spent in bed. Durango, she had discovered, had extraordinary stamina. "Yes," she said finally, thinking just how much she had liked spending time at the Rolling Cascade with him. "It was a very rewarding experience."

"And you didn't once have morning sickness," he pointed out.

She grinned. "And I did enjoy the break. Maybe this bracelet works after all."

He lifted her hand and kissed her wrist. Then he smoothed his hands over her stomach, massaging gently, liking the thought that his child rested there. "And I take it our baby is well?"

"Yes, she's doing just fine."

"That's good to know. Now I can turn my full attention to her mother." He whispered the words in her ear and the sound was so low and seductive that it made every muscle in her body quiver.

"And how will you do that?" she asked innocently, knowing the answer but wanting him to expound anyway.

"I can show you better than I can tell you."

Cocking her head, and with a seductive glint in the depths of her hazel eyes, she said, "Then show me."

And he did that night. Numerous times.

"That's it. Move a little to the right. Oooh, yes. Now tilt your head a little back. Just a little. That's perfect, now hold it right there."

It was at that moment that Savannah took Durango's picture, just one of several she had taken already that day after he'd come in from work. She had convinced him that she needed to use up the rest of her film and that he would make the perfect model.

"Now open your shirt and let me see your chest."

He frowned. "Hey, just what kinds of photos are you taking?"

She grinned. "I told you. I want to sell my boss on the idea of doing a calendar of park rangers. They do them of firemen and policemen all the time. It's about time we honor American heroes."

He crossed his hand over his chest, ignoring the fact that Savannah and her camera were still clicking. "And just who will be buying these calendars?" he asked, thinking about a calendar that his cousin Thorn had done for charity a couple of years ago. They had sold like hotcakes.

She chuckled. "Anyone who appreciates good art… as well as a good-looking man. Besides, I think it would be a great idea for a charity fund-raiser. I can see you as Mr. February."

He lifted a brow. "Why Mr. February?"

She shrugged, and then said, "I think of you as Mr. February because that's the month this is, and so far it's been a good one—morning sickness and all. Also, February makes you think of hearts, and it was this month I heard a heart…the one belonging to our baby… so, you being Mr. February makes sense even if what I just said doesn't."

Durango looked at her with understanding because to him everything she said *did* make sense. No matter how long their marriage lasted or when it ended, the month of February would always have a special meaning to them. Without saying anything else he undid the top button while she snapped away with her camera.

"Sexy. Yes, that was one sexy pose," she said, looking up at him, deciding she'd taken enough pictures of him for now. Just then her pulse quickened due to the totally male look he was giving her.

"You think so?"

"Yes," she said, unzipping the case to put her camera in.

"I have to admit it was fun. When did you decide to get into photography?" he asked, leaning against the wooden rail of the outside deck.

Savannah glanced up at him. A great expanse of mountain range was in the background and for a heartbeat of a minute she was tempted to pull her camera out again. He was giving her another sexy pose.

"When I was a teen…sixteen, I think," she said. "My grandparents bought me my first camera and I drove everybody crazy with it by taking pictures whether I had their permission or not. I caught Mom, Rico and Jessica in some very embarrassing moments."

"Um, should I be worried?" he asked, grinning.

Savannah laughed. "No, I've grown up a lot since that time. Now I'm harmless."

Harmless? Durango wasn't so sure about that. Since Savannah had come into his life, nothing had been the same. The people he worked with couldn't believe it when he'd made the announcement that morning that he had gotten married. A number of them thought he was joking until Savannah had shown up at the ranger station at noon for their lunch date. Then he'd seen both understanding and envy in a lot of the guys' eyes. He wondered what those same coworkers would think a year from now when he and Savannah went their separate ways.

"I hope you like what I cooked for dinner."

Savannah's words intruded, reclaiming his thoughts. "I'm sure I will. But you didn't have to go to any trouble. I could have fixed something when I got in."

She laughed. "It's the least I can do while you're at work every day. I'm not used to being home all day. In fact, I pitched the calendar idea to my boss. If he approves the project, I'll be busy. Do you think your coworkers will mind having their pictures taken?"

Durango shook his head and grinned. "No, they'll probably get a kick out of it. The thought of being featured on a calendar will boost a few of their egos, I'm sure."

He studied her, sensing something was bothering her. He hadn't picked up on it earlier, but now without a camera in her hand it was becoming obvious. He couldn't help wondering if she oftentimes used her camera as an emotional shield.

"Did something happen today that I should know about, Savannah? Does it have anything to do with your mother or your brother?"

He knew her mother was still in Paris and Savannah had spoken to her the day before. She hadn't reached her brother until later in the day. He had been surprised but happy with her news and was looking forward to their visit to Philly.

Durango watched as she took a deep breath and said, "No, it's not about my family."

He nodded. That could only mean one thing. It was about *his*. "Did someone in my family call you today?"

"Yes."

"Who?"

He saw the small smile that touched her lips before she said, "It would probably be easier to ask who didn't. You have a rather large family."

Large and overwhelming, Durango thought, giving her his full attention. "And?"

"And…er…everyone, although surprised by the news we had gotten married, seemed genuinely sincere in wishing us the best, which made me feel like a phony."

He understood her ambivalence because he'd felt the same way at work today. "You're not a phony. Our decision to have a temporary marriage is our business and no one else's."

"Yes, I know…but."

He lifted an eyebrow. "But what?"

"But everyone was so nice. Even your cousin Delaney called all the way from the Middle East. And all the Westmoreland spouses, those married to your cousins and brother, called to welcome me into the family. They said from this day forward we would all be sisters. It was the same welcome Jessica told me they gave her. Do you know how that made me feel?"

She was staring at him with a strained expression on her face. He smiled at her. "No, how did that made you feel?"

"Special. I've always dreamed of belonging to a huge family, but it's not for real. Do you know what I'm saying? Am I making much sense?"

Yes, he knew what she was saying and she was

making plenty of sense. He remembered that one of the main reasons she had agreed to marry him was that she wanted their child to have something she'd never had—a chance to belong to a large family; a family who would always be there for you through the good times or bad; a family who stuck together no matter what; a family that instilled strong values in future generations and a family who proved time and time again that when the going got tough, they didn't cut and run. They rallied around each other and gave their support.

"Yes, I understand," he said, after expelling a deep breath. "No matter what, there will always be a bond between us because of our child. You know that, don't you?"

"Yes, I know it, but I still feel like I'm being deceitful and that bothers me."

Not for the first time, Durango compared Savannah with Tricia. The more he did so, the more he was discovering there was no comparison. Both were city girls for sure, but where being deceitful actually bothered Savannah, Tricia hadn't shown any remorse when she'd looked him dead in the eyes and told him that she'd played him for a fool.

"I'm going to put dinner on the table now, Durango. I'll let you know when everything is ready."

Feeling her need to change the subject, he asked, "Need my help?"

"No. I can manage."

Moments after Savannah left, Durango turned to gaze out at the mountains. Today was a clear winter day and what he saw was breathtaking, a sight to behold, and it provided such a picturesque view that it made him appreciate his decision to settle down in these parts years ago.

He'd always found comfort in looking at the mountains when something weighed heavily on his mind and today Savannah was weighing heavily on his mind.

Although he had decided that Tricia and Savannah weren't anything alike, he still felt as though he was reliving the past. It had been so quick, too easy to fall in love with Tricia, and he had done so, proudly wearing his heart on his sleeve. But once she had ripped that sleeve, he had decided it could never be repaired. Under no circumstances would he allow himself to be that vulnerable again.

Durango knew the difference between lust and love and right now what he felt for Savannah was nothing more than lust. She had caught his eye from the first; they had made love, made a baby, and now they were married. But still the very thing that had drawn them together from the start was good old-fashioned lust. And they were taking it to a whole other level. Just the thought of what they had shared over the past few days made his breath catch, and last night, through the wee hours of the morning, had been the epitome of perfection.

He would be the first to admit that during one of those moments, a part of him had analyzed, fantasized, even had gone so far as to consider the idea of more than a year with her. But then that rip in his sleeve, that deep gash in his heart, had reminded him that there were some things in life that a man never got over. The pain he had suffered that one time had completely closed his mind to the prospect of ever loving again.

That's the way it was and that's the way it would stay.

Later that night Durango and Savannah sat cross-legged on the floor in front of the fireplace. They had eaten and showered and were ready to relax.

"Dinner tasted wonderful tonight, Savannah."

She smiled over at him. "Thanks. That's my grand-mother's favorite dish," she said of the steak and baked potatoes she had prepared.

"So," Durango said, stretching out to lie on his side. "How do you suggest we spend the rest of the evening?"

She grinned at him and said teasingly, "I could take more pictures."

"I don't think so. Let's think of doing something else."

"Something like what?"

"Something like finding out just how hot things can get between us."

His words made her pulse quicken and she watched his mouth tilt into a very seductive smile. "Um, what do you have in mind?" she asked, meeting his gaze and holding it tight.

"Come here and let me show you," he said, reaching out and gently snagging her wrist to bring her on the floor beside him. She watched his every move as he took off her robe. "Aren't you curious about the next step?" he asked.

She glanced down at his lap and saw the size of his arousal through his robe and immediately, her feminine muscles clenched in appreciation and anticipation. "No, I have an idea how this is going to play out," she said, her breath almost catching in her throat.

"Good."

"But I do have one request," she said, wrapping her arms around his neck.

"What?"

"Let me take off your robe."

He smiled. "Go for it."

When she had removed his robe she took her tongue and licked a section of his shoulder before she drew back and looked at him. "You have a beautiful body."

He chuckled. "You think so?"

"Yes."

"Thanks, and I think you have a beautiful body, as well, and it's a body that I want to get all into."

"Well, in that case…"

He moved closer to her, growled low in his throat as he nudged her on her back. Like a leopard on the prowl, he cornered his prey and when he had her just where he wanted her he whispered softly, "Now it's my turn to lick."

And he did just that, starting with the insides of her thighs before moving to savor another part of her.

"Durango!"

Only when he was nearly intoxicated with the taste of her did he ease his body over hers to take her hard and fast, putting everything he had into each mind-wrenching thrust and watching her features glow with the pleasure he was giving her. And when he felt the quivering deep in her womb where his child nestled, he threw his head back and rocked furiously against her the same way she was rocking against him.

It pleased him immensely to know she was on fire, but only *for* him and *with* him. And when she arched against him and groaned from deep within her throat, he felt those same sensations that engulfed her rip through him as one hell of an orgasm slammed into him, lifting him to a place he'd never been before, pushing him high above the clouds, the earth, the entire universe.

And when he drove into her again and then again, he was met with an immense feeling of satisfaction. Knowing she was reaching the same level of mind-shattering pleasure as he was put him in total awe of everything they were sharing. He couldn't get enough of her. She was simply amazing. A city girl by day and a mountain wildcat by night.

And as she continued to pull everything out of him, take what he'd never given another female, he could only think of the remaining months they would be together and knew when she left, his life would never be the same.

"Get some rest, baby. I'm going to my office for a while," Durango whispered in Savannah's ear. After making love in front of the fireplace, he had picked her up in his arms to carry her into the bedroom and tucked her into bed. Quietly closing the door behind him, he went downstairs to his office.

He immediately walked over to the window. The moon's light cast a beautiful glow on the mountains, giving him a feeling of warmth, and for a while he stood there thinking that things couldn't get any better than this. He loved where he lived, he enjoyed his job and for a short while he wasn't living alone.

Sharing dinner with Savannah had been wonderful and afterward they had showered together as if it was the most natural thing to do. But nothing could top the lovemaking that had come later. It seemed that each and every time they came together was better than the last, and that thought was beginning to bother him.

Deciding he didn't want to dwell on it any longer, he was about to take a seat behind his huge desk when the phone rang. So it wouldn't disturb Savannah, he quickly picked it up, not bothering to check caller ID as he normally did. "Hello."

"What the hell is going on, Durango?"

He leaned back in his chair, recognizing his oldest brother's voice immediately. "Jared. And how are things with you?"

"Cut the crap and answer my question."

Durango rolled his eyes. Jared, the attorney, was his no-nonsense brother. Marriage had softened him some, but he was still a hard case. "What makes you think something is going on?"

"You got married."

Durango smiled. Yes, that would say it all. "It was time, don't you think? You seemed happy, so I decided to try it."

"And you want me to believe that?"

"That would be nice."

"Well, I don't."

"Figures."

"And Ian isn't talking."

Durango smiled. "That's good."

"Mom's overjoyed, of course," Jared Westmoreland went on to say. "I think she emailed every single family member those pictures she got over the internet."

"Okay, Ian's not talking, but Mom's happy, so what's your problem, Jared?"

"I want to know why you did it."

"The reason I told you earlier wasn't good enough?"

"No."

He wasn't surprised. Of his five brothers, it was Jared who knew him the best. He could never pull anything over the brother who was nearly three years older and to Durango's way of thinking, plenty wiser. Whereas other relatives would cautiously buy the story that he and Savannah had fabricated, he immediately thought of three members of the Westmoreland family who would not. Jared and his cousins Dare and Stone.

The attorney in Jared would put up an argument no matter what Durango said, and because Dare—the current sheriff of College Park, Georgia—was a former FBI agent, he had a tendency to be suspicious of just about everything.

And Durango dreaded the call he knew he would eventually get from his cousin Stone. He and Stone were only months apart in age and had always been close. Durango figured the only reason Stone hadn't called yet to give him hell was because he and his wife, Madison, were somewhere in Europe on a book promotional tour.

"Are you going to tell me what I want to know, or will I have to take drastic measures and start an investigation?" Jared asked, breaking into Durango's thoughts.

"Um, what drastic measures would those be?"

"How does catching the next plane to Montana to check out things for myself sound?"

Not too good. Durango sighed, knowing Jared was dead serious and because of that he decided to come clean. "Savannah is pregnant."

He heard his brother's deep sigh. Then for a few moments Jared was silent, evidently taking it all in.

"How far along?" Jared finally asked.

"Going into her third month."

Silence again. Then Jared said, "It happened Christmas night."

Durango lifted an eyebrow. "How did you know?"

"For Pete's sake, Durango, do you think you weren't missed at the card game that night? Hell, we'd all been counting on winning all your money. And besides that, I couldn't help but notice you were attracted to the woman and we all saw you leave the reception to walk her to her room."

Durango smiled, remembering. "You all saw too much that night."

"Whatever." Then moments later Jared asked, "The two of you made a decision to get married for the baby's sake?"

"Yeah, that just about sums it up. But our marriage is only temporary."

"Temporary?"

"Yes, until the baby is around six months old. I didn't want my child born illegitimate and I wanted to be around during Savannah's pregnancy to bond with it and spend some time with them for a while afterward."

"And what happens after that?"

"Then we part ways. But Savannah and I have

agreed to always be there for the baby. She knows I want to be a part of its life and Savannah wants that, too. It won't be easy with us living so far apart, but we'll manage."

There was another long pause and then Jared asked, "And you're okay with the temporary setup?"

Durango frowned. "Why wouldn't I be?"

"I saw those pictures Mom is so proudly brandishing about town. At your wedding, you and Savannah looked good together, actually happy. If I didn't know better, then I—"

"But you do know better, which is why you made this call. Don't let those pictures fool you, Jared. The only thing going on between the two of us is the baby. Six months after it's born Savannah will go her way and I'll go mine."

"And until then the two of you will live together happily as man and wife?"

"More or less." And at the moment he was thinking more because he was discovering that Savannah was such a giving person, he couldn't imagine her giving less.

"Be careful, Durango."

Durango's eyebrow lifted higher. "Be careful of what?"

"Discovering the fact that your heart isn't really made of stone and that it might be putty in the right woman's hands."

Durango frowned. "Trust me, it won't happen to me."

Jared laughed. "I thought the same thing. Although I'm not complaining now, mind you. I discovered the hard way that the worst types of affairs are the pretend kind."

"What are you talking about?"

There was another pause and Durango thought he heard the sound of his brother sipping something. Probably a glass of wine. He could imagine Jared doing so in that million-dollar home he owned. Jared was a hotshot Atlanta attorney who over the years had made a name for himself by handling high-profile divorce cases involving celebrity clients. Up until a year ago, Jared had been determined to stay a bachelor like Durango, and then Dana Rollins happened, surprising the hell out of everyone in the Westmoreland family who'd known Jared's stand on marriage. He'd always claimed it wasn't for him. He was a divorce attorney who ended marriages, not initiated them. But now he was a happily married man who didn't care if the world knew how much he loved his wife.

"My engagement to Dana," Jared finally said, pulling Durango's thoughts to the present then jettisoning them back to the past when he remembered Jared's surprised announcement of his engagement at their father's birthday party last Easter.

"What about your engagement?"

"There never was one, at least not a real one."

Durango frowned, wondering what the hell his brother was saying. He was too tired, not in the right frame of mind to try to figure out anything tonight. "What do you mean there never was one? I was there when you announced it."

"I never announced anything. Mom did."

Jared's words made him think. Jared was right. Their

mother had been the one who'd made a big fuss about Jared's engagement. Jared hadn't really said much. But then he hadn't denied it, either.

"Are you saying you went along with an engagement because Mom put you on the spot?"

"There was more to it than that, Durango. If you recall, soon after that we found out about that lump in Mom's breast. She'd made it up in her mind I was getting married and the last thing I wanted to do was to burst her bubble, considering everything."

Durango nodded. "So you pretended to be engaged? And you actually got Dana to go along with doing something like that?"

"Yes, but in the midst of it all we fell in love."

Durango shook his head, thinking how his brother had effectively pulled the wool over their eyes. "Who else knew the truth?"

"Dare. No one else needed to know. The only reason I'm even telling you is that I want you to see how things can happen."

"Things like what?"

"How you can enter into a situation thinking one way and in the end, your thinking can change. The more I got to know Dana and spent time with her, the more I wanted more out of our relationship. I saw Savannah that night and I sensed the attraction between the two of you. She's a woman a man can easily fall in love with. I could see that happening to you."

Durango sat up straight in his chair. "Well, I can't," he snapped. "I'm happy things turned out that way for you and Dana, but it won't for me and Savannah."

"Can you be sure of that?"

"Yes, I can be sure. You were evidently capable of loving someone. I'm not. At least not now. If I had met Savannah before Tricia, then I—"

"When will you let go of what she did to you?"

"I have let go, but that doesn't mean I want to open myself up to the same kind of hurt again."

"And you think that you will be?"

"I'm thinking that I'm not willing to take the risk."

"And what about Savannah?"

"What about her?"

"What if she feels differently?"

"She doesn't and she won't. She was more against us marrying than I was. In fact, I had to convince her it was the right thing to do. She only agreed to do it for the baby's sake. She'll stay for six months and then she's out of here."

"And the two of you have agreed to all of this?"

Durango rolled his eyes. "Yes, but we haven't put it in writing, if that's what that attorney's mind of yours is driving at. Hey, maybe that isn't such a bad idea. I want her to know I will continue to do right by her even after the baby is born. Draw me up something, will you?"

"Draw you up what?"

"I don't know. Some legal document that spells out that I will continue to support her and the baby after the marriage is over. I want to set up a college fund and I intend to provide generous monthly financial support for my child, which I'll be able to afford thanks to that business venture I'm in with McKinnon."

"Are you sure you want to bring a legal document into the picture now?"

"Why not? I'd think she would appreciate knowing

I will support her, something her father didn't. She has this thing about how her old man treated her pregnant mother when they got married and he never did right by her, Jessica and her brother. I want to assure Savannah that I have no intentions of treating her that way."

A half hour later Durango ended the call with Jared after telling him everything he wanted to put in the document. Whether his brother wanted to accept it or not, his marriage to Savannah was only temporary and Durango did not intend to ever forget that fact.

Chapter 11

The next two weeks were busy ones for Savannah. It helped tremendously that her bouts of morning sickness were infrequent and she woke each day seeing it as another adventure.

Her boss was excited about the idea of a calendar to commemorate Yellowstone National Park and the men who protected its boundaries. In addition to the calendar, he also envisioned something bigger and he had suggested a documentary film. She was excited about the idea and spent most of her days shooting footage that might be used for the project.

Her nights belonged to Durango. After dinner she would read to him from the baby book, keep him abreast of all the changes that were taking place with her body, and then they went to bed. Each night Durango did his own investigation, getting firsthand knowledge by going deep inside her body. And each time he entered her, after bringing her to a feverish pitch, she was fully aware that the private moments they shared would remain a part of her, even after they had parted ways. But then she realized that something had happened that she hadn't counted on.

She had fallen in love with Durango.

As she stood looking out the window, a part of her wondered at what point it had happened. Had it been just last night, when they had showered together and he had made love to her in such a beautiful way that it had brought tears to her eyes? Or had it been last week, when he had taken her hiking up the mountain, and they had stopped at the hunting cabin that he and McKinnon had built and had enjoyed the packed lunch he'd made for them. Or later, before coming back down the mountain, when they had enjoyed each other, making love outside near a beautiful stream under a beautiful Montana sky. She would always relish the tender, loving moments they shared and knew that deep down she would miss Durango.

She turned when she heard the phone ring, and quickly crossed the room, thinking it was Durango, but the caller ID indicated it was her brother, Rico, instead.

"Hello."

"I know, Savannah."

Savannah lifted a brow having an idea of what he knew. Evidently her mother had let something slip. "You know what?" she asked innocently.

"That you're pregnant."

Savannah smiled wryly. That was Rico for you.

Straight to the point. "I had planned to tell you when I thought the time was right."

There was silence for a moment and then he asked, "Are you okay with it?"

Savannah chuckled. "I'm more than okay with it. I'm ecstatic. Of course, I wasn't at first because I was nervous and scared more than anything. Then I decided since I never planned to marry anyway, at least I'd have a baby. I always wanted one."

"But you *did* get married."

"Only for the baby."

"Which is something you swore you'd never do."

She sighed deeply. Leave it to Rico to remind her of that. "This is different. Durango and I went into this marriage with our eyes open. We want what's best for our child and we'll do whatever it takes to make sure that happens."

"Even if it means sentencing yourselves to a loveless marriage?"

"Yes, but in our case it will only be temporary. We've agreed to a divorce when the child is six months old."

"And you're okay with that?"

"Sure. Why wouldn't I be?" she asked simply.

"No reason, I guess. When are you coming home?"

She shrugged. "Not sure. I had thought of coming to Philly to check on things, but all my bills are paid up, so there's no rush. Besides, I like it out here."

"And your husband?"

"What about him?"

"How's he treating you?"

In all the right ways that a man should treat a

woman. That very thought came to the tip of Savannah's tongue and she hesitated, thinking of just how true it was. Maybe it was because they knew that things between them were only temporary, but whatever the reason, she enjoyed every second, every moment she spent with Durango.

But then it would be easy for her to do so anyway, because she'd fallen in love with him, and could now admit that she had done so the first time she had seen him at Jessica and Chase's wedding.

"Savannah?"

"Durango is treating me well, so don't worry yourself by thinking anything different. He's a good man."

"He got you pregnant."

She heard the anger in Rico's voice. "And he wasn't in that bed alone, remember that," she replied tersely. "Nor did he have my hands tied behind my back. Remember that, too," she added. "I'm a big girl, Rico."

He chuckled. "And you'll be getting even bigger in the coming months."

She smiled, glad the tension between them had passed. "Yes, and multiple births run in the Westmoreland family. So we might be getting double."

"Finding out that you're pregnant and the possibility of you having twins. That's a lot for me to deal with, Savannah."

Her smile deepened. "But I'm more than certain that you will."

"It was really nice of your coworkers to give this party in our honor," Savannah whispered to Durango while glancing around the room. Beth Manning, one of the female park rangers, had contacted her at the beginning of the week to tell her of the rangers' plans to host a postwedding party for her and Durango.

At first Savannah had felt dishonest, but then, like Durango had said, the terms of their marriage were nobody's business.

"Yes, it was nice of them," he agreed, placing his arm around her shoulders to pull her closer to his side. They were at the home of Beth and her husband, Paul. Paul was a veterinarian in the area.

Savannah thought that Beth and Paul had a beautiful house that was located not far from Durango's ranch, on the other side of the mountains. Inside the decor was different from Durango's. Instead of it having two stories, the rooms were spacious and spread out on one level. And one side of the living room was a huge picture window that had no curtains, blinds or shades to block the beautiful panoramic view of the mountains.

Savannah had met most of the park rangers who worked with Durango when she had joined him for lunch one day, but this was the first chance she'd gotten to meet their spouses. Already she liked everyone. She thought they were genuinely friendly and appreciated them for making her feel welcome and at home.

Everyone had brought a covered dish and they were enjoying themselves, having a good time basking in the decent weather as well as the delicious food. One thing Savannah noticed was that Durango rarely left her side. He was always there, either holding her hand or placing his arms around her shoulders. She knew to everyone who observed them they appeared to be a very happy couple.

"Are the two of you ready to open the gifts now?" a smiling and exuberant blond-haired, blue-eyed Beth came up to them and asked.

Durango glanced at his watch. It was nearing midnight. "Now would be good. It's getting late."

"When did you ever care about time, Durango? I've known you since college and you've never been known to leave a party early," Beth's husband Paul came to join them and asked with twinkling green eyes and a charming smile.

"Oh, but he's a married man now, Paul," Beth reminded her husband, grinning. "We're seeing a new Durango Westmoreland."

Savannah could only imagine how the old Durango had been. She'd known the first moment she'd seen him that he was irresistible to women. Any man with his dark, striking good looks and strong, masculine body had to be. She wasn't naive to assume that before she'd met him he had lived a quiet life that hadn't included women. In fact, Jessica had been quick to tell her that he was a playboy and chances were once he regained his freedom he would revert to his womanizing ways.

A short while later she and Durango found themselves seated in chairs that were in the middle of a circle. Everyone else sat around them.

One by one Beth handed Savannah a gift that she excitedly opened. She and Durango received wineglasses, bath towels, plants, throw rugs and various other gifts. Durango had watched the happy enthusiasm on Savannah's face as she opened each present. But it was the huge, beautiful blue satin bedspread that had caught everyone's attention, including his.

The lower part of his body actually stirred when Savannah unwrapped it. Immediately, he could envision it on his bed with them buried beneath it while they made love. He met her gaze and knew she had had the same thought, and that made his body stir even more. Lucky for him that was the last gift that needed to be opened.

"I'm going to load everything in my truck and Savannah and I are going to call it a night," he said to everyone while glancing at his watch again. "It's officially Sunday morning."

Paul chuckled. "Nobody made you the time keeper, Durango, but I understand. I've been married four years longer than you have."

Savannah didn't know what to say other than thanks and good night to everyone once the guys had helped Durango load all the packages into his truck.

"I never thought I'd live to see the day that Durango Westmoreland fell so hard for a woman," Penny Washington, another park ranger, came and whispered in Savannah's ear. "The two of you look so happy together."

It was on the tip of Savannah's tongue to say that looks were deceiving, but then she changed her mind. She wasn't sure how Durango actually felt about being with her, but she could inwardly admit she was very happy being with him. And that, she thought, was beginning to be the root of a very serious problem. It was all fine and dandy when the two of them had wanted the same thing out of their marriage—no emotional ties. But now she loved him, and it was getting harder and harder to pretend otherwise.

"Ready?"

She glanced up and noticed Durango had come back

inside the house. She saw the look in his eyes. She recognized it. She was becoming used to it. But still, that didn't stop the sensation of air being ripped right out of her lungs. Already she felt her entire body melting.

She cleared her throat. "Yes," she said.

"Wait a minute, Durango. You know how these types of gatherings are supposed to end. You have to kiss your bride for us," one of the rangers called out.

Durango smiled and hollered back, "Hey, that's no problem." And then he leaned down and kissed her in front of everyone, taking her mouth as passionately and as thoroughly as he'd done when they'd been alone. His kiss made her want and desire him...and love him even more. The cheers, catcalls and whistles went unnoticed. She was too busy drowning in the taste of the man who was her temporary husband.

Durango had only made it partway to the ranch when he couldn't take it any longer. Pulling his truck over to the side off the road, he cut off the ignition then, after unsnapping their seat belts, he reached across the seat and pulled Savannah into his arms. He needed another kiss.

Her lips parted instantly, eagerly. She was full of fire and heat and the more he devoured her mouth, the more she returned his passion.

He liked the sound of her whimpering in pleasure; he liked the feel of her wiggling in his lap, trying to get even closer; and he liked the scent of her scintillating perfume.

He reluctantly withdrew his mouth from hers. If he didn't stop now they would wind up making love in his truck and he didn't want that. He wanted a bed. "As soon as we get home I'm going to teach you a skill every woman should know."

A quick surge of heat rushed through Savannah at his words. "And what skill is that?"

He gently squeezed her nipples through her blouse and grinned ruefully. "You'll find out soon enough." He then placed her back in her seat and snapped her seat belt in place.

Sitting beside him the rest of the way to the ranch was torture for Savannah. He had turned her on and there was no way she could get turned off. In silence she glanced over at him. It was a moonless night but the glow from the SUV's console was all the light she needed to study his profile and note the intensity that lined his features. She quickly realized that he was as turned on as she was.

When they reached the ranch he brought the truck to a stop, got out, strode over to the passenger side, opened the door, unsnapped her seat belt and lifted her into his arms. Walking swiftly, he headed for the house.

"What about the gifts?" she asked, pressing her face into his chest, relishing the masculine scent of him.

"I'll unload everything tomorrow. There's no time tonight."

She smiled, thinking he was certainly making time for something. He opened the door and, after kicking it back shut with the heel of his boot, he carried her up the stairs to his bedroom.

She didn't have to wonder what would happen next. Durango undressed her in record time and then proceeded to undress. Soon he had her on her back and purring like a cat.

He touched her everywhere, with his hands and then with his mouth, first tugging gently on her nipples, letting his tongue bathe them as he licked away. She heard herself moan, groan and whisper his name several times. Her legs felt weak. Her body ached. And her mind was being blown to smithereens.

No man could touch her and make her feel the way Durango was making her feel. She was certain of it. He could stroke her desire and fill all of her needs and only with him could she give her entire being, and share the very essence of her soul. Her love.

At the thought of how much she loved him, a pulse began beating deep inside of her, close to her heart. And when his mouth released her breasts to move lower, she nearly stopped breathing.

He touched her intimately and her body responded immediately. Her back arched and her hips bucked the moment his fingers slipped inside of her. His fingers stroked her, expertly, seductively, intently, and moments later, when his mouth replaced his fingers, her entire body nearly jumped off the bed at the same time that a small, hoarse gurgle of pleasure found its way up her throat. If she could be granted one wish for them, besides wanting a healthy baby, she wanted this. Him. For the rest of her life.

"You make me think crazy stuff, Savannah," he whispered when he covered her body with his own and swiftly entered her, making her breath catch. She wondered what crazy stuff he was thinking because he was making her think crazy stuff as well. And the craziest was that she didn't want their marriage to end. But she knew there was no future for them. She loved him, but he didn't love her. But tonight, she wanted it all and if she couldn't have the real thing, then she would pretend.

They had made love plenty of times but something about tonight was different. She felt it in his every stroke, his every thrust into her hot and responsive body. Whatever fever that was consuming him began consuming her, as well.

And she couldn't take it anymore.

A deep-rooted scream tore from her lips and she felt it, the smoothness of his engorged flesh as it jetted a hot thickness deep inside her, getting absorbed in her muscles, every hollow and every inch of her womb. And when he leaned down and kissed her, the urgency of that kiss melted her further. She knew if she lived to be a hundred, Durango was the only man who would ever have her heart.

A short while later, bathed in the room's soft lamplight, she exhaled a satiated sigh as he pulled her closer into his arms. He kissed her gently as one hand possessively cupped her breast. "I can't get enough of you," he whispered huskily.

She couldn't get enough of him, either, and knew she never would. "What skill did you want to show me?" she asked, barely able to get the words out.

He shifted on his back, lifted her, smiled and said, "Now I want you on top."

"Tell me about your brothers," she said, bending her head toward his and whispering against his lips. After several hours of practicing her new skills, she couldn't move an inch even if she needed to.

He wrapped his arms around her waist, keeping her there, on top of him with their bodies connected. "I guess you should know something about them as you'll get to see them soon. I found out today that I'll be able to take two weeks off now that Lonnie is back at work," he said.

"That means we can fly to Atlanta and Philly?"

"Yes, within a week's time."

She snuggled closer. "I met all your brothers at Chase and Jessica's wedding, but I don't know much about them and I want to be prepared."

"Okay, then let me prepare you," he said. "At thirty-eight, Jared is the oldest and the only one who's married. He's the attorney in the family. Next comes Spencer. He's only eleven months younger than Jared. He's a financial planner. I always admired his ability to keep both his profession and personal life from falling apart a few years ago when his fiancée drowned. He took Lynette's death hard, and I doubt to this day that he has fully recovered. Spence lives in California and is the CEO of a large financial firm there."

He looked at her and gave her his disarming smile and said, "I'm the third oldest and you know everything there's to know about me. But if there's more you think you need to know, then I'd rather show you than tell you."

"No, I think I have a pretty good idea of what you're all about," she said, determined not to be sidetracked. "What about the others?"

His smile widened to touch the corners of his lips.

"Then there are the twins, Ian and Quade. They're thirty-three. You spent time with Ian at our wedding. He was seriously involved a few years ago with a woman who worked as a deputy for Dare, but they broke up. I don't know the reason they split, and as far as I know, he hasn't gotten serious about another woman since then."

He shifted their bodies and placed her on top of him. She felt his staff had grown as he entered her. She felt stretched, hot and ready. "My brother Quade works for the Secret Service. We barely know where he is most of the time, and when he comes home we know not to ask any questions. And last but not least, there is Reginald, whom we call Reggie. He'll be turning thirty later this year. He owns his own accounting firm in downtown Atlanta."

Savannah lifted her head. She had heard the love, the respect and the closeness in Durango's voice when he'd spoken of his brothers. "Now what about your—"

"I'm through talking for a while."

She raised an eyebrow. "Are you?"

"Yes."

She smiled. "So what would you like to do?"

He grinned and the sexual chemistry between them was immediate and powerful. "I'd like you to perfect that skill I taught you earlier."

Chapter 12

Durango woke up on Monday morning with an ache in his right knee. Although a glance out the window indicated a clear day he knew the ache was a sign that a snowstorm was coming.

Being careful not to wake Savannah he eased out the bed and went into the bathroom. The moment the door closed behind him he took a deep breath and met his dark gaze in the vanity mirror. Except for the remnants of sleep still clinging to his eyes, he looked the same. Okay, he admitted he did need a shave. But there was something going on inside him that he couldn't see. It was something he could feel and it was something the depth of which he had never felt before.

Not even for Tricia.

At the thought of the one woman who had caused him so much pain, he felt…nothing. Not that ache that used to surround his heart, nor the little reminders of the heartbreak that he had survived. What he felt now was an indescribable fulfillment, one that was new but welcome. It was a fulfillment that Savannah had given him. A warm feeling that she had miraculously placed in his heart.

In a short period of time, being around her, spending time with her and getting to know her, Savannah Claiborne had done something no other woman had been able to do. She had taken his heartache away. She had opened new doors for him, passionate doors, doors filled with trust, faith, hope and love.

Love.

That one word suddenly made him feel disoriented. But just as quickly, he came to the realization that he did love Savannah. He loved everything about her, including the baby she was carrying. And he wanted them both, here with him, and not just temporarily, but for always. He didn't want their marriage to end. Ever.

He sighed deeply, admitting that Jared had been right. His heart had been putty in the hands of the right woman.

Savannah's hands.

Now, the big question was, what was he going to do about it? He'd had a hard enough job selling her on the idea of a temporary marriage; she would probably fight him tooth and nail if he brought up the idea of a permanent one. But he would. Tonight. If he had to he would catch her at one of her weakest moments.

He would do whatever it took to win Savannah's heart.

Savannah waited for the mail with excitement. Her boss had indicated that he would be sending the contract for her to sign for the proposal she had submitted for the calendar and documentary. Already, several of Durango's coworkers, eager to participate, had volunteered.

As she sat at the table and sipped her tea she thought about the phone calls she had gotten from Durango. He'd called twice to warn her about a snowstorm that was headed their way. In the second call, he had informed her that he wanted to talk to her about something important when he got home. Although he wouldn't go into any details, she could tell by the tone of his voice that whatever he wanted to discuss was serious.

She heard the mail truck pull up and quickly placed her teacup aside and grabbed her coat off the rack. As soon as she stepped outside, she felt the change in the weather.

After getting all the mail out of the mailbox, she quickly went back inside to the warmth. Tossing all the letters aside that were addressed to Durango, she came across two that were addressed to her.

The first was the one she'd been waiting for, from the company where she worked. The second, however, caused her to lift an eyebrow. It was a letter from Jared Westmoreland's law firm. Curious, she ripped into the letter Durango's brother had sent her and pulled out the legal-looking document.

Tears began forming in her eyes when she read it. In his ever-efficient way, Durango was taking every precaution by reminding her of the terms of their agreement, as well as putting in writing what he intended to do for her and the baby after their marriage ended. The purpose of the paper she held in her hand was to remind her of their agreement. Their marriage was nothing more than a business arrangement.

She wondered if that was what he wanted to talk to her about when he got home. Had he detected the change in her? Had she not been able to hide the fact that she loved him? Maybe he wanted to get everything out in the open, and back into perspective? Was the document his way of letting her know he was beginning to feel smothered and wanted her to leave?

A sudden pain filled her heart and she knew she could never stay where she wasn't wanted…or loved. Her mother had remained in such a situation, but Savannah had vowed that she never would. Tossing the document on the table, she went into the bedroom to pack. If she was lucky, she would be able to catch a plane to Philadelphia before the bad weather set in.

She was going home.

Durango glanced up at his office door and saw Beth standing there. He smiled. He hadn't had a chance to thank her for hosting the party the past weekend.

Before he could open his mouth, she quickly said, "Paul just called and said that an SUV resembling yours passed him on the road."

Durango lifted an eyebrow and sat up straight in his chair and frowned. He had begun using one of the park's SUVs so that Savannah wouldn't be without transportation at the ranch. "And he thinks he saw my Durango?"

"He said it looked a lot like yours and that it was headed toward Bozeman. He was concerned with the storm coming in."

So was Durango. He had called Savannah twice earlier to tell her about the bad weather coming their way and she hadn't mentioned anything about going out. Why on earth would she drive to town?

"Maybe it wasn't your truck, but one that looked like yours."

Durango knew Beth was trying to keep him from worrying, but he was already reaching for the phone to call home. Most people around these parts knew his truck when they saw it because of the custom chrome rims.

He began to panic when no one answered the phone at his place. He then tried Savannah's cell phone. When he didn't get an answer he hung up the phone and glanced back at Beth, who had a worried look on her face. A snowstorm in Montana wasn't anything to play with and the thought of Savannah out in one wasn't good. He stood, already moving toward the door. "I'm out of here. I need to find Savannah before the storm hits."

"Call me when you do."

"I will." He tossed the words over his shoulder as he quickly left.

No need to panic now, Savannah told herself as she continued to drive although she could barely see the road through the snow. It seemed the huge flakes had begun coming all at once, blanketing everything, reducing visibility to zero.

Knowing it was no longer safe to move Durango's truck another foot, she pulled to the shoulder of the road and killed the engine. She reached into her purse for her cell phone and tried several times without success to reach Durango. Without the heat in the truck, she soon began to feel chilled. She reached for the blanket Durango kept under the seat. Savannah wrapped it around her shoulders, grateful for the warmth it provided, but knew it was only a temporary measure. She wasn't sure how long she could sit here like this, but she also knew to get out of the truck in this type of weather would be suicidal. She wasn't far from the ranch but she wasn't familiar enough with the area to venture out on foot. She decided to stay put.

The best thing to do would be to wait and turn on the engine for heat every so often. She hoped and prayed that the storm would let up or that someone would find her.

Durango drove the road that led from Bozeman to his ranch. Within eight miles of his home he spotted his truck on the side of the road. Pulling up beside it, he quickly got out of the Jeep, ignoring the snowflakes that clung to his face. His heart was beating rapidly as he ran to his SUV.

His heart leaped in his chest the moment he opened the door. Savannah was wrapped in his blanket and curled up on the seat. He reached out and touched her and the first thing he noticed was that she was cold as ice. The second thing he noticed was her overnight bag and camera case on the floor. *Where was she going? Why was she leaving?*

"Savannah? Baby, are you okay? What's going on?"

When she didn't respond he panicked. He pulled her gently into his arms, sheltering her face in his thick, fur-lined parka.

His first inclination was to get her to a hospital and fast. But that was a fifteen-mile trip. He was adequately trained in first aid and made a quick decision to get Savannah to a warm place.

Since they were close to the ranch, he decided to go there. Once at home he would call Trina. He had spoken to her earlier and knew she was at the Marshalls' place on a medical call. The Marshalls' baby had picked the day of what looked to be one of the biggest snowstorms of the year to be born.

Trina would have to pass by his place on the way home. If she hadn't left already, he would have her stop at his ranch. As he slogged through the deep snow to the SUV, he couldn't help worrying about his wife and child.

He didn't know why she had tried leaving him, but now that he had found her, there was no way he would ever let her go.

"And you're sure Savannah and the baby are going to be all right, Trina?"

Trina motioned for them to step out in the hallway before she began speaking. "Yes, they are both doing fine. I checked the baby's heartbeat and it's as strong as ever. That's a tough kid the two of you are going to have."

Durango had nearly been a basket case when she'd arrived. Any assumption she'd had that the only reason he had gotten married was because Savannah was pregnant had gotten blown out the window, smothered in the snow. What she saw in Durango was a man who truly loved his wife.

Seeing that her words had relaxed him somewhat, Trina continued by saying, "You did the right thing by bringing her here and getting her warm. Giving her that tea really did the trick. But I'm glad you found her when you did. I don't want to think about what would have happened if you hadn't. She knew the risk of carbon monoxide poisoning which is why she hadn't kept the truck's heater running and I'm glad she didn't."

Durango nodded. He was glad, as well. "How long will she be sleeping?"

"For another couple of hours or so. Just let her rest," Trina said, slipping into her coat.

"Are you sure you want to go out in this? You can stay and wait for things to clear up."

Trina smiled. "Thanks, but I know my way around these parts pretty good. Have you forgotten that I grew up here? I only live a few miles away. I'll be fine. And I promise to call you when I get home."

Durango nodded, knowing there was nothing he could say to Patrina Foreman that would make her change her mind. Perry had always said that stubborn was her middle name. "Thanks for everything, Trina. How can I repay you?"

"You already have, Durango. From the day you moved into the area, you were always a true friend to me and Perry, and then, after I lost him, you, McKinnon, Beth and everyone else in these parts were there for me, giving me the shoulder I needed to cry on and helping me keep the ranch running. For that I will always be grateful."

She smiled and continued by saying, "Perry and I were married for five happy years, and my only regret is that we didn't have a child together. Then I would have something of his that would always be with me. But you have that, Durango. You got the best of both worlds. You have a wife you love and the child she is giving you. Take care of them both."

An hour or so later, Durango stood at the window, barely able to see the mountains for the snow. It was falling thicker and faster. At least Trina had called to let him know she had made it home and he was glad of that. He had also called the rangers' station to let everyone know Savannah was safe and doing fine.

He sighed deeply and lifted the document he held in his hand and reread it. It had included all the things he had told Jared he wanted in it, and now after reading it he could just imagine what Savannah had thought, what she had assumed after reading it herself. How would he ever convince her to stay now?

He glanced around the room. The house would be cold, empty and lifeless without Savannah there. No matter what he needed to do, get on his knees and beg if he had to, he refused to let the woman he loved walk out of his life.

Savannah forced her eyes open although she wasn't ready to end her dream just yet. In it Durango had just removed her clothes, had begun kissing her. But a sound made her come awake.

She glanced across the room, and there he was, the man she loved, kneeling in front of the fireplace, working the flames and keeping her warm. She breathed in deeply as pain clutched at her heart. She recalled packing, trying to make it to the airport before the storm hit. How had she gotten back here, to a place where she wasn't wanted? That agonizing question made her moan deep in her throat and it was then that Durango turned around and stared at her, holding her gaze with his and with a force that left her breathless.

She watched as he stood and slowly came over to the bed, his gaze still locked on hers. "You were leaving me," he said in a low, accusing tone. "You were actually leaving me."

Savannah sighed. Evidently he wasn't used to women leaving him and the thought of her abandoning him hurt his pride. "You didn't want me anymore," she said softly, not knowing what else to say. "I thought it would be best if I left."

"Did you think that I didn't want you anymore because of that document Jared sent?" When she didn't respond to his question quickly enough, he said, "You assumed the wrong thing, Mrs. Westmoreland."

Savannah blinked. In all the weeks they had been married, he had never called her that, mainly because they'd both known the name was only temporary. So why was he calling her that now? "Did I?"

"Yes, you did. I thought having everything spelled out in a document was what you'd want. I guess I was wrong."

"It doesn't matter," she said softly, trying to hold back her tears.

He came and sat on the side of the bed and took her hand in his. "Yes, it does matter, Savannah. It matters a lot because you matter. You matter to me."

She shrugged, weakly. "The baby matters to you."

"Yes, and the baby matters to you, too. But you also matter to me. *You* matter because I love you."

She blinked again and those beautiful hazel eyes of hers stared at him with disbelief. He was determined to make her believe and accept his love. "I do love you. It would be a waste of time to figure out exactly when it happened, but since we have all the time in the world you can go ahead and ask me anyway," he said, smiling and stretching out beside her on the bed.

"When?" she asked, barely able to get the single word out.

He paused, as if searching for the right words. "I think it was when I arrived late at the rehearsal dinner and saw you standing there talking to Jessica. And when you looked up and met my gaze, something hit me. I assumed it was lust, but now I know it was love. Lust would not have driven me to have unprotected sex with any woman, tipsy or not, Savannah. But when we made love I was driven by an urgency I'd never felt before to be inside you and feel the full impact of exploding inside you."

He grinned. "Pill or no Pill, no wonder you got pregnant. Now when I think about it, it would have really surprised the hell out of me if you hadn't gotten pregnant. I was hot that night and so were you. Mating the way we did was just a pregnancy waiting to happen. It wasn't intentional, but it was meant to be. And regardless of how you feel about me, I love you."

He shifted a little to get closer to her. "A few weeks ago, before we married, you asked why I had an aversion to city girls and I never gave you an answer. Maybe it's time that I did."

And then he spent the next twenty minutes or so telling her about Tricia, the one woman he'd actually thought he'd loved and how she had used him and tossed his love back in his face. "And I actually thought I could never love another woman for fear of getting hurt that way all over again, especially a woman who was a city girl."

He chuckled in spite of himself, remembering the first night he'd seen her. "The moment I saw you I knew you were a city girl and as much as I didn't want to, I couldn't help falling in love with you anyway, Savannah."

He looked down at her, held her gaze. "And no matter what that document says, I do love you. I love you very much."

Savannah felt her cheeks getting wet and tried furiously to wipe at them. But Durango took over, and leaned down and licked them dry. When he pulled back his dark eyebrows rose, clearly astonished. "I thought all tears were salty but yours are sweet. Is there anything that's not perfect about you?"

Savannah let out a small cry and threw her arms around Durango's neck and whispered, "I love you, too, and I fell in love the exact moment that you did."

He chuckled softly and eased from the bed. "Then that leaves only one thing to do," he said, reaching to retrieve the legal document from the nightstand.

Savannah watched as he stood and walked over to the fireplace and tossed it in, and watched with him as the flames engulfed it, burning it to ashes.

"Now that that is taken care of," he said.

Savannah kept her eyes on Durango as he slowly removed his shirt. Her heartbeat quickened when he then proceeded to take off his jeans. "I know you're probably too exhausted to make love, but I need to hold you in my arms, Savannah. I need your warmth, I need your love and I need your promise that you won't ever leave me."

She swallowed thickly when he came back to the bed and slipped under the covers with her. She turned to him when he pulled her into his arms. "I won't leave you, Durango. I want forever if you do…and I'm not tired."

He smiled. "I want forever, too, and you are tired. You just don't know it."

He captured her lips with his, kissing her with all the intensity of a man who had found love by first having an affair—the Durango affair. It was definitely his last.

"So, Mrs. Westmoreland, will you stay married to me? For better or for worse?"

She smiled through her tears. "Yes, I'll stay married to you, but I have a feeling all my days will be for the better."

He leaned over and kissed her after whispering, "I'll make sure of that."

Epilogue

Savannah glanced around the room. There were more Westmorelands than she remembered from Jessica's wedding. She'd known Durango's family was big but she had no idea it was this large.

The wedding reception given in their honor had turned out to be a beautiful affair. To Savannah's surprise, even her grandparents from Philly had come down to be a part of it.

"I know how you feel," Dana Rollins Westmoreland said as she eased up beside her. "The first time Jared took me to meet them I thought that this wasn't a family, it was a whole village."

Savannah smiled, thinking the very same thing. She glanced around the room again and it was Tara Westmoreland, who was married to Durango's cousin Thorn, who came up and said, "It seems that Durango called a meeting with the menfolk."

"Oh," Savannah said, wondering the reason why.

Upon seeing her concern, Tara said, "I'm sure whatever they need to talk about won't take long. In the meantime, has anyone ever told you how I met Thorn?"

Savannah smiled. "No, but after meeting him I'm sure it was very interesting."

"Yes, it was. Come on, let me, you and Dana grab the others and go into the kitchen for a talk. If the guys can have a little chat time then so can we."

After gathering up Delaney, Shelly, Madison, Jessica, Casey and Jayla, the Westmoreland women headed for the kitchen. The married women would tell Savannah how they met their husbands and fell in love.

"Okay, I can see all of you have questions, so what is it that you want to know?" Durango asked the men who had cornered him and demanded this meeting.

It was Stone who spoke up. "I know it's really none of our business, Durango, but we know you. What's the real reason you got married?"

Durango shook his head. He'd known his marriage would be hard for a lot of his family to believe, so he decided to be up-front with them, since he suspected a few had their suspicions anyway.

"Savannah is pregnant. However," he went on to say before any unnecessary speculation could get started, "although her pregnancy might have been the reason we married initially, it's not now."

Spencer Westmoreland raised a dark eyebrow. "It's not?"

"No. I'm in love with her. She's in love with me. We're having a baby in September and we're happy."

The men in the room stared at him. A few, those who knew how easy it was to fall in love if the right woman came alone, accepted him at his word. But Durango saw a few skeptical gazes.

"And you want us to believe that just like that, a die-hard bachelor can fall in love?" Quade Westmoreland said.

"It can happen," Durango said, smiling.

"I agree," added the man who'd once been such a confirmed bachelor that the women had pegged him the *Perfect Storm.* Storm Westmoreland met the gazes of his brothers and cousins and one lone brother-in-law, Sheikh Jamal Yasir. "All of you know my history and yet Jayla was able to capture my heart," he reminded them.

Thorn Westmoreland chuckled. "And all of you know what Tara did to me."

The men in the room doubted they would ever forget. Tara had been Thorn's challenge and had lived up to the task.

"And you're really happy about being married, Durango? No regrets?" Reggie Westmoreland asked, needing to be certain.

Durango met all the men's gazes. "Yes and there aren't any regrets. You've all seen Savannah. What man wouldn't be happy married to her? But her beauty isn't just on the outside. It's on the inside, as well. I need her in my life and she has single-handedly opened my heart to love."

All the men in the room finally believed him. As

miraculous as it seemed, Durango Westmoreland had fallen in love. Unfortunately that didn't bode well for the remaining single Westmorelands, who didn't have falling in love on their agendas. The thought of doing so was as foreign to them as a six-legged bear.

"Congratulations and welcome to wedded bliss," Chase Westmoreland said, clapping Durango on the back.

"Thanks, Chase."

Other congratulations followed. It was Ian who had a serious question to ask. "What about us? The ones who have no desire to follow down that path?"

Durango grinned at his brother and said, "I hate to tell you this, but I doubt any man is safe. I'm going to tell it to you like someone older and wiser told me. No matter how much your heart is made of stone, it can turn to putty in the right woman's hands."

Jared Westmoreland grinned and raised his wineglass in the air and said, "With that said, gentlemen, I rest my case."

Dare Westmoreland, who had been quiet all this time, smiled and said after glancing around the room at the remaining six Westmoreland bachelors, "Now we're faced with that burning question again. Which one of you will be next?"

* * * * *

IAN'S ULTIMATE GAMBLE

Prologue

"**I** won't do it, Malcolm!" Brooke Chamberlain said sharply as she absently pushed a dark-brown dread that had fallen in her face back behind her ear. If she'd had any warning about the reason she'd been summoned to her boss's office, she would have found an excuse not to come.

As far as she was concerned what he was asking her to do was totally unreasonable. First, she had just come off one assignment, involving a successful vineyard that had been caught producing more than wine, and second, he wanted her to go back out west and literally spy on the one man who hated her guts—Ian Westmoreland.

Malcolm Price rubbed a frustrated hand down his face before saying, "Sit down, Brooke, and let me explain why I decided to give the assignment to you."

Brooke gave an unladylike snort. As far as she was concerned there was nothing to explain. Malcolm was more than just her boss. He was a good friend and had been since their early days with the Bureau when he'd been a fellow agent. Because they had been good friends, he was one of the few people who knew of her past relationship with Ian as well as the reason they had parted ways.

"How can you of all people ask me to do that to Ian, Malcolm?" she said, pacing the room as she spoke, refusing to sit down.

"Because if you don't, Walter Thurgood will be assigned to do it."

She stopped moving. "Thurgood?"

"Yes, and once he is, it will be out of my hands."

Brooke sat down in the chair Malcolm had offered her earlier. Walter Thurgood, a hotshot upstart, had been with the Bureau for a couple of years. The man had big ambitions, and one was to be the top man at the FBI. After several assignments he'd earned the reputation of being one of those agents who got the job done, although there were times when how he'd gone about it had been questionable.

"And even if Ian Westmoreland is clean, by the time Thurgood finishes with him, he'll make him seem like the dirtiest man on this planet if it makes Thurgood look good," Malcolm said with disgust in his voice.

Brooke knew Malcolm was right. And she also knew what Malcolm wasn't saying—that when you were the son of someone already at the top, the people around you were less likely to slap your hand when you behaved improperly.

"But if you think Ian is running a clean operation and you don't suspect him of anything, why the investigation?" she asked.

"Only because the prior owner of the casino, Bruce Aiken, was found guilty of running an illegal betting operation there, and we don't want any of his old friends to come out from whatever rock they hid under during Aiken's trial and start things up again without Westmorland's knowledge. So in a way you'll be doing him a big favor."

Brooke's gaze dropped from Malcolm's to study her hands, clenched in her lap. Ian would not see things that way, and they both knew it. It would only widen the mistrust between them. But still, she knew there was no way she could allow Thurgood to go in and handle things. It would be downright disastrous for Ian.

She lifted her head and met Malcolm's gaze once again. "And this is not an official investigation?"

"No. You'll be there for a much-needed vacation, while keeping your eyes and ears open."

She leaned forward as anger flared in her eyes. "Ian is one of the most honest men I know."

"In that case you don't have anything to worry about."

She stared at Malcolm thoughtfully for a moment and then said, "Okay."

Malcolm lifted a dark brow. "That means you're going to do it?"

She narrowed her eyes. She was caught between a rock and a hard place and they both knew it. "You knew I would."

He nodded and she saw another certainty in the

depths of his dark blue eyes. The knowledge that four years after their breakup she was still in love with Ian Westmoreland.

Chapter 1

Ian Westmoreland sat at his desk, knee-deep in paper-work, when for no apparent reason he felt a quick tight-ening in his gut. He was a man who by thirty-three had learned to trust his intuition as well as his analytical skills. He lifted his head to glance at the wood-paneled wall in front of him.

He reached out, pressed a button and watched as the paneling slid back to reveal a huge glass wall. The people on the other side who were busy wandering through the casino, taking their chances at the slot ma-chines, gambling tables and arcades, had no idea they were being watched. In certain areas of the casino they were being listened to, as well. More than once the se-curity monitors had picked up conversations best left unheard. But when you operated a casino as large as the Rolling Cascade, the monitors and one-sided mirror were in place for security reasons. Not everyone who came to a casino was there to play. There were those who came to prey on others, and those were the ones his casino could do without. His huge surveillance room on the third floor, manned by top-notch security experts viewing over a hundred monitors twenty-four hours a day, made sure of it.

Since the opening, a lot of people had made reservations merely to check out the newly remodeled casino and resort and to confirm the rumors that what had once been a dying casino had been brought back to life in unprecedented fashion. *People* magazine had announced in a special edition that the Rolling Cascade had brought the ambience of Las Vegas to Lake Tahoe, and had done it with class, integrity and style.

Ian stood and sat on the corner of his desk, his eyes sharp and assessing as he scanned the crowd. There had to have been a reason he was feeling uptight. The grand opening had been a success and he was glad he'd made the move from riverboat gambling casino owner with ease.

A few minutes later he was about to give up, and chalk it up to having an off day and get back to work, when he saw her.

Brooke Chamberlain.

He stood as his entire body tensed. What the hell was she doing here? Deciding he wasn't going to waste time trying to figure that out, he reached for the phone on his desk. His call was quickly answered by the casino's security manager.

"Yes, Ian?"

"There's a woman standing at the east-west blackjack

table wearing a powder-blue pantsuit. Please escort her to my office immediately."

There was a pause when his security manager asked a question. And in a tight voice Ian responded, "Yes, I know her name. It's Brooke Chamberlain."

After hanging up the phone, his full attention went back to the woman he'd once come pretty damn close to asking to be his wife…before her betrayal. The last time he'd seen her had been three years ago in Atlanta at his cousin Dare's wedding. Since she'd once worked for Sheriff Dare Westmoreland as one of his deputies, she'd been invited, and Ian had deliberately ignored her.

But not this time. She was on his turf and he intended to let her know it.

Ian was watching her.

Brooke wasn't sure from where but the federal agent in her knew how. Video monitors. The place was full of them, positioned so discreetly she doubted the crowd of people who were eager to play the odds knew they were on camera.

"Excuse me, Ms. Chamberlain?"

Brooke turned to stare into the face of a tall, husky-looking man in his late forties with blond hair and dark blue eyes. "Yes?"

"I'm Vance Parker, head of security for the casino. The owner of this establishment, Ian Westmoreland, would like a few words with you in his office."

Brooke's lips curved into a smile. She seriously doubted that Ian had just a "few words" to say to her. "All right, Mr. Parker, lead the way."

And as Vance Parker escorted her to the nearest elevator she prayed that she would be able to survive the next two weeks.

With his gaze glued to the glass, Ian had watched the exchange. He had known the exact moment Vance had mentioned his name. Upon hearing it, Brooke's reaction hadn't been one of surprise, which shot to hell the possibility that she hadn't known he owned the place. She had knowingly entered the lion's den, and he was determined to find out why.

He stood and moved around his desk, suddenly feeling that knot in his gut tighten even more. And when he heard the ding, a signal that someone was on their way up in his private elevator, the feeling got worse. Although he didn't want to admit it, he was about to come face-to-face with the one woman he'd never been able to get out of his system. Whether deliberately or otherwise, during the two years they were together, Brooke had raised the bar for his expectations about women. Deputy by day and total woman at night, she had made any woman that had followed seem woefully lacking. He'd had to finally face the fact that whether he liked it or not, Brooke Chamberlain had been the ultimate woman. She was the one woman who had killed his appetite for other women. The one woman who'd been able to tame his wild heart.

Not only tame it, but capture it.

The memory brought a bitter smile to his lips. But today he was older and wiser, and the heart she once controlled had since turned to stone. Still, that didn't stop his breath from catching in his throat when he turned at the sound of the elevator door opening.

Their gazes connected, and he acknowledged that the chemistry they'd always shared was still there. Hot. Intense. Soul stirring. He felt it, clear across the room, and when he felt the floor shake, he placed his hand on his desk to keep his balance.

This was the closest they'd been to each other since that morning when he'd found out the truth and had walked out of her apartment after their heated argument. At Dare and Shelly's wedding, Ian had kept his distance, refusing to come within ten feet of her, but those gut-wrenching feelings had been strong then, nonetheless.

Over the years it had been hard to let go of the memory of the day they'd met in Dare's office, when she'd been twenty-two. Even in her deputy's uniform she had taken his breath away, just as she was doing now at twenty-eight.

Despite their separation and the circumstances that had driven him to end what he'd thought was the perfect love affair, he had to admit that she was the most beautiful woman he'd ever set eyes on. She had skin the color of sweet almond; expressive eyes that turned various shades of brown depending on her mood; lips that could curve in a way that made every cell in his body vibrate; and a mass of dreadlocks that came to her shoulders, which he loved holding on to each and every time he entered her body.

His hand balled into a fist at his side. The thought that Brooke could dredge up unwanted memories spiked his anger, and he forced his gaze away from her to Vance. "Thanks, Mr. Parker. That will be all."

Ian watched his good friend lift a curious brow and shrug big wide shoulders before turning back to the elevator. As soon as the elevator door closed, Ian's attention returned to Brooke. She had moved across the room and was standing with her back to him, staring at a framed photo of him and Tiger Woods and another of him and Dennis Rodman.

She surprised him when she broke the silence by saying, "I heard Tiger and Dennis have homes in this area."

Ian arched a brow. So she wanted to make small talk, did she? He shouldn't have been surprised. Brooke had a tendency to start babbling whenever she was nervous. He'd actually found it endearing the night of their first date. But now it was annoying as hell.

He didn't want her to make small talk. He didn't want her there, period, which brought him back to the reason she was here in his office. He wanted answers and he wanted them now.

"I didn't have Vance bring you here to discuss celebrity homes. I want to know what the hell you're doing here, Brooke."

The moment of reckoning had finally arrived. Brooke had grabbed the chance to take her eyes off Ian when he'd all but ordered Vance Parker to leave them alone. Although she had prepared for this moment from the day she'd left Malcolm's office, she still wasn't totally ready for the encounter. Yet there was nothing she could do but turn around and hope that one day, if he ever found out the truth, he would forgive the lie she was about to tell.

On a sigh, she slowly turned, and the moment she did so their eyes locked with more intensity than when Vance had been present. Her internal temperature suddenly shot sky high, and every cell in her body felt fried from the sweltering heat that suddenly consumed her.

Words momentarily failed her since Ian had literally taken her breath away. He had always been a good-looking man, and today, three years since she'd last seen him, he was doubly so; especially with the neatly trimmed beard he was sporting. He'd always had that drop-dead-gorgeous, let-me-bed-you-before-I-die look. He'd been a man who'd always been able to grab the attention of women. And now this older Ian was a man who exuded raw, masculine sexuality.

When she had returned to Atlanta to take the job as one of Dare Westmoreland's deputies, she had heard about the two Westmoreland cousins who were the same age and ran together in what women had called a wolf pack. Ian and his cousin Storm had reputations around Atlanta for being ultimate players: Storm had been dubbed the Perfect Storm and Ian, the Perfect End.

It was rumored that any woman who went out with Ian got the perfect ending to their evening, after sharing a bed with him. But all that had changed when he'd begun showing interest in her. He'd called her a hard nut to crack; she'd been one of the few women to rebuff his charm.

Instead of willingly falling under his spell like other women, she'd made him earn his way into her bed. The result had been two years of being the exclusive recipient of his special brand of sexual expertise.

The rumors hadn't been wrong, but neither had they been completely right. She had discovered that not only was Ian the Perfect End but he was the Perfect Beginning as well. No one could wake a woman up each morning the way he could. The memories of their lovemaking still curled her toes and wet her panties. He had been her first lover and, she thought, her only lover.

"Are you going to stand there and say nothing or are you going to answer my question, Brooke?"

Ian's question reclaimed Brooke's attention and reminded her why she was there. And with the angry tone of his voice all the memories they'd ever shared were suddenly crushed. Placing her hands on her hips she answered with the same curt tone he'd used on her. "I'll gladly answer your question, Ian."

Ian folded his arms across his chest. How could he have forgotten how quick fire could leap into her eyes whenever she got angry, or how her full and inviting lips could form one perturbed pout? Over the years he had missed that all-in-your-face, hot-tempered attitude that would flare up whenever she got really mad about something.

The women he'd dated after her had been too meek and mild for his taste. They'd lacked spunk, and if he'd said jump, they'd ask how high. But not the woman standing in front of him. She could dish it out like nobody's business and he had admired her for it. That was probably one of the reasons he had fallen so hard for her.

"The reason I'm here is like everyone else. I needed time away from my job and decided to check in here for two weeks," she said, intruding into his thoughts.

Ian sighed. As far as he was concerned her reason sounded too pat. "Why here? There are other places you could have gone."

"Yes, and at the time I booked the two weeks I didn't know you were the owner. I thought you were still running a riverboat casino."

For a few seconds he said nothing. "Hurricane Katrina brought an end to that. But I'd decided to purchase this place months before then. It was just a matter of time before I settled on land."

He studied her for a moment, then asked, "And when did you find out this place was mine?"

Brooke gave a small shrug. "A few days ago, but I figured what the hell, my money spends just as well as anyone else's, and I can't go through life worrying about bumping into you at the next corner."

She released a disgusted sigh and raked her hands through her dreads, making them tumble around her shoulders. "Oh, for heaven's sake, Ian, we have a past, and we should chalk it up as a happy or unhappy time in our lives, depending on how you chose to remember it, and move on. I heard this was a nice place and decided it was just what I needed. And to be quite honest with you I really don't appreciate being summoned here like I'm some kind of criminal. If you're still stuck on the past and don't think we can share the same air for two weeks let me know and I can take my money elsewhere."

Anger made Ian's jaw twitch. She was right, of

course—he should be able to let go and move on; however, what really gripped his insides more than anything was not the fact that they had broken up but why they had. They'd been exclusive lovers. She was the one woman he had considered marrying. But in the end she had been the woman that had broken his heart.

Even when she had moved away to D.C. to take that job with the Bureau, and he had moved to Memphis to operate the *Delta Princess,* they'd been able to maintain a long-distance romance without any problems and had decided within another year to marry.

But the one time she should have trusted him enough to confide in him about something, she hadn't. Instead she had destroyed any trust between them by not letting him know that a case she'd been assigned to investigate had involved one of his business partners. By the time he'd found out the truth, a man had lost his life and a family had been destroyed.

As far as her being here at the Rolling Cascade, he much preferred that she leave. Seeing her again and feeling his reaction to her proved one thing: even after four years she was not quite out of his system and it was time to get her out. Perhaps the first step would be proving they *could* breathe the same air.

"Fine, stay if you want, it's your decision," he finally said.

Brooke lifted her chin. Yes, it would be her decision. There was no doubt in her mind if it was left up to him, he would toss her out on her butt, possibly right smack into Lake Tahoe. "Then I'm staying. Now if you'll excuse me I want to begin enjoying my vacation."

She went to the elevator and without glancing back at him pushed a button, and when the doors opened she stepped inside. When she turned, their gazes met again, and it was during that brief moment of eye contact before the doors swooshed closed that he thought he saw something flicker in the depths of her dark eyes. Cockiness? Regret? Lust?

Ian drew his brows together sharply. How could he move on and put things behind him when the anger he felt whenever he thought of what she'd done was still as intense as it had always been?

Moving around his desk he pushed a button. Within seconds Vance's deep voice came on the line. "Yes, Ian?"

"Ms. Chamberlain is on her way back down."

"All right. Do you want me to keep an eye on her while she's here?"

"No," Ian said quickly. For some reason the thought of someone else—especially another man—keeping an eye on Brooke didn't sit well with him. Deciding he owed his friend some sort of explanation he said, "Brooke and I have a history we need to bury."

"Figured as much."

"And another thing, Vance. She's a federal agent for the FBI."

Ian heard his friend mutter a curse word under his breath before asking, "She's here for business or pleasure?"

"She claims it's pleasure, but I'm going to keep an eye on her to be sure. For all I know, some case or another might have brought her to these parts, and depending on what, it could mean bad publicity for the Cascade."

"Wouldn't she tell you if she were here on business?"

Ian's chuckle was hard and cold. "No, she wouldn't tell me a damn thing. Loyalty isn't one of Brooke Chamberlain's strong points."

Knowing video monitors were probably watching her every move, Brooke kept her cool as she strolled through the casino to catch the elevator that connected to the suite of villas located in the resort section. All around her crowds were still flowing in, heading toward the bar, the lounge or the area lined with slot machines.

It was only moments later, after opening the door to her villa and going inside, that she gave way to her tears. The look in Ian's dark eyes was quite readable, and knowing he hated her guts was almost too much to bear. If he ever found out the real reason she was there…

She inhaled deeply and wiped her cheeks, knowing she had to check in with Malcolm. Taking the cell phone from her purse, she pressed a couple of buttons. He picked up on the second ring.

"I'm at the Rolling Cascade, Malcolm."

He evidently heard the strain in her voice and said, "I take it that you've seen Ian Westmoreland."

"Yes."

After a brief pause he said, "You know this isn't an official investigation, Brooke. Your job is to enjoy your vacation, but if you happen to see anything of interest to let us know."

"That's still spying."

"Yes, but it's beneficial to Westmoreland. You're there to help him, not hurt him."

"He won't see it that way." Her reply was faint as more tears filled her eyes. "Look, Malcolm, I'll get back to you if there's anything. Otherwise, I'll see you in two weeks."

"Okay, and take care of yourself."

Brooke clicked off the phone and returned it to her purse. She walked through the living room and glanced around, trying to think about anything other than Ian. The resort was connected to the casino by way of elevators, and the way the villas had been built took advantage of paths for bicyclers and joggers, who thronged the wide wooden boardwalk that ran along the lake's edge. Since this was mid-April and the harsh winter was slowly being left behind, she could imagine many people would be taking advantage of those activities. The view of the mountains was fabulous, and considering all the on-site amenities, this was a very beautiful place.

After taking a tour of her quarters, she felt a mix of pleasure and excitement rush through her. Her villa was simply beautiful, and she was certain she had found a small slice of paradise. This was definitely a place to get your groove on.

The view of Lake Tahoe through her living room and bedroom windows was breathtaking, perfect to capture the striking colors of the sunset. Brooke was convinced the way her villa was situated among several nature trails was the loveliest spot she had ever been. This was a place where someone could come and leave their troubles behind. But for her it was a place that could actually intensify those troubles.

Pushing that thought from her mind, she entered her bathroom, still overwhelmed. It was just as large as the living room and resembled a private spa. This was definitely a romantic retreat, she thought, crossing the room to the Jacuzzi tub, large enough to accommodate four people comfortably. Then there was the trademark that she'd heard was in every bathroom in the villa—a waterfall that cascaded into a beautiful fountain.

She breathed in deeply, proud of Ian and his accomplishments, and recalled the many nights they would snuggle in bed while he shared his dream of owning such a place with her. When he got the opportunity to purchase the *Delta Princess,* a riverboat that departed from Memphis on ten-day excursions along the Mississippi with stops in New Orleans, Baton Rouge, Vicksburg and Natchez, she had been there on his arm at the party his brothers and cousins had thrown. And when his cousin Delaney had married a desert sheikh, she had been the one to attend the weddings with him in the States and the Middle East.

She sighed, knowing she had to let go of the past the way she'd suggested that he do. But the two years they were together had been good for her, the best she could have ever shared with anyone, and she had looked forward to the day their lives would be joined together.

She frowned. Four years ago Ian had refused to hear anything she had to say, had even refused to acknowledge that if the FBI hadn't discovered Boris Knowles's connection to organized crime when they had, all of the man's business dealings would have come under scrutiny, including his partnership with Ian.

Common sense dictated that she tread carefully where Ian was concerned. He was smart and observant. And he didn't trust her one iota. There was no doubt in her mind that he would be watching her.

Brooke's breathing quickened at the thought of his eyes on her for any amount of time, and moments later a smile curved the corners of her lips. Then she laughed, a low, sultry sound that vibrated through the room. Let him watch her, and while he was doing so maybe it was time to let him know exactly what he'd lost four years ago when he'd walked out of her life.

Ian glanced at the clock on his office wall and decided to give up his pretense of working, since he wasn't concentrating on the reports, anyway. He had too many other things on his mind.

He resisted the urge, as he'd done several times in the past couple of hours, to push the button and see what was going on in the casino, in hopes he would get a glimpse of Brooke. His hand tightened around the paper he held in his hand. He thought he was downright pathetic. And just to think, she was booked for two weeks.

It took him a minute to notice his private line was blinking, and he quickly picked up his phone. "Yes?"

"Ian, how are you?"

He smiled as he recognized Tara's voice. A pediatrician, she was married to his cousin Thorn, a nationally known motorcycle builder and racer. "Tara, I'm doing fine. And what do I owe the pleasure of this call?"

"Delaney's surprise birthday party. Shelly and I are finalizing the guest list and we wanted to check with you about someone who's on it."

Ian leaned back in his chair. It was hard to believe that his cousin Delaney would be thirty. Her husband, Prince Jamal Ari Yasir, wanted to give his wife the celebration of a lifetime and he wanted it held at the Rolling Cascade. It seemed only yesterday when he, his brothers and cousins had taken turns keeping an eye on the woman they'd thought at the time was the only female in the Westmoreland family in their generation.

Delaney hadn't made the job easy, and most of the time she'd deliberately been a pain in the ass, but now she was princess of a country called Tahran and mother of the future king. And to top things off, she and Jamal were expecting their second child.

"Who do you want to check with me about?"

"Brooke Chamberlain."

Ian rubbed a hand down his face. Talk about coincidences. Hearing Brooke's name brought a flash of anger. "What about Brooke?"

"I know Delaney would love to see her again, but we thought we'd better check with you. We don't want to make you uncomfortable in any way. I know how things were at Dare and Shelly's wedding."

Ian leaned back in his chair. He doubted anyone knew how difficult things had been for him at that wedding. "Hey, don't worry about it. I can handle it."

There was a slight pause. "You sure?"

"Yes, I'm sure." He decided not to bother mentioning that Brooke was already there in the casino and they were sharing the same air, as she'd put it. "I got over Brooke years ago. She means nothing to me now."

Ian sighed deeply and hoped with all his heart that the words he'd just said were true.

Chapter 2

Sitting at a table in the back that afforded him a good view of everything that was going on, Ian saw Brooke the moment she walked into the Blue Lagoon Lounge. Under ordinary circumstances he would have given any other beautiful woman no more than a cursory glance. But unfortunately, not in this case. Brooke was, and always had been, a woman who warranted more than a glance, and her entrance into any room could elicit looks of envy in most women's eyes and a frisson of desire down many men's spines.

Taking a deep breath, he frowned in irritation when he saw the look of heated interest in several masculine gazes as she wove her way through the crowded room with confidence, sophistication and style. And what bothered him more than anything was the fact that the same heated interest in other men's eyes was reflected in his, as well. And her outfit wasn't helping matters. Talk about sexy....

She was wearing her hair up in a knot on her head but had allowed a few strands to fall downward to capitalize on the gracefulness of her neck and the dark lashes that fanned her eyes. And her luscious lips were painted a wicked, flaming-hot red.

But it was that sensuous black number draping her body that had practically every male in the room drooling. Emphasizing every curve as well as those long, beautiful legs, the short dress had splits on both sides, and Ian actually heard the constricting of several men's throats when she slid onto a bar stool and exposed a generous amount of thigh. Before she could settle in the seat, he watched as several men stood, eager to hit on her.

Ian took a leisurely sip of his drink. Unless she had changed a lot over the past four years, the poor fools who were all but knocking over chairs to get to her were in for a rude awakening. Although she probably appreciated a compliment as much as the next woman, Brooke was not someone who fawned over male attention. He had learned that particular lesson the hard way the day they'd met. From that day forward he had never underestimated her as a woman again.

And after being deeply involved with her, he also had a more intimate view of the woman who was the center of every man's attention in the lounge tonight. Without a doubt he was probably the only man in the room who knew about the insecurities that had plagued her most of her young life. Her father and two older brothers had been known as the Chamberlain Gang, robbing banks as they zigzagged across state lines before the FBI brought an end to their six-month crime spree.

As a teenager, Brooke and her mother had moved to Atlanta to start a new life and find peace from the taunts, ridicule and insensitivity of those less inclined to put the matter to rest. It was then, while in high school, that Brooke decided to bring honor and dignity back to the Chamberlain name by working on the right side of the law.

The scene at the bar reclaimed Ian's attention, and he chuckled as one man after another was treated to Brooke's most dazzling smile, followed by her more than courteous refusal. He lifted his drink, and before taking another sip he muttered quietly, "Cheers."

There must be a full moon in the sky, Brooke thought, idly sipping her drink. The wolves were definitely on the prowl and had mistakenly assumed she was easy prey.

What woman didn't enjoy knowing a man thought she was attractive? But there were some men who thought beauty went hand in hand with stupidity. One man had even offered her the chance to be his second wife, although he claimed he was still happily married to the first.

"I see you haven't lost your touch."

Brooke glanced over at the man who slid into the seat beside her. The smile in his eyes threw her for a second, but that was only after a flutter of awareness inched up her spine. "Thanks. I'll take that as a compliment," she said, sipping her drink when her throat suddenly felt dry.

She fought to keep her body from trembling and, in an attempt at control, studied her reflection in the glass she held instead of placing her full attention on Ian, the way she wanted to do.

"I really thought I wouldn't see you anymore tonight," he said, taking a sip of his drink.

With that Brooke cocked a brow and turned to him, first taking in how he was dressed. He had changed out of the business suit he was wearing earlier and was wearing another one, just as custom-made and just as appealing. And, like all his attire, it represented his status as a successful businessman. Whether he wanted to or not, he stood out as the impeccably dressed owner of this casino and did so in style.

"Why?" she asked, her concentration moving back to his comment. "Why did you think you wouldn't see me anymore tonight? Did you assume I'd hide out in my villa, Ian, after our meeting earlier? Like I told you, I can't go through life worrying about running into you as if I did something wrong."

Ian's eyes narrowed. "A man's life was lost," he said in a tight voice.

"Yes," she said coolly. "But Boris Knowles should have considered the consequences. He didn't get involved with a group of amateur criminals, Ian. He was involved in organized crime. Don't try and make me feel guilty for the choices he made."

"But had I known, I—"

"Had you known, there wouldn't have been anything you could have done. He was in too deep. Why is it so hard for you to believe that? Telling you would not have changed a thing, other than involve you in a situation you didn't need to be involved in."

Brooke didn't know what else she could say to get through that thick skull of his. He refused to believe he wouldn't have made a difference, and that not knowing about Boris had been a blessing.

She heard his muttered curse and knew it was a mistake to have come to the lounge, a place where she figured he would be. "Look, Ian, evidently you and I will always have a difference of opinion about what happened and why I kept things from you. And I'm tired of you thinking I'm the bad guy."

She stood and threw a couple of bills on the counter. "See you around. But then, maybe it would be better if I didn't."

Ian muttered another curse as he watched Brooke disappear through the door, leaving her sensuous scent trailing behind. He felt that familiar stab of pain he encountered whenever he thought of her betrayal. But Brooke's words reminded him of the same thing Dare, a former FBI agent himself, had told him. Organized crime wasn't anything to play with, and regardless of the outcome, Boris had made his choices.

Dare had also tried to make Ian understand that when Brooke had taken the job as a federal agent, she had also taken an oath to uphold the law and to maintain a vow of confidentiality. Had she told him about the case, and security had been breached, it would have risked not only Brooke's life but the lives of other federal agents.

Ian had understood all of that. But still, he believed

that when two people were committed to each other, there weren't supposed to be any secrets between them. So in his mind she had made a choice between her job and him. That, in a nutshell, was what grated on his ego the most. Yet at some point he had to let go and move on or the bitterness would do him in. He couldn't continue to make her feel like the "bad" guy, especially when he of all people knew how much becoming an agent had meant to her. Twice her application had been turned down when background checks had revealed her family history—namely her father and brothers. It had taken Dare, who'd still maintained close contacts inside the Bureau, to write a sterling letter of recommendation to get her in.

Ian drew in a deep breath. It was time for him and Brooke to finally make peace. He knew that because of all that had happened between them, the love they once shared could never be recovered, but it was time he put his animosity to rest and make an attempt at being friends.

Brooke angrily stripped out of her dress. Ian Westmoreland was as stubborn as any mule could get. He refused to consider that she had been doing her job four years ago and if she had told him anything about the case, her own life could have been in jeopardy. No, all he thought about was what had happened to a man who'd been living a lie to his family, friends and business associates.

Fine, if that was the position Ian wanted to take, even after four years, let him. She refused to allow him to get on her nerves, and somehow and in some way she would wipe away the memories she found almost impossible to part with. More than anything she had to erase him from her heart. But in the meantime she planned to enjoy herself for the next two weeks and wouldn't let him stand in the way of her doing just that.

She slipped into the two-piece bathing suit, thinking a late-night swim might make her feel better. Swimming had always relaxed her, and she was seriously considering adding a pool to her home in D.C. The question was whether or not she would have the time to enjoy it. In a few months she would have made her five-year mark with the Bureau and it was time to decide if she wanted to remain out in the field or take on administrative duties. Her good friend and mentor, Dare Westmoreland, had cautioned her about Bureau burnout, which was what had happened to him after seven years as an agent.

Brooke had just grabbed her wrap when she heard the knock at her door. Evidently room service had made a mistake and was at the wrong villa. Making her way across the room, she leaned against the door and glanced through the peephole, and suddenly felt a sensation deep in the pit of her stomach. Her late-night caller was Ian.

She tensed and shook her head. If he thought he would get in the last word he had another thought coming. After removing the security lock she angrily snatched open the door. "Look, Ian, I—"

Before she could finish, he placed a single white rose in her hand. "I come in peace, Brooke. And you're right. It's time to put the past behind us and move on."

* * *

Ian's heart slammed against his chest. He had been prepared for a lot of things, but he hadn't been prepared for Brooke to open the door in a two-piece bathing suit with a crocheted shawl wrapped around her waist that didn't hide much of anything.

There were her full, firm breasts that almost poured out of her bikini top and a tiny waist that flared to shapely hips attached to the most gorgeous pair of legs any woman could possess. And her feet—how could he possibly forget her sexy feet? They were bare, with brightly painted toenails, encased in a pair of cute flat leather sandals.

Her unique scent was feminine and provocative and the same one he had followed out of the lounge. It was the same scent that was filling her doorway, saturating the air surrounding him, getting under his skin. She was and had always been a woman of whom fantasies were made. And seeing her standing there was overwhelming his sense of self-control.

He sighed deeply, inwardly wishing he could focus on something other than her body and her scent. He wanted to concentrate on something like the rose he had given her, but instead his gaze lowered to her navel, which used to be one of his favorite spots on her body. He could recall all the attention he used to give it before moving lower to…

"Ian?"

He snatched his attention back to her face and cleared his throat. Damn, he had come to make peace, not make love. They would never share that type of relationship again. "Yes?"

"Thanks for the rose, and I'm glad we can move forward in our lives, and I hope that one day we can be friends again," she said.

Brooke was watching his eyes, probably noting the caution within their dark depths when he said, "I hope so, too."

She nodded. "Good."

He leaned in the doorway. "You're going out?"

"Yes, I thought I'd go for a swim at one of the pools. The one with the huge waterfall looks inviting."

Ian nodded. It was. He had passed the area on his way here, and another thing he noted was that it was crowded with more men than women. He then remembered that the Rolling Cascade was hosting a convention of the International Association of Electricians. There were over eight hundred attendees, eighty percent of them men who probably thought they were capable of finding a woman's hot spot and wiring her up in a minute flat. He drew his dark brows together sharply. Not with this woman.

"That pool is nice, but I know of one that's a hundred times better," he said, when an idea suddenly popped into his head.

"Really, where?"

"My penthouse."

She met his eyes then, and he could imagine what thoughts were going through her mind. Hell, he was wondering about it himself. He had no right to feel possessive, as if she was still his. But just because she wasn't didn't mean he shouldn't have a protective instinct where she was concerned, did it?

Feeling better about the reason he was inviting her

to his suite, he reached out and took her hand in his. "Look, it was just an invitation for you to use my private pool. Besides, I'd like to catch up on how things have been going for you. But if you prefer we don't go any further than the rose, that's fine."

Brooke took a second to absorb Ian's words. He wanted them to become friends again and nothing more. He had given her a peace offering and now he wanted them to catch up on what had been going on in their lives. She doubted that he knew she asked about him often, whenever she and Dare spoke on the phone. She knew Ian was back at the top of his game, had reinstated his role of the Perfect End and now claimed he would never, ever settle down and marry. With his cousin Storm happily married, Ian much preferred being the remaining lone wolf of the Westmoreland clan.

"I'd love to go swimming in your private pool and get reacquainted," she said, and hoped and prayed she could get through an evening alone with him in his private quarters.

The smile that touched his lips sent heat spreading through her. "Good. Are you ready to leave now?"

"Yes. I just need to grab a towel."

"Don't bother. I have plenty."

"Okay, let me get my door key."

Moments later she stepped out and closed the door behind her. As they walked together, side by side, toward a bank of elevators, she was fully aware that Ian was looking at her, but she refused to look back. If for one instant she saw heated desire in his eyes, she would probably do something really stupid like give in to the urgency of the sexual chemistry that always surrounded them and ask him to kiss her. But knowing what ironclad control Ian could have, he would probably turn her down.

"Welcome to my lair, Brooke Chamberlain."

Ian stepped aside to let her enter, and Brooke's breath caught the moment she stepped into the room. His personal living quarters were a floor above his office, and both were connected by a private elevator, an arrangement he found convenient.

The moment Brooke crossed the threshold it was as if she had walked into paradise. She had figured that, as the owner of the Rolling Cascade, Ian would have a nice place, but she hadn't counted on anything this magnificent, this breathtaking.

His appreciation of nature was reflected in the many plants around the penthouse, which encompassed two floors connected by a spiral staircase.

The first things she noticed were the large windows and high ceilings, as well as the penthouse's eclectic color scheme—a vibrant mix of red, yellow, orange, green and blue. She was surprised at how well the colors worked together. For symmetry, the two fireplaces in the room were painted white, and then topped with a hand-painted tapestry.

It appeared the furniture had been designed with comfort in mind, and several tropical-looking plants and trees gave sections of the room a garden effect.

"Come on, let me show you around," he said, taking her hand in his.

The warmth of the strong hand encompassing hers sent a wave of sensation rippling through her. She tried not to think about what expert hands they were and how he used to take his thumb and trail it over her flesh, starting at her breasts and working his way downward, sometimes alternating his thumb with his tongue.

His silky touch could make her purr, squirm, and elicited all kind of sounds from her. And when he would work his way to her navel—heaven help her—total awareness of him would consume her entire body, making her breathe his name in an uncontrolled response to his intimate ministrations.

"You okay?"

His words snatched her back to reality, and she glanced up at him. "Yes, why do you ask?"

"No reason," he murmured, and the tone sent a shiver all through her.

Brooke raised a brow. Had she given something away? Had she made a sound? One he recognized? One he remembered?

They walked together while he gave her a tour. French doors provided a gracious entry from room to room, and the kitchen, with its state-of-the-art cabinets and generously sized island, reflected a wise use of space. The skill of an interior designer touched every inch of Ian's home, and Brooke thought this was definitely the largest penthouse she'd ever seen. It encompassed more square footage than her house back in D.C.

Ian told her that Prince Jamal Ari Yasir was his primary investor, and that his brothers, Spencer and Jared, and his cousin Thorn had also invested in the Rolling Cascade. The one thing Brooke had always admired about the Westmoreland family was their closeness and the way they supported each other.

When he showed her his bedroom a spark of envy ran through Brooke at the thought of the other women who'd shared the king-size bed with him. But then she quickly reminded herself that Ian's love life was no business of hers.

"So, what do you think?" he asked casually.

His question momentarily froze her, and she shifted her eyes from the bed and met his gaze. "I'm really proud of you, Ian, of all your accomplishments. And you are blessed to belong to a family that fully supports what you do. They are really super."

Ian smiled. "Yes, they are."

"And how are your parents?"

"They're doing fine. You do know that Storm got married?" he asked, leading her out of the bedroom, down the spiral stairscase, to an area that led to an enclosed pool.

She smiled up at him. "Yes. I can't imagine marriage for the Perfect Storm."

The corners of Ian lips curled in a smile. "Now he's the Perfect Dad. His wife Jayla and their twin daughters are the best things that ever happened to him. He loves them very much."

When there was a lull in the conversation, Brooke said, "And I heard about your uncle Corey's triplets."

He chuckled. "Yeah, can you believe it? He found out he had fathered triplets around the same time he was reunited with a woman who'd always been his true love. He's married now and is a very happy man on his mountain."

Brooke nodded. She had visited Corey's Mountain

in Montana with Ian and knew how beautiful it was. "I also heard that Chase got married and so did Durango."

He nodded, grinning. "Yes, both were shockers. Chase and Durango married two sisters, Jessica and Savannah Claiborne. Durango and Savannah eloped and had their wedding here."

He then looked over at her. "I see Dare's been pretty much keeping you informed."

She shrugged. She detected a smile in his voice, although she didn't see one in his face. "Yes. Do you resent knowing Dare and I keep in touch?"

"No, not at all," he said, his tone making it seem as if such a notion was ridiculous. "Dare knew you for a lot longer than I did. You used to be his deputy and the two of you were close. I didn't expect you to end your friendship with him just because things didn't work out between us, Brooke. The Westmorelands don't operate that way."

Moments later he added, "And I also know that you've kept in touch with other family members." He shook his head, grinning. "Or should I say they kept up with you. Delaney let me know in no uncertain terms that our breakup had no bearing on your friendship."

"Did she?" Brooke asked, attempting to conjure up an air of nonchalance she was far from feeling. She and Delaney had remained friends, and a few years ago when Delaney had accompanied her husband to an important international summit in Washington, the two of them had spent the day shopping, going to a movie and sharing dinner.

"Here we are."

They stopped walking, and Brooke's breath caught.

Now this was paradise. Ian's enclosed pool was huge, and included a cascading waterfall and several tropical plants, and was connected to his own personal fitness center and game room.

"You like it?"

"Oh, Ian, it's wonderful, and you're right—it's better than the one by the villas."

He reached behind her and handed her a couple of towels off a stack. "Here you are, and I meant to ask earlier, how's your mom?"

Brooke smiled. "Mom's doing fine. Marriage agrees with her. While Dad was living—even though he was incarcerated—she refused to get involved with anyone. She was intent on honoring her wedding vows, although she'd always deserved better. She refused to divorce him."

Ian nodded. "I heard about your father. I'm sorry."

Brooke shrugged. "He was a couple of years from being up for parole and what does he do?" she asked angrily. "He causes a prison riot that not only cost him his own life but the lives of four other inmates, as well."

"And how are your brothers?"

"Bud and Sam are okay. Mom stays in contact with them more than their biological mother," she said of her father's first wife. When her mother had married Nelson Chamberlain, her brothers were already in their teens.

"I write them all the time and have taken Mom to see them on occasion. I think they've finally learned their lessons and will be ready for parole when the time comes," she said.

Brooke appreciated Ian asking about her family. She

had loved her dad and her brothers even though they had chosen lives of crime. And she simply adored her mother for having had the strength to leave her husband to provide her daughter with a better life.

She was about to remove her wrap when she nervously glanced over at Ian. "Will you be taking a swim, too?"

He smiled, shaking his head. "No, not tonight. The pool will be all yours. There are a couple of calls I need to make, so I'm going to leave you alone for a while. Do you mind?"

"No, and I appreciate you letting me use your pool."

"Don't mention it."

"And I enjoyed our chat, Ian."

"So did I." He glanced at his watch. "I'll be back in around an hour to walk you to your villa."

"All right."

After Ian left, Brooke licked her suddenly dry lips, remembering how quickly he had exited the room. Was she imagining things? Had the thought of her undressing in front of him—doing something as insignificant as removing the wrap of her bathing suit—sent Ian running? Um. Maybe that ironclad control he used to have wasn't as strong as she'd thought.

The possibility that the attraction they'd once shared was just as deep as before sent a warm feeling flowing through her. And suddenly feeling giddy, she removed her wrap, walked over to the deep end of the pool and dived in.

Ian's hand trembled as he poured wine into his glass. Talk about needing a drink. It had taken everything within him not to pull Brooke into his arms several times during their conversation. And even worse, he had picked up on that vibe, the same one she always emitted whenever she wanted him to make love to her.

It had been awkward to stand beside her and know what her body wanted and not oblige her the way he would have done in the past. Angrily he slammed down the glass on his coffee table. *This is not the past, this is the present and don't even think about going back there, Westmoreland. The only thing you and Brooke can ever be is friends, and even that is really pushing it.*

He muttered a curse, and at the same time the phone rang. It was his private line. "Yes?"

"Hey, you're okay?"

Hearing his cousin Storm's voice, Ian shook his head and smiled. It had always been the weirdest thing. His brother Quade was his fraternal twin like Chase was Storm's. But when it came to that special bond he'd heard that twins shared, it had always been he and Storm and Quade and Chase.

Quade worked for the Secret Service, and half the time none of the family knew what he doing or where he was. But they could depend on Chase to know if Quade was ever in trouble with that special link they shared. Likewise, Ian knew that only Storm could detect when something was bothering him, even thousands of miles away.

"And what makes you think something is wrong?" Ian asked, sitting down on a leather sofa. This spot gave him a view of Brooke whenever she swam in the shallow end of his pool.

Storm chuckled. "Hey, I feel you, man. The one night I should be getting a good night's sleep, now that the girls are sleeping through the night, I'm worried about you."

Ian lifted a brow. "Worried about me?"

"Yes. What's going on, Ian? What has you so uptight that I can sense it?"

Ian's attention was momentarily pulled away from his phone conversation when Brooke swam to the shallow end of the pool. He shifted slightly on the sofa to get a better view and knew from where he sat that he could see her but she couldn't see him.

He watched as she stood up, emerging from the water like a sex goddess as she tossed her wet hair back from her face. But it wasn't her hair that was holding his attention. *Have mercy!* She had a body that made men drool, curves in all the right places—and he was familiar with those curves, every delectable inch. And that bikini, wet and clinging to her, looked good on her. Too good. He could only imagine the reaction she would have gotten from other men. But just the thought that he had once touched her all over, licked her all over, made love to that body in more ways than he could count, sent blood surging through his veins. "Damn."

"Hey, man. Talk to me. What's going on?"

Storm's words reminded Ian he was still holding the phone in his hand, and it was taking every ounce of strength he had to continue to do so. He suddenly felt weak, physically drained.

"Brooke," he finally said, whispering her name

softly, drawing out the sound deep from within his throat on a husky sigh. "She's here."

"What do you mean she's there?"

Ian rolled his eyes upward. "Just what I said, Storm. She checked into the Rolling Cascade for two weeks for some R and R. But at this moment she happens to be in my penthouse, using my pool. We're trying to put the past behind us."

"Brilliant. That's just brilliant, Ian," Storm chuckled. "Don't tell me, let me guess. You and Brooke are trying to put the past behind you and become friends. Come on, Ian. Think about it. Do you actually believe you can be just friends with the only woman who's ever had your heart?"

Ian frowned. "Yes, since the key word is *had*. I stopped loving Brooke years ago."

"So you say."

"So I mean. Good night, Storm."

Chapter 3

Ian stood and walked across the room to the wall-to-wall, floor-to-ceiling window that gave a breathtaking view of Lake Tahoe.

When he had reopened the casino after extensive remodeling, he'd given it more than just a new name and a new face. He had given the place a new attitude. He had painstakingly combined the charm of the Nevada landscape with the grandeur of a world-class casino, then added an upscale nightlife whose unique ambiance appealed to a sophisticated clientele.

His penthouse had the best view of the lake. Strategically set on the west side of the casino and covering portions of both the eighth and ninth floors, his domain was away from the villas, the various shops and restaurants, the golf courses with cascading waterfalls and the tennis courts. He considered his personal quarters his very own private hot spot, although between the hours he'd spent making sure things were perfect for the grand opening nine months ago, his time had been too consumed in business matters to pursue any intimate pleasures, and he had not yet invited a woman up to his lair, other than members of his family and now Brooke.

Brooke.

He cocked his head, and a smile touched his lips when he heard the sound of her splashing around in the pool. For some reason, he liked knowing she was there, and regardless of what Storm thought, he and Brooke held no emotional ties. The most they could ever be again was friends.

Brooke swam back and forth through the calming water as she did another lap around Ian's pool. After several more laps she pulled herself up on the ledge thinking that she'd had a wonderful workout. She felt rejuvenated in one sense and exhausted in another. Beside the pool was a long padded bench that looked absolutely inviting, and she decided to rest a while.

She lay flat on her back and stared up at the ceiling. All she could think about was Ian's dark eyes and the way they had looked at her moments before he'd left her alone. Swim or no swim, she'd been fantasizing about him ever since. She was trying to keep her distance, especially knowing how quickly she could be consumed by desire for him. Though she hadn't been completely honest with him about the real reason she was there, she couldn't control her attraction to him. Basic urges were exactly what they were. Basic. And she knew firsthand how skilled Ian was in taking care of anything that ailed her.

She flipped onto her stomach and studied a nearby plant. Anything to get Ian off her mind. But it wasn't working. As her eyes closed, her mind shifted back to a time when he had moved his mouth all over her breasts, sucking and lapping at her nipples while his fingers skimmed the edge of her panties....

Ian wasn't sure how long he stood at the window looking out, idly sipping his wine observing various yachts, sailboats and schooners cruising the lake below, resembling fireflies as they went by. Tomorrow was another busy day. He had meetings with Nolen McIntosh, his casino manager, Vance on security matters and Danielle on PR. Then of course there was that discussion with his event planner regarding the final details for Delaney's surprise birthday party.

It took Ian only a minute to notice something was different. There was no sound coming from the pool. He set his wineglass on a nearby table, moved away from the window and headed toward the room where he'd left Brooke almost an hour earlier.

The pool was empty, so he glanced around the room and then saw her. She lay flat on her stomach on the padded bench, asleep. The intensity of the emotions he felt at that moment hit him from every angle. When was the last time Brooke had slept at his place? It had been years. Their angry parting words—mostly from him—still burned fervently in his ears. She had tried to explain, tried presenting her side of things. But he hadn't wanted to listen. He hadn't wanted to ever see or talk to her again.

So what was happening here? Why was he talking to her, seeing her again? Why had he let her into his space, the only place free of memories of her?

She moaned in her sleep, and hearing the sound he stepped closer, allowing his gaze to rake over her shapely body, feeling a rush of adrenaline. A deep swallow made its way down his throat as his gaze moved to the tie that held the top part of her bikini in place, the smooth curve of her back, the flare of her hips under the thin scrap of material that was supposed to be a bikini bottom. Her skin looked soft, inviting and warm to the touch. He wanted his hands all over her thighs, and he would do anything to cup her delicious bottom. And he didn't want to think about how he wanted to use his mouth on her breasts.

He sighed deeply. Considering their history, it was only natural that he would feel this heated lust, this mind-searing desire. There was a time when, if he'd found her like this, he could have awakened her by making love to her, gently flipping her on her back and using his hands and his mouth to show her what real moans were all about. His stomach began trembling at the memories, and hot liquid fire filled his body at the very thought. But he knew things were different. They no longer had that kind of relationship, and he doubted they ever would again. She was no longer his to touch at will.

That realization dictated his next move. Reaching to a table behind him he grabbed a huge towel and gently covered her. He would not wake her. He would let her rest. But neither would he leave her. He wanted to be there when she awoke. Call it pure torture, but he wanted to look into the depth of those eyes, catch her drowsy, sleepy, tousled look, the sexy one she got whenever she roused from sleep. That look used to stir up everything male within him and arouse him to no end. And that look would drive him to take her with a passion that could never be duplicated with any other woman.

Removing his jacket, he folded it neatly and placed it across the back of a wicker sofa before settling down in a wicker chair and stretching his legs out in front of him. From this position he could watch her while she slept and see her when she woke up.

And as he sat there, his mind went back to that day six years ago when they had met. He had walked into Dare's office, and from that day on his life had never been the same.

Slowly released from the throes of a deep sleep, Brooke kept her eyes closed as she drowsily inhaled gently and then yawned. There was nothing like a swim to work the aches and pains out of her muscles, and that thought made her recall where she was and why the familiar scent of one particular man was surrounding her.

She slowly opened her eyes and they immediately connected to the dark penetrating ones of Ian Westmoreland. Sitting in a chair across the room, he looked slightly disheveled, as if he'd been sitting there for a while, but nothing could erase that sexy look he wore so well. What had been a crisp white shirt now had a few buttons undone, and the sleeves were rolled up. With his legs stretched out in front of him, his trousers were pulled tight against muscular, well-defined thighs.

A sensual shiver ran down her body and she felt the huge towel covering her and knew he had placed it there. The thought of him being that close to her, placing a towel over her body, stoked her insides, creating a heavy warmth.

A part of her wanted to sit up, stretch her legs, apologize for falling asleep, but she couldn't do any of those things. She couldn't move, could barely breathe. His gaze was holding her in place and making her remember happier times, passionate times, and she wondered if he was doing the same.

She watched his eyes darken even more, and in re-sponse a rush of hormones that had been dormant for four years rushed through her system. Awareness churned in her stomach, and her entire body suddenly felt sensitive, acutely aware of him as a man. However, not just any man.

He was the man who had first introduced her to the pleasures that a couple could share; the man who used to wake her up each morning by using his hands and lips on every part of her body; a man who, besides being the best lover any woman could possibly have, had become her confidant and her best friend.

Brooke blinked, was caught momentarily off guard when he stood and began walking toward her, showing telltale proof of how much he wanted her. The bulge in his pants couldn't lie. Her body instantly responded, recognizing the sexual chemistry that emanated from him and quickly overpowered her.

She raised her body to a sitting position, stretched

out her legs and braced her hands on both sides of her. She couldn't help wondering what he was thinking. She definitely knew her thoughts. The heated look in his eyes, the hot familiarity, gave her an idea. There was still a lot unsettled between them. There were some things that could never be as they used to be. But there would always be a level where they would be in accord. And this was it.

Deep down a part of her wished otherwise, wished she could expunge him from her heart as she knew he had done her. He might still want her, desire her, but he no longer loved her. But right now, at this moment, heaven help her, it didn't matter. She needed to feel his body pressed close to hers, needed to once again feel his arms holding her, his mouth tasting hers.

He came to a stop in front of her and the light that poured down from overhead highlighted the darkness of his skin in contrast to his white shirt. She stared up at him, as blood throbbed through her veins, and she took in his broad chest and strong lean body.

She slowly stood, wondering if her legs could hold her weight, but that concern quickly vanished from her mind when she heard a sensual moan escape his clenched teeth, and she knew he was trying to resist her, fight what they were both feeling.

But when he began to lean closer, she knew he had given up the battle and was giving in to temptation. Common sense was being overwhelmed by lust. And when their mouths connected and their tongues mingled, flames sparked inside of her and she completely lost whatever control she'd had. This is Ian, her mind and body taunted. And she did what seemed so natural, which was to kiss him back in all the ways he had taught her to.

Ian made love to Brooke's mouth with as much skill as he possessed. *Mercy.* He wanted this. He needed this. Four years hadn't eliminated the yearning, the urgency or the hunger. She wasn't out of his system, and maybe this would be the first step in ridding her from it. But the more their tongues consorted, fused and intertwined, the harder it was to regain control. And when he brought her body closer to his, let his hands slide over her backside with a possessiveness he had no right to feel, he wanted to do more than taste her. He wanted to place her back on the bench, further stoke the heat between them, remove his clothes, straddle her body, remove her bikini bottom and make her his again.

His again.

That thought made him lift his head sharply, knowing that was the last thing he wanted. Things could never go back to being the way they were. He refused to let them. There were some things you could never recover from, and one was a broken heart. He'd loved and he'd loved hard. And whether she had intended to or not, she had destroyed that love.

He looked down and his gaze swept over her features. His eyes touched each and every part of the face he would always cherish. But that was as far as things would ever go. He would want her, lust after her, but he would never love her again.

"Come on and let me walk you back to your villa," he said in a husky voice tinged with regret.

As if he had kissed any and every word from her mouth, Brooke merely nodded, gathered the towel around her and followed him as he led her to his private elevator.

"I didn't mean to overstay my welcome," she finally was able to say when the elevator doors opened.

He looked down at her, his features tight. "You didn't."

For some reason she didn't believe him. One thing she knew about Ian was that he was a man who didn't forgive easily, nor was he quick to forget. He claimed he wanted them to move on and be friends, but she wondered if that's what he really wanted, or if that was something he would ever be willing to tolerate. Brooke opened her mouth to say something and then closed it. Chances were he would be keeping his distance for the remainder of her stay.

When they reached her door he stepped aside to let her unlock it. She thought this was where he would tell her good-night, and he surprised her when he took her hand and followed her inside, closing the door behind him.

"Hidden video cameras in the halls," he whispered in a throaty voice before gently pulling her into his arms. He then leaned down and kissed her again, the connection slow and lingering, but just as thorough as before. The kiss sent shudders all through her.

Moments later his mouth left hers to trail heated kisses along her neck and jaw. The feel of his beard rubbing against her skin was eliciting sensations deep in the pit of her stomach. A man like Ian was deadly in more ways than one.

"Will you go sailing with me tomorrow, Brooke?"

She raised her chin, still shuddering, surprised at his request. "Are you sure that's what you want?" she asked.

He was silent for a moment and stared deep into her eyes. It was all Brooke could do not to melt right there on the spot from the heat generating in his gaze. "Yes, I'm sure." He stepped back. "I'm beginning to realize something, Brooke."

"What?" she asked, having a difficult time swallowing.

"Moving beyond what we once shared isn't going to be as easy as I thought."

She lifted her brow and fought back the thick lump of emotion that clogged her throat, almost kept her from breathing. "What do you mean?"

"Mere friendship between us won't ever work."

"You don't think so?"

"No." His voice was clipped, cool and confident. "And since things can never be like they were, we need finality. Closure. A permanent end."

She knew that what he was saying was true, considering the kisses they had shared, but still, hearing him say it hurt deeply. "So, how do you suggest we go about it? Do you want me to leave?" she asked, knowing that wasn't an option even if he wanted her to.

He stared at her for a long moment, then answered by saying, "No. I don't want you to leave. What I want, what I need, is to have you out of my system, and I know of only one way that can be accomplished."

Brooke sighed deeply. She knew of only one way that could be accomplished, as well, and she wasn't going for it. It might get her out of his system, but it would only embed him deeper into hers.

She shook her head vehemently. "It won't work."

"Trust me, it will."

She lifted her chin and glared at him, trying to ignore the way her inner muscles clenched in response to the huskiness of his voice. "It might work for you, but not for me."

Ian leaned in closer to her, his voice low and deep, his lips just a hair away from touching hers. "I'd love to prove you wrong, Brooke. Even now you feel it, the heat, the urge, the cravings. You remember how things used to be between us as much as I do. You remember our out-of-control pheromones, wild nights when we couldn't wait to make love, going so far as to start stripping naked as soon as the door closed behind us."

"Ian."

"And how I would take you right then and there, wherever—on the wall, the floor, the sofa, giving you everything you wanted, whatever you needed. And how you would practically—"

"Stop it, Ian," she said sharply, stepping back away from him to halt the trembling that had begun in her stomach. "I won't let what you're suggesting happen."

She read his expression, saw the challenge in his eyes, the deep-rooted stubbornness. "Okay," he said with a smile that said he didn't believe her any more than she believed herself. "I'll be by to pick you up to go sailing at noon. See you later, Brooke."

Brooke tilted her head, watched him cross the room, open the door and walk out without looking back. She pulled the towel tighter around her body when a chill touched it. After spending so much time in the pool tonight she should be smelling of chlorine. But she smelled of Ian. His manly scent seemed to be all over her.

She dropped the towel and quickly moved toward her bathroom, needing a shower. She would send him a message, letting him know she had changed her mind about going sailing with him.

He might like the idea of playing with fire, but she did not.

Chapter 4

"We have reason to believe one of our guests is smoking in his room," Joanne Sutherlin, resort manager, said to the employees around the conference table during the resort's regular status meeting.

"We haven't been able to find any proof, but a housekeeper reports she's smelled smoke. It seems the guest has been trying to disguise his smoking by spraying heavy cologne in the air," she said.

"If we can prove he's breaking a hotel policy, then we can end his stay with us."

Everyone at the table nodded. They knew Ian had very low tolerance when it came to anyone not abiding by the Rolling Cascade's smoke-free policy.

The next item up for discussion by the management team was entertainment. The activities director confirmed that he had booked deals with top performers for the next eighteen months. Highlights of the upcoming schedule included a two-week billing for Mariah Carey in June, Michael McDonald in September and Phil Collins in December. Smokey Robinson opened tonight for a two-week engagement that was already sold out every night.

Nolen, the casino manager, indicated security had alerted him that a couple of prostitutes had tried soliciting guests in the casino. Although Nevada had legalized prostitution, it was only allowed in licensed brothels. Unfortunately, casinos were a prime target for call girls looking for potential "dates." Ian was committed to keeping the Rolling Cascade prostitution-free.

"We have the matter taken care of," Nolan assured him.

Ian nodded. That's what he wanted to hear. He glanced at his watch. He had ordered a picnic basket from one of the restaurants for his lunch date with Brooke. He had left a message for her that he would be picking her up at noon and couldn't wait to get her on his boat.

He remembered their conversation last night. He had deliberately walked out the door without looking back. To say he had ruffled a few of her feathers would be an understatement. But then, he had merely been upfront with her. It was too late to start playing games. He knew what they needed and she did as well. In order to bring closure, they needed to purge each other from their systems, and until that was done there would always be this emotional tug-of-war between them.

He suddenly felt goose bumps cover his body at the thought of seeing her again and of the afternoon he had planned. A hint of a smile tugged at his lips. She might be resistant now, but once he got her on his sailboat and made her remember all the things she was trying to forget, their day would end the way they both wanted it to.

His pulse began beating wildly an hour later as the status meeting ended. He quickly headed toward his penthouse to change into more comfortable clothes.

"Mr. Westmoreland?"

He turned before stepping into his private elevator. "Yes?" he asked Cassie, a young woman who worked in the resort's business center.

"This message was left for you this morning."

He took the sealed envelope she handed him. "Thank you." He tore it open and read the note.

I've changed my mind about going sailing with you, Brooke.

Ian frowned. If Brooke thought she could dismiss him just like that, she had another thought coming.

"Is there anything you need me to do, sir?"

It was then that Ian realized Cassie was still standing there. He lifted his head and met her gaze. This wasn't the first time he'd seen the heated look of lust in the depths of her dark eyes, and he could recognize a flirtatious comment when he heard one. He recalled what he knew about her. She was a recent college graduate with a degree in hotel management. He had decided long ago, after operating his riverboat, that he would never become sexually involved with his employees. And even though, due to his busy schedule, it had been almost a year since he'd slept with anyone, the only woman his body craved had just canceled their lunch date.

Brooke propped a hand on her hip and stared at the outfits she had placed on the bed. Both were suitable for an afternoon of shopping, but which one should she wear?

The capri pant set was what she would have worn had she gone sailing with Ian. It had a bit more style than the cotton shorts set, and was a designer outfit she'd purchased while in San Francisco last month. The shorts set would provide better comfort of movement as she walked from store to store making purchases. She was about to hang the capri set back in her closet when she heard a knock on her door.

Leaving her bedroom, she wondered if it was housekeeping. The lady had come earlier, but since Brooke had ordered room service for breakfast she had asked the woman to come back later.

Brooke didn't want to think of herself as a coward, but she had dined in her room this morning because she hadn't wanted to run into Ian. They needed at least a couple of days of distance for him to rethink that preposterous suggestion he'd made. In the meantime she would avoid him by taking advantage of all the amenities the resort had to offer. He needed time to cool off, and the interlude would give her the opportunity to assess his operation.

She glanced out the peephole and her heart slammed against her ribs the moment she did so. It was Ian. Did he not get her message canceling their date to go sailing?

When she opened the door, she wasn't quite ready for

the fluttering sensation she felt in her chest. He stood in the doorway casually dressed in a pair of khakis and a blue polo shirt and holding a picnic basket. She'd forgotten how good he looked in everyday clothes. He looked sexy in a suit, but in casual wear he was drop-dead gorgeous.

"You ready?" he asked, cutting into her thoughts.

She raised a brow and pulled her robe tighter around her. "Didn't you get my message?"

He smiled as he walked around her, entering the room without an invitation. "Yes, I got it, but I assumed there must have been a mistake."

She glared at him, wondering why he would think that. "Well, you assumed wrong. There is no mistake. I'm not going sailing with you."

He set the basket on the table, crossed his arms over his chest and asked, "Why? Are you afraid to be alone with me?"

"I'm not afraid, Ian, just cautious," she said as she struggled to maintain her composure.

"And why do you feel the need to put your guard up, Brooke?"

Ha! He had the nerve to ask her that!

Irritation settled in her spine. "I'm not new to this game of yours, Ian."

He cast her an innocent look. "What game?"

She didn't hesitate in answering. "Your game of seduction."

His lips quirked. "Since you think you know me so well, why are you so uptight about spending time with me? You used to know how to handle me. At least you thought you did."

A soft chuckle escaped Brooke's lips. "I didn't think anything. I did handle you. I proved that I wasn't like those half-wit tarts you used to mess around with," she said, crossing the room to him and lifting her chin.

"And furthermore, Ian Westmoreland," she added, reaching out and tapping him on the chest with her finger, "your brand of seduction won't work with me."

"And why won't it?" he asked, grabbing her finger before she jabbed a hole in his chest. "It's always worked before."

"Always worked before? Oh really, well we'll just see about that," she said over her shoulder after turning toward the bedroom. "I'll be ready in five minutes."

"Need any help getting dressed?"

"No, thank you. And if I remember correctly your expertise was in getting me undressed."

When she slammed the bedroom door shut, Ian couldn't help but smile. He remembered that fact, as well. It appeared that he would have to change his strategy a bit today, but eventually he'd have her right where he wanted her.

It was a beautiful day for sailing. The last time she had been on a boat was a couple of years ago when Malcolm had tried fixing her up with an old college pal of his. They had double dated on a deep-sea fishing trip. Unfortunately, she and the guy didn't hit it off, had nothing in common and she'd spent the entire two hours comparing him to Ian. Luckily for her, but unluckily for Malcolm, his date got seasick, and they had to return to shore earlier than planned.

"So what do you think?"

Ian's words intruded into her thoughts, and she glanced over at him and then wished she hadn't. He stood tall next to the railing, silhouetted against the noonday sun, looking every bit the sexy captain. She dismissed that image from her mind and tried concentrating on the sailboat instead. According to Ian, the boat was owned by the casino, which in essence meant it was his. "This boat is a beauty, Ian."

He had surprised her by how expertly he handled the sailboat and all the sleek maneuvers as it glided across the waters of Lake Tahoe with ease. Whether Brooke wanted to admit it or not, it was the perfect day for an afternoon sail, and so far Ian had been the most gracious host in addition to being a well-behaved gentleman. The latter really surprised her.

The food had been delicious yet simple: ham and cheese sandwiches, chips, wine and cheesecake. Nothing fancy, nothing meant to impress. And because it shouldn't have, it did anyway. Sharing lunch with him had been wonderful. He had told her how Stone and his wife had met when they'd been on a plane together bound for Montana. He also told her of his uncle's three children. The cousins had forged a family bond with their newfound Westmoreland cousins from Texas, Uncle Corey's triplets—Clint, Cole and Casey.

"You'll like Casey if you ever get the chance to meet her," he said, taking a sip of his wine. He smiled when he added, "Her brothers had just as much trouble keeping the guys away from her as we did Delaney when she was growing up."

Brooke lifted her eyes toward the sky and breathed in the fresh April air. It was a beautiful day and being out on the lake was exactly what she needed. Had she remained at the resort she would have probably spent way too much money shopping. "I bet it was hard on the three of them, already adults before finding out their father was alive and not dead as they'd thought."

Ian nodded. "Yes, Clint and Cole are handling things okay. It's harder for Casey to come around. She was close to her mother and when Casey found out her mother had lied to them all those years, it hurt."

Ian surprised Brooke by sliding closer to where she sat. "We've talked enough about my new cousins. Now it's time to play," he said, leaning toward her with a hint of mischief in his eyes. It was then she thought that maybe she'd given him credit for being well behaved and a gentleman too soon.

"What sort of game?" she asked, suddenly feeling off balance by his closeness.

"I watched you the other night."

She had an idea where this was going and decided to see if she was right. "And?"

"You were sitting at the blackjack table."

"Go on," she encouraged.

"And I noticed something about you."

"Which was?"

"You can't play worth a damn."

Brooke's eyes widened just seconds before she burst out laughing. This definitely wasn't where she'd thought the conversation was going. And he'd said it so seriously that she quickly agreed he was telling the truth. She couldn't play worth a damn, but playing blackjack wasn't anything she did on a regular basis. "You plan on giving me a few pointers?"

He surprised her by saying yes and pulling out a deck of cards. "It's the only fair thing to do," he said grinning. "I can't have you losing all your money in the casino. It might be bad for business. So pay attention, Ms. Chamberlain."

And he spent the next hour trying to make a proficient gambler out of her.

"I really had a nice time, Ian," Brooke said later that afternoon when they had returned to the casino and he walked her to her villa.

"Prove it by going to a show with me later tonight," he said, taking her hand in his as they continued to walk toward her door.

"A show?"

"Yes, Smokey Robinson opens tonight."

Brooke's eyes widened. "*The* Smokey Robinson?"

At Ian's nod, she smiled and said, "I think he was the only other man my mother loved besides my father."

"In that case, the least you can do is go and swoon in her honor?" Ian said with a grin. He knew his mother felt the same way.

"That would be the daughterly thing to do, wouldn't it?" she asked with a teasing glint in her eyes.

He chuckled. "Of course."

"All right. Then I'll go."

They stopped in front of her door. He studied her for a long moment before saying, "I'll be by to get you for the second show at ten."

"Wouldn't it be easier for me to meet you downstairs somewhere?"

He gave her a smooth grin. Not hardly, he wanted

to say. If she looked anything tonight like she had the other night when she'd shown up at the lounge, the last thing he wanted was other men hitting on her. "It's no problem. I need the exercise, anyway," he said smiling.

"Okay."

When they just stood there a minute, she gave in and asked, "Would you like to come in for a minute?"

He continued to look at her, knowing if he were to go into that room with her, it wouldn't be for just a minute. Patience, he'd discovered, was the key. He hadn't stirred up any stimulating memories like he'd originally planned to do today, but he had enjoyed the time they had spent together. And there would be other times, other opportunities. He would make sure of it.

"No, there're a couple of things I need to do before tonight," he said, stepping back. "But I dare you to ask me that same question after the show," he said, his expression suddenly turning seductive.

She grinned up at him and he knew she was taunting him when she said, "Um, I'll think about it."

He chuckled. "Yeah, you do that." And then he turned and walked away.

When Smokey sings...

The room was packed. People were even crowded around the wraparound bar in the back. But everyone's attention was on the man who'd taken center stage and was belting out "The Tracks of My Tears." His falsetto was his calling card, and the lyrics had meaning. They filled the room with love and romance.

He then did a medley of his Motown tunes and when he began singing "Oh Baby Baby," Brooke's gaze shifted to Ian. She found him staring back at her. Was he thinking the same thing she was? That in the relationship they'd once shared they had both made mistakes, or did he still blame her for everything?

She was so deep in thought that she was startled when everyone stood, began clapping and gave Smokey Robinson a standing ovation. Moments later he went into his final number, "Going to a Go-Go," and the place came alive. Older couples, who remembered the song and the popular dances during that time, got on the floor and began moving their bodies in all kinds of ways. Brooke couldn't help remembering her mom doing those same dances around the house when Brooke was a little girl.

"You want to go out there and try it?" Ian asked, leaning over to her. When he evidently saw the hesitancy in her eyes, he chuckled and asked, "Hey, what do we have to lose?"

She glanced at the crowd on the dance floor and then back at him. "Parts of our face if we got in the way. They're doing a dance called 'the jerk' and I'd hate to be on the receiving end of one of their elbows."

Ian laughed, and although it could barely be heard above the loud music, Brooke felt the richness of the sound of hi voice and was suddenly hit with a feeling of nostalgia, remembering other times they had gone out on the town together, dancing, partying, having fun. If anyone had told her a couple of days ago that the two of them would be able to put their anger, hurt and resentment on hold for an evening, she would not have believed them. The pain had been too deep on both sides.

He leaned forward again and took her hand in his.

"Come on. Let's show these old folks how to really get down."

The next thing Brooke knew they were out on the dance floor, shaking their bodies like everyone else. Ian had complimented her earlier on her choice of attire, a short, chocolate-brown silk chiffon dress with a swirling, handkerchief hemline. It gave her all the ease she needed as she moved to the music.

She couldn't recall the last time she'd gone dancing, let herself go, allowed herself to feel free. Only with Ian could she be this way. Only with him.

When the music came to an end, he pulled her closer to him, lowered his head, keeping their mouths separated by a mere inch and said, "Come with me for a moment. I want to show you something."

She knew she should ask what he wanted to show her, and just where he was taking her when he led her out of the lounge. But she didn't. She couldn't. The only thing she could do was walk by his side as they held hands and pray that wherever they were going, she would still be in control when they got there.

Brooke tried not to feel nervous as they rode up in Ian's private elevator. He was leaning on the opposite wall and looking positively delicious in one of his designer suits. He stared at her and sent a torrent of heat through her body. The man could make everything inside of her flutter with those dark eyes of his, and she was doing everything within her power not to succumb.

"So where are you taking me?" she asked after they passed the floor to his penthouse.

He smiled before pushing off the wall. "Be patient. We'll get there soon enough."

That's what had her worried. "And just where is there?" The elevator was still going up and although she knew they were on his private side of the casino, she had no idea where they were going. Already they had gone beyond the eighteenth floor.

Before he could respond—not that he would have anyway—the elevator came to a stop. She hated admitting it but he had aroused her curiosity. He had also aroused something else. Being confined in an elevator with Ian wasn't a good idea and it was taking a supreme effort on her part to downplay his sexiness. His charisma was touching her in all kinds of places, causing her body to feel hot. What she needed was a splash of cold water. The elevator door opened and she turned to follow him when he stepped out.

Her breath caught. Ian had brought her to his private conservatory. From up here, she could see everything. It was a beautiful April night, and when she glanced up she saw the sky was a beautiful shade of navy blue. The stars sparkled like glistening diamonds above and the half moon provided a warm glow and a feeling of opulence.

Ian's conservatory was the ideal place to create a relaxing sanctuary surrounded by the beauty of God's universe. The lighting inside the conservatory created pools of soft illumination. It was an intimate setting that framed the moon and stars to their best advantage. The room was furnished with rattan furniture. Each piece was richly detailed, intricately patterned out of woven banana leaf with a natural finish. The cushions on the sofa and chair looked too comfortable for words, and the other accessories—the coffee table, side table and foot stool, completed the seating arrangement. Everything in the room seemed to fit. Even the tall, handsome man standing beside her.

"So what do you think?" he asked, breaking into her thoughts.

To say she was impressed was an understatement. He never ceased to amaze or surprise her. But then, she really should have known that. Ian was a very smart man who'd graduated from Yale University, magnum cum laude, at twenty-two with a degree in physics. But he definitely wasn't your ordinary geek. After working for a year at NASA's Goddard Space Flight Center, he had returned home when his grandfather died. He began working for a research firm in Atlanta to be close to his family and it was there that the gambling bug hit him. The way Ian saw it, beating the odds was based on statistical probability. To him it was a matter of mathematic calculations rather than a game of chance. And, he was very good at math.

"I think this place is beautiful, Ian. The furniture and plants enhance everything. There's nothing like having a beautiful environment with the outside all around and the sky up above."

Ian nodded. That's exactly the way he felt. He'd always loved looking at the sky at night, and when he got older it had seemed the most natural thing to choose a career studying it. Although he no longer worked in that profession, he hadn't given up his love of astronomy.

"Come look through this," he said, taking her hand and leading her over to a huge telescope.

Brooke peered through the telescope at the moon, the stars and the other celestial bodies that were visible in the sky. She smiled when she saw a shooting star. According to myth, shooting stars fell to the earth creating a flower with each impact.

She straightened, suddenly feeling Ian's heat, and knew he had come to stand directly behind her, so close she could feel the warmth of his breath on her neck. A long, tense moment passed before she could draw in enough air to ask, "You come here often?"

"Whenever I need to get away or just to think."

Ian knew he would never tell her that although this was the first time she had been in his conservatory, he thought of her often when he was up here. It was the only place he allowed himself to let the memories of the love they'd once shared slip through the wall he had built around his heart.

At one time she had been his own special star. She had shone brightly even when the skies had been gray for him and menacing dark clouds had appeared on his horizon. Brooke had been his sun after every storm.

His career change from scientist to casino owner hadn't been easy, but she, along with his family, had motivated and encouraged him to pursue his dream. Brooke had been there by his side when he had celebrated the purchase of the *Delta Princess.*

He sighed deeply, knowing two things for sure. Brooke was still deeply embedded in his system, and no matter what it took he was going to get her out of it. Just the thought of having her in his bed one last time sent a wave of heat coursing through him. But it wouldn't be fair to rush her into a night of hot, wild passion, even though that might be what they both needed.

He had to be patient.

Brooke pointed up toward the sky, trying to deflect the sensations she felt flowing through her body as a result of Ian's closeness. "Look at that star," she said.

Ian grinned and wrapped his arms around her waist, pulling her body closer to his, and whispered, "I hate to disappoint you, but that's a satellite."

"Oh." Her heart jumped, and heat suddenly flooded her spine where his chest was pressing against it. Then there was the feel of her backside pressed against the zipper of his pants. She felt the firmness of his arousal, getting thicker by the minute, and wished there was some way to defuse the tension steadily growing between them. Of course she knew that Ian would have his own ideas of how they should go about rectifying the problem.

Deciding she couldn't take much more of what she realized was his sly attempt to seduce her, Brooke turned around to suggest they go back to the lounge. Her move was a huge mistake. Turning around placed her face-to-face and body-to-body with him. When she gazed up into his eyes, she suddenly had a memory lapse, and every coherent thought froze in her brain. At that moment nothing mattered but the man staring down at her.

He reached out and traced the pad of his thumb across her jaw, and when he did, currents of electricity shot to every part of her. He leaned down and brought his face closer to hers. Up this close, underneath the beauty of a moonlit, star-filled sky, her gaze swept over his features and her heart reaffirmed her love for him.

"Do you know what it means when a couple kisses under a shooting star?" he asked, his voice low and husky.

"No, what does it mean?" she asked.

"According to Greek mythology, Zeus bestows upon the couple the gift of uncontrollable passion."

Uncontrollable passion? Brooke swallowed deeply, thinking they must have kissed under a shooting star once before because whenever it came to passion it seemed they'd cornered the market. Back in the old days, he had been able to draw her to him with a magnetic force. Her hormones would go haywire each and every time. She felt her bones melting just thinking about those times.

"In that case I suggest we don't kiss under a shooting star," she said, trying to get a grip on her senses.

"I disagree." He moved his thumb from her jaw to her neck. "Nothing's wrong with a hefty amount of passion every once in a while," he said, leaning closer to her.

Not if you haven't had any in four years, she wanted to say, but the only thing she could do was stand and watch his mouth get closer and closer and…

Her eyes drifted shut when his lips touched hers, and when he deepened the kiss she thought there was nothing like being kissed under the beauty of a night sky, especially when the person doing the honors was the man you loved.

Brooke's insides sizzled as Ian's tongue gently, unhurriedly mated with hers. Kissing was something she'd always enjoyed doing with him and she couldn't help but recall how they had even gone so far as to develop their own technique of French kissing. And the way Ian was using his tongue on her now jarred her senses, melting her insides. She felt heat spread up her thighs, settle between her legs, and she felt the first sign of that special brand of titillation only he could stir within her. When it came to passion, they didn't need a shooting star. Their fiery chemistry came naturally.

The room felt like it was beginning to spin when he intensified the kiss, delved deeper into her mouth, making the taste of him explode against her palate. She grabbed ahold of his shoulders, felt the fabric of his jacket underneath her fingers, holding on tight lest she be swept away.

When Ian finally released her mouth she could barely breathe, and a moan slipped from between her lips although she fought to hold it back. She felt the solid length of him cradled against her middle and knew what his body wanted. She tilted her head and looked at him, gazed into those dark eyes that could make a woman swoon. She was getting in deeper by the minute.

He continued to stoke the fire within her as he slid his hand up her arms, over her shoulders and leaned closer to place butterfly kisses around her nose and mouth. "I need to leave town for a few days," he said softly against her lips.

She felt her jaw go slack. "What?"

He pulled back just a little, enough for her to see the darkness of his eyes. "I need to leave in the morning for Memphis to finalize the sale of the riverboat. I'll be gone for two days."

"Oh." She tried hiding her disappointment and couldn't. Her pouty expression must have given her away.

He looked somewhat amused when he asked, "Are you going to miss me?"

She gave him a weak smile. Oh, yes, she would miss him, but then the separation would give her a chance to screw her head back on straight. "Not at all," she said teasingly.

"Um, then maybe I should give you a reason to miss me…and to look forward to my return."

Before Brooke could draw her next breath she was swept off her feet into Ian's strong arms.

Chapter 5

Ian didn't have to go far to the sofa, which was a good thing because he was so terribly aroused his zipper was about to burst. Only Brooke could do this to him this quick and fast, with an urgency that made him want to tear the clothes off her body and do it then and there.

But he knew with Brooke he could never just do *it*. Oh, yeah, in the past they would mate like rabbits several times over, and he would take her in every position known to man—even some he'd conjured up that actually defied the laws of gravity—but still, in his mind they had never just done it. Each time they'd come together, intimately connected, it had meant something emotionally, too. They had always made love and never just had sex. Even now when he wanted to work her out of his system, he knew it would mean something.

And that was the gist of his dilemma.

Although he wanted to believe otherwise, making love to Brooke would be more than a means to an end. His best-laid intentions could backfire, and she could get even deeper under his skin. That thought was unnerving.

And yet that possibility hadn't lessened his desire for her, hadn't stopped his testosterone from kicking into overdrive or from giving him the most intense arousal he'd had in four years. In other words, he needed to "do it," like, yesterday, but only with this woman.

He leaned back on the sofa with her in his arms, and before she could open her mouth to utter a single word, his tongue was there, lapping her next breath from her parted lips. He kissed her deeply. His heart throbbed, his pulse was going haywire and his hands seemed to be everywhere, but mostly working their way under her dress.

When he realized that in less than five seconds flat he had his fingers right smack between her legs, he snapped his head up and stared at her. This was madness. This was crazy. This was typical Ian and Brooke.

He drew in an unsteady breath when these thoughts rang through his mind. They had always been hot for each other, and nothing had changed. Together they were spontaneous as hell. Whenever their bodies joined as one all they had to do was think orgasm and it happened.

He saw the darkening of her eyes, a signal that she wanted him as much as he wanted her. But he needed to hear her say it. He had to know before he went any further that whatever they did tonight, she would be with him all the way and there would be no regrets.

"Brooke?"

She heard her name whispered from his lips in a tone so raspy and sensual it made her breath hitch in her throat. She knew what he wanted. She also knew what he was asking, and at the moment she couldn't deny Ian Westmoreland a single thing. It had been four years for her, and the abstinence had taken its toll. She felt out of her league, something she'd never felt with Ian before. She didn't know how to react. The only thing she did know was that she wanted him.

She reached out and clutched the lapels of his jacket. "I don't understand the intensity of this, Ian," she whispered truthfully, pulling his mouth down closer to hers.

"Then let me explain it to you without words," he said silkily against her lips.

And then he was kissing her again, and with their mouths still connected he slid to the edge of the sofa. Shifting her in his arms he changed her position in his lap and brought her legs around his waist. With her dress bunched up around her waist, she felt the thickness of his arousal pressed against the juncture of her legs. There was no way she could regain her senses now even if she wanted to. She was a goner.

Heat flared through her when she felt the straps of her dress fall from her shoulders, and then he was no longer kissing her. He had turned his attention to her breasts. Being braless left her bare and exposed for his pleasure, and when his mouth latched on to a nipple she knew this was just the beginning. When it came to breast stimulation he was as skilled as they came.

"Ian."

Ian pulled away, deciding he would take more time with her breasts later. He knew exactly what they both wanted and needed now. He stood with her in his arms when the ring of his cell phone intruded.

"Damn," he muttered as he placed her on her feet while working the phone out of his jacket. "What?" he barked after answering the call.

"Domestic dispute," Vance said, the security manager's words washing over Ian like a pail of cold water. "One of those electricians got a surprise visit from his wife."

"And?"

"She caught him in bed with..." After a brief pause Vance added, "...another electrician. Male."

"What?"

"You heard me right. And now the woman is hysterical."

Ian rubbed his hand down his face. He couldn't very much blame her for that. Because of the satellite floating overhead, the reception was clear, and standing close in front of him he knew that Brooke had heard Vance's words. Ian met her gaze and, regardless of the situation, he was tempted to sweep his mouth down for another tongue-tingling kiss. Instead he said to Vance, "Go on, I'm sure there's more."

"Yes. She's threatened to sue everyone—the electricians' union, the airline that flew him here, the guy he was caught with, as well as this casino for allowing such behavior and conduct."

Ian didn't like hearing the word *sue*. "Where are you?"

"On the fourteenth floor."

"I'm on my way." He flipped the phone shut and gazed into Brooke's face thinking how damn sexy she looked with her hair mussed and her lips swollen from his kisses.

"I need to go," he said regretfully, straightening his jacket.

"I understand how it is when duty calls."

A small smile tugged at his lips. "I appreciate that." Straightening out the situation might take a while, and since it was almost two in the morning, Ian knew it would be two days before he saw Brooke again.

He took her hand in his as he led her toward the elevator. "Enjoy yourself while I'm in Memphis."

She smiled over at him. "I will."

He frowned. "But not too much."

She chuckled. "Okay, I won't."

When the elevator closed behind them, he pulled her into his arms. He thought of asking her to come to Memphis with him but quickly pushed the idea from his mind. Instead he said, "Have dinner with me in my penthouse when I get back."

He thought it was better to ask now. He had a feeling the two-day separation would have her thinking that tonight had been a mistake, and he didn't intend to let that happen.

"Ian, I—"

He kissed the words off her lips. "No, Brooke. We owe it to ourselves to finish what we started."

She stared up at him. "Do we?"

"Yes." And then he kissed her again, liking the feel of her in his arms, her warmth, her closeness and definitely her taste.

When he released her mouth she sighed deeply and said, "All right."

Tension that had been building inside of him slowly left his body. "I'll see you to your suite."

She shook her head. "That's not necessary, Ian. You have a matter that needs your immediate attention. Besides," she said, smiling, "I think I'll stop at one of the blackjack tables and try out some of those skills you taught me today."

He chuckled. "Okay."

"Have a safe trip, Ian."

"Thank you."

As the elevator arrived on the lobby floor, he released her. When she stepped away he suddenly felt a rush of loss through every part of his body. And when she began walking off he called out to her before she was swallowed by the crowd. "Don't forget about dinner Friday night."

She turned around and smiled. "I won't."

"My place. Seven sharp."

She nodded and continued to stare at him until the elevator door closed.

Brooke sat idly at a table in one of the cafés sipping her coffee and thinking of her telephone conversation with Tara Westmoreland that morning. Tara was Delaney's best friend and was married to Delaney's brother Thorn Westmoreland. Tara had invited Brooke to the surprise thirtieth birthday party being planned for Delaney next weekend at the Rolling Cascade.

Brooke was surprised Ian hadn't mentioned anything about the party to her. Perhaps he didn't want her there. She could remember how tense things had been at Dare and Shelly's wedding. But at that time the relationship between her and Ian had been very strained. Now, although they weren't back together or anything like that, at least they were talking…and kissing, she thought, smiling to herself. However, he might not want to give his family the wrong impression, and if they were seen together she could certainly see that happening.

"Enjoying your stay, Ms. Chamberlain?"

Brooke glanced up and met Vance's less-than-friendly eyes. On more than one occasion she had caught the man staring at her as if he was deliberately keeping her within his scope, and more than once she had wondered if Ian had asked him to keep an eye on her while he was gone. If he had, that meant he suspected her of something. It also meant he still didn't trust her.

Her heart quickened and she inwardly scolded herself for jumping to conclusions. This man was head of security at the casino and he was probably programmed to be suspicious of everything and everyone.

"Yes, I'm enjoying myself. This is a beautiful casino."

"I think so, too."

"And please, call me Brooke."

"Okay, and I'm Vance."

Brooke nodded. She was very much aware of who he was. He was the man who had taken her to Ian's office that first day. She had a feeling that had she refused he would have found a way to get her up there anyway with minimum fuss. He had that air about him, a no-nonsense, get-the-job-done sort of guy, and she wondered if he'd had a history at some point with the Bureau.

"Would you like to join me for coffee, Vance?" she asked, nodding to the huge coffeepot sitting in the middle of the table.

He surprised her when he said, "Don't mind if I do." And then he took the seat across from her. She leaned back in her chair. He had asked his question and now it was time to ask hers. He was former military; that was a given from his demeanor. But she needed to know something else about him.

"What Special Forces or federal agency were you affiliated with, Vance?"

His blue eyes, sharp and clear, riveted to hers as he poured a cup of coffee. "What makes you think I was part of the military or an agency?"

She shrugged. "Your mannerisms."

He chuckled. "I guess it takes one to know one."

She raised her brow, and before she could say anything, he said, "Don't bother denying it. Ian told me. Only because he knew he could trust me. So your secret's safe."

She took a sip of her own coffee and then said, "It's not a secret. It's just that my profession isn't anybody's business."

He moved his massive shoulders in a shrug. "Like I said, Ian mentioned it. As head of security here he felt I should know."

She nodded and wondered what else Ian might have told him. "You still haven't answered my question," she decided to remind him.

"I didn't, did I," he said, smiling coyly. "I was in the Corp and then I worked for the Bureau awhile before taking a position in the Secret Service."

The executive branch, Brooke mused. "I take it you know Quade," she said of Ian's twin brother.

Vance grinned fondly. "Yes, I know Quade. In fact I'm the one who trained him for his first assignment. Quade and I worked together for years and that's how I met Ian. When I decided to retire after twenty-five years in the service, Quade knew I wasn't one to sit idle and twiddle my thumbs. He mentioned Ian had a position here that I might be interested in. The rest, as they say, is history."

Brooke smiled. "And from what I can see, the way you run things indicates you're the right man for the job," she said honestly.

"Thanks."

She seriously meant the compliment. Her eyes and ears had been open and she'd seen how he had expertly and professionally, with the authority that could only come from someone with his years of experience, handled several potentially troublesome incidents.

"If I didn't know better I'd think you were a member of my staff, Brooke."

Brooke met his gaze over the rim of her cup after catching his meaning. He was no rookie and although she had tried to be discreet in her inquiries, he had been alert and had picked up on her interests. "Part of the job."

"Yes, but you're not working, are you? At least, that's what Ian told me. He said you were here for rest and relaxation."

She placed her cup down and straightened in her seat, deciding this wily old fox missed nothing. "Ian was right. What I meant when I said part of the job was that after a while, once you've been an agent, certain things become second nature."

"Oh, like being observant and noticing every little thing?"

"Yes, like being observant and noticing every little thing." She couldn't help but wonder if he believed her.

She watched as he leaned forward and then he said, "I guess a second pair of eyes never hurt. But I think we need to clear the air about something. Ian is a good man. Although he's a lot younger than most casino owners, he has a good sense for business. Somehow with that kind of mind he has the ability to play the odds and come up a winner. This place is a testimony to that. Investors trust him with their money because he has a proven track record of running a clean, profitable operation. My job is to be his eyes and ears as well as to protect his back. And, more important, Ian is not just my boss, I consider him a good friend."

Brooke picked up her coffee cup and stared down into the dark liquid a moment before meeting Vance's gaze and asking, "Is there a reason you're telling me this?"

He chuckled softly. "Only you can answer that, Brooke."

She held Vance's gaze. "No matter what you or anyone else might think, I trust Ian implicitly."

"But…"

"But I think we should end this conversation," Brooke said frowning, thinking she might have said too much already. Vance was no fool. He was as sharp as they came, and with his history he probably knew she had lied through her teeth when she claimed she was at the casino for rest and relaxation.

Vance laughed, breaking into her thoughts. "You're good, Brooke, and because I like you, I'm going to show you just how good an operation Ian runs," he said as he stood. "How about coming with me."

Two hours later Brooke had returned to her room to rest up a bit before changing for dinner. Vance had given her a tour of the casino's security surveillance center upstairs, and she'd had to agree with him that not too much went on in the casino that he wasn't aware of, including the lovers tryst between those electricians. Although there weren't any video cameras in individual rooms, they were installed in the elevators, hallways, lobby and every other inch of the casino. Security had noticed the excessive amount of time the two men had been visiting each other's rooms during the late-night hours.

Vance had also told her that being the born diplomat Ian was, he had brought a semblance of order to the situation last night, although there was only so much one could do after a woman discovered her husband had been unfaithful, and with someone of the same sex.

Brooke was just about to walk into the bathroom to run her shower when the phone rang. She quickly crossed the room to pick it up. "Hello."

"Miss me yet?"

Although Ian's voice sounded cool and in control, Brooke felt shivers tingle up her spine, anyway. His call had definitely caught her off guard. He had to have been thinking about her to have called. The mere fact that he had brought a smile to her lips. "No, I've been too busy to miss you," she said teasingly.

"Oh, and what have you been doing?"

Brooke glanced out of the window. The view of the mountains was breathtaking, but the mountains weren't the main thing on her mind now. The man she was talking to was.

She thought back to his question, doubting he would appreciate knowing Vance had given her a tour of his security setup. "I've been doing a lot of things but mostly perfecting my blackjack skills."

His laugh sent a warm feeling all through her stomach. "I hope you won't be breaking the casino before I return."

"I'll try not to, but I have been lucky a few times."

"Luck has nothing to do with it. Like I've told you, it's merely a matter of calculating the odds."

"If you say so. Will you still be returning tomorrow night?"

"Those are my plans and so far things are on schedule. I should be able to wrap up the deal in the morning and arrive there by late afternoon."

Brooke nodded. She didn't want to admit it but she *had* missed him. The mere fact that until this week she hadn't seen him in four years meant nothing. Once she'd seen him her heart had remembered; unfortunately, so had her body.

"What are your plans for the rest of the day?"

His question pulled in her thoughts. "To shop until I drop." She then decided to mention something that had been bothering her all day. "I got a call from Tara this morning inviting me to Delaney's surprise birthday party. Why didn't you mention it?"

"I really didn't think about it much. Besides, I figured sooner or later you would hear from some member of my family."

"And how do you feel about me being there?" she questioned.

"Why are you asking me that? Is there a certain way I should feel, Brooke?"

"I don't know," she replied quietly. "I know how tense I made you feel being at Dare's wedding."

"At the time, considering everything, I think a certain degree of discomfort for both of us was understandable."

"And now?"

"Now I think we're a lot more at ease with each other, don't you?"

Considering how they'd been spending a lot of their time while they'd been together she would definitely say yes. "I just don't want you to get bent all out of shape if your family starts assuming things about us."

"I'm used to my family, Brooke. Maybe the real question is whether or not you'll get bent out of shape. My mom refuses to believe that you and I won't ever work out our problems and get back together, no matter what I've told her to the contrary. She likes you. Always has."

Brooke smiled. She'd always liked his mom, as well.

"So are you thinking about going?"

"Probably," she replied, hoping that making an appearance wouldn't cause a big commotion. Unfortunately, there didn't seem to be any way to avoid it. Everyone had known how serious her and Ian's relationship was at one time, and she was sure some of them didn't know the reason for their breakup. Although he was close to his family, Ian was a private person when it came to his personal life.

"And you're sure you won't have a problem if I decide to go?" she asked again.

"Yes, I'm sure I won't have a problem with it." He chuckled. "Besides, it's about time I give the family something to talk about. Things have been pretty quiet since Durango got married a few months ago, and I'll be the first to admit that we Westmorelands need a little craziness every once in a while."

A half hour later Ian sat and reflected on his conversation with Brooke. He'd asked her if she'd missed him and before they'd hung up he'd gotten her to admit she had. That meant he was making progress. But the truth was that he wasn't faring much better. He missed her, too.

He should never have let her back into his life, but now that she was, he was in a bad way. It was crazy what mere kisses could do to a man.

It had been more than just the kisses, though. It had been her presence and the heated attraction that enveloped them each and every time they were together.

"Would you like anything else to drink, sir?"

Ian glanced up at the waiter. He had dined alone at

a restaurant known for its sizzling and delicious steaks. The food had been excellent, but the only sizzling and delicious thing on his mind during the entire meal had been Brooke.

"No, that will be all for now."

What Ian wanted was a quiet moment to just sit, sip his wine and pine for the woman he desired more than anything else. He longed to see her again, take her into his arms, make love to her on his bed or hers—which technically was also his because he owned the casino—and take her to a place he hadn't been since they'd separated. A place that had his insides coiling just thinking about it. It had been a place they'd discovered years ago; it had been their own universe, their own solar system, a personal space only the two of them occupied.

The hand holding his wineglass tightened as he felt that same squeeze in his groin. How could one woman stir up his passion, his desire and his lust to such unprecedented proportions?

"Ian?"

Snatched from his heated musings, Ian glanced up at the very attractive woman standing beside his table. He smiled at her. "Casey, what are you doing here in Memphis?" he asked his cousin as he came to his feet. The last time he'd seen her was at his brother Durango's wedding reception in Atlanta.

"I'm on a buying trip for my store," she said smiling back at him. "I'll be here for a couple of days. What about you?"

"I'm here on business and I'll be flying out in the morning." Ian knew she owned a fashion boutique back in Beaumont, Texas. "Come join me," he invited, pulling out a chair for her. "Would you like to order something?" he asked, not sure if she'd eaten yet.

"Thanks," she said as she sat down. "But, no. I've just finished eating and was about to leave. I thought it was you from across the room, but I wasn't sure, and for a moment I was hesitant about coming over to ask. You seemed deeply absorbed in thought."

He sat back down and chuckled. "I was," he said without any further explanation. It was best she didn't know what he'd been thinking about. "So are you coming to Delaney's surprise party next week at the casino?"

He saw her grimace slightly and knew she hadn't yet made up her mind. Whereas her brothers Clint and Cole had quickly meshed into the Westmoreland family fold, Casey was still a little reserved. Evidently after thinking for years that her family consisted of only her and her two brothers, the multitude of Westmorelands overwhelmed her.

"Do you know if my father is coming?" she asked.

"Yes, as far as I know Uncle Corey's coming," Ian said, taking another sip of his drink. "I can't see him missing it."

He knew Casey was still struggling to develop a relationship with the father she hadn't known she had. All those years she'd thought he was dead.

"I'm thinking about taking him up on his offer and spending a month in Montana," Casey said.

Ian raised a brow. He'd heard his uncle extend the invitation, but Ian hadn't been sure Casey would accept it. For her to consider making a visit was a huge step in building a relationship with her father.

"I think that's a wonderful idea, Casey," Ian said. "And I'm sure Uncle Corey and Abby would love having you spend some time with them."

While kicking back and enjoying the taste of his wine, Ian listened as Casey brought him up to date on her brothers, who were both Texas Rangers. She knew for certain they would be at Delaney's party, but Ian noticed she still hadn't answered his question as to whether or not she would make an appearance.

An hour or so later, Ian opened the door to his hotel room. He glanced across the room. His bags were all packed and he was ready to go. Hell, he would leave tonight if he could get a flight out. To say he was eager to return to Lake Tahoe was an understatement.

Even now he wanted to pick up the phone and call Brooke but he kept reminding himself he had spoken to her earlier. He shook his head as he began undressing, wondering what in the hell was happening to him. Brooke walks back into his life and his mind goes bonkers. Okay, she was the sexiest thing he'd ever laid eyes on, both then and now, but still, that wasn't a good enough reason to get carried away.

But he *was* getting carried away. He was beginning to feel emotions that he hadn't felt in years. He raked his hand over his head thinking that wasn't a good thing, but for now there wasn't anything he could do about it.

Not a damn thing.

Chapter 6

Brooke had spent the past two days shopping and enjoying a lot of the amenities the resort had to offer and, of course, keeping her eyes and ears open while doing so. Now the day Ian was scheduled to return had arrived, and as she lowered her body into the warm water of the Jacuzzi tub in her bathroom, excitement filled her to a degree she hadn't known in a long time. She submerged her body deep into the tub and let the jets provide a deep massage for the muscles she had overworked during her two-day shopping spree.

She laid her head back and closed her eyes as the jets and the bubbles whisked her away to another place, tantalizing as well as soothing her state of mind, sharpening her focus and her outlook.

Another moan escaped her lips when she shifted her body and doing so shot a jet of water to the area between her legs. She smiled thinking that was some kind of massage therapy. But she was realistic enough to know that the only way the deep-rooted tension and urgency that had settled in that part of her body could be removed was by the skill of one man.

Ian Westmoreland.

As her eyes remained closed she contemplated how their dinner that evening would go. She remembered sharing meals with him before and how things ended. The memories sent shivers all through her body. He hadn't earned the nickname the Perfect End for nothing.

A couple of hours later, after her bath and a short nap, Brooke began getting dressed. Although she didn't agree that one more time between the sheets would get them out of each other's systems, she did agree that they needed one last time together to put an ending chapter to what once had been a beautiful relationship.

The thought of finality tightened the muscles surrounding her heart but she knew it had to be. She had to finally move forward in her life. She was young and believed that sooner or later she would get over Ian, no matter how hard such a thing would be. When she returned to D.C. she would ask Malcolm for a couple of weeks off.

She needed time alone to sort things out and to put her life in order. She also needed to make some decisions regarding her future. If she decided to leave fieldwork, she needed to know what other opportunities the Bureau had to offer. When she had mentioned such a possibility to Vance, he had suggested a job at the White House. Apparently, there were always places for capable women on the first lady's security detail.

A smile touched her lips when she thought of the time she'd spent with Vance. In the end, she'd decided that she liked him because he had Ian's best interest at heart and he was loyal to those he cared about. Ian was like that, too. Ian's sense of loyalty was the main reason he couldn't get past the Boris Knowles case.

She glanced at the underthings she had placed on her bed, items she had purchased that day. Ian always loved black lace on her, and she was going to make sure that tonight he saw a lot of it.

She squared her shoulders after dabbing perfume on her pulse points and between her breasts. The outfit she had bought to wear was an attention getter. It was meant to tease, tantalize, to impress and undress all in one. She intended to make their last time together special.

Tonight she would be the one to give them the perfect end.

It felt good being back, Ian thought, as he walked into the penthouse a little later than he'd wanted. His connecting flight had been hell, with enough turbulence to make even a grown man weep.

The first thing he'd wanted to do when he had arrived at the casino was to find Brooke, but Vance had mentioned he had seen her leave the resort earlier. She had been headed for the shops in town. It looked as if she intended to do some serious shopping. Ian ended up going to his penthouse a disenchanted man. He unpacked with the thought that he was preparing for a night he intended Brooke would remember for a long time.

Ian checked his watch a few hours later. It was ten

to seven. Where was she? He distinctly remembered Brooke always showed up at any destination a few minutes earlier than scheduled. Of all the nights for her to change her routine and—

His breath caught when he heard the ringing of his elevator alerting him he was about to have a visitor. Deciding this would be a special night, he had changed into a pair of black trousers and a white button-up shirt. But to give his outfit a casual spin he had left his shoes off. He wanted to look totally at home, totally relaxed and completely in control.

He walked over to the elevator and was standing there when it opened. As soon as it did, his throat suddenly felt tight and he could only stare, almost tongue-tied as he feasted his eyes on Brooke. She was wearing a short, lacy black concoction that seemed to scream, strip me. His fingertips began to itch, wanting to do that very thing.

"I know I'm early, but aren't you going to invite me in?"

Hell, he planned to do better than that, he thought, edging backward so she could take a step forward. When she did, the elevator door swooshed close. "Welcome back, Ian."

God, he'd missed her. In just a couple of days she had gotten back under his skin. Deep. He opened his mouth to reply but no sound came out. His mind couldn't get beyond the fact that she was standing there wearing black lace. She of all people knew how he felt about black lace; especially on her. She could wear it like no other woman. He was aroused to the nth degree from just seeing her in it.

The itching in his fingers intensified and a need he tried to ignore gripped him, made his blood sizzle and his heart pound in his chest. He took a step forward. It was then that he studied her face; a face that had invaded his dreams so many times over the past four years; a face he couldn't forget no matter how he tried.

Ian quickly accepted the fact that it wasn't about the dress Brooke was wearing or how sexy she looked in it that made him so attracted to her. Brooke, the unique individual she'd always been, had captured his interest from the first and still held it tight.

But still…he had to give kudos to the dress. It made a provocative statement, and seeing her in it did the things to him she'd known it would.

"Ian?"

His gaze returned to her face. He watched her mouth quiver and decided to kiss that quiver right off her lips. He intended to give her a proper hello, Ian Westmoreland style. Leaning over, he ran his fingertips along her jaw and then, leaning closer still, he began gently nibbling on her lips, savoring the moment and relishing the sweet taste of her and the feel of her full lips beneath his.

He had wanted to linger, but the need hammering inside of him wouldn't let him. It drove an urgency he couldn't control, and when her moan filled his mouth he indulged her by taking the kiss deeper. All the long-denied needs he'd pretended weren't there were hitting him full force, begging for the kind of release only she could give.

He tightened his hold on her as his mouth mated with hers, slowly yet torridly, taking his breath away with every return stroke of her tongue while it moved sensuously in his mouth, hitting those spots she knew from the past could drive him mad with desire.

One thing he and Brooke had enjoyed doing as a couple was exploring new things in the bedroom, and on one occasion they'd had a kiss-a-thon. By the time it was over, they had explored every kind of kiss known to man and had gone further by inventing some of their own.

And she remembered, he thought, as his hands on her hips tightened and he pulled her closer to him. Not only had she remembered but she was putting some of those techniques into action, making blood pulse through his veins and sending heat spreading all through him; especially his loins. With a mastery and skill that almost made him weak in the knees, she was taking over the kiss, making him groan into her mouth and reminding him why he had fallen so hard for her years ago. Brooke had a way of taking him by surprise.

And she was doing it now.

He definitely hadn't expected this, a kiss that went far and beyond any fantasy he'd ever had. He had figured she would be reluctant, would fight the intensity of the chemistry they were feeling. But she wasn't. In her own way she was letting him know that she needed to move on with her life just as he needed to move on with his. She accepted that there could never be a reconciliation. They needed closure, and this was the only way they would get it. She was kissing him with a passion that sent shivers vibrating through his body and he was greedily lapping it up.

"Brooke," he whispered when she finally released his

mouth. But before she could take a step back, he swept her into his arms and once again covered her lips with his.

She could go on kissing him forever, Brooke thought, as Ian kissed her and she greedily kissed him back with equal fervor. And moments later when he released her mouth and began walking with her in his arms, her breath caught in her chest as he moved up the stairs to his bedroom.

She glanced up, saw the smoldering look of desire in his eyes, and the pressure mounting inside her escalated.

When he came to a stop, she glanced around and he slowly placed her on her feet, sliding her body against his in the process, letting her feel the bulge in his pants, evidence of his intense desire for her.

He tipped her chin up and met her gaze. "I want you."

His words made her draw in a shaky breath. It had been four years since she had been with a man, and her body was attuned to Ian in a profound way. He was the one and only man she'd ever been intimate with. Something deep within her began to prepare her for the pleasure she knew only he could give with those wonderful hands, that skillful tongue and that big strong body. Just thinking about what was to come had sensations erupting all the way inside her womb.

"And I want you, too, Ian," she said breathlessly as she felt her center begin to quake with a longing she hadn't felt in a long time. "Tonight, I need you," she added.

"Not as much as I need you," he replied, reaching out to remove her dress.

A hiss escaped between Ian's teeth when he pulled the dress over her head and tossed it aside only to reveal more black lace—a sexy bra and silky high-cut panties. Unable to help himself, he dropped to his knees right there in the middle of the room and buried his face in her belly, needing the scent of her in his nostrils and the taste of her on his tongue.

He leaned forward and began licking the hollow of her navel while easing her panties down her legs. He paused only long enough for her to step out of them before nipping at her belly and moving lower.

He pulled back for a moment and looked up at her. He continued to hold her gaze as he reached out and slipped one hand between her legs, letting his fingers go to work in her damp flesh. And when she grabbed hold of his shoulders and began moaning and grinding against his hand he knew she was on the brink of an orgasm so explosive she would have it right there if he didn't do something.

And so he did.

He broke eye contact with her and dipped his head and glided his tongue over her, into her, exploring, probing and loving her in a way he hadn't wanted to do with any other woman. His hands held tight to her thighs as his tongue continued its assault with hard, steady strokes, needing the taste of her in each and every part of his mouth.

He tasted her shivers, felt a shudder shake her body and heard her moan his name as she automatically bucked against his mouth, but he refused to pull back. Instead his tongue seemed to go into a frenzy, and it took her with a greediness that sent tremors through him.

A strangled growl escaped his lips when her spasms ended. He stood and quieted her aftershocks with his mouth on hers, needing to kiss her again. And then he was sweeping her into his arms and taking her to his bed and placing her on his satin bedspread.

He slid a hand to her chest and undid the front clasp of her bra and eased her out of it, tossing it aside. He'd always thought that her breasts were the most beautiful in the world and automatically he leaned forward and rubbed his face against them, licking the area between her breasts before latching his lips onto a hardened nipple and drawing it into his mouth.

Ignoring her moans, he suckled hard, deep, relentlessly, one then the other, once again mesmerized by her taste, and when he couldn't hold back any longer, he stood and hurriedly stripped off his clothes, needing to be joined with her with such an intense need that his entire body was throbbing. And when he came back to the bed, she reached out and her hands captured his engorged flesh as if she needed to touch it, become reacquainted with the feel of it. When she began stroking him, he almost lost it.

"Easy, baby," he murmured as his knee pressed into the mattress. "Too much of that and I'm a goner." He moved to position his body over hers and nudged her legs apart with his knee.

His gaze locked on hers. He knew she'd been taking the Pill for years to regulate her periods, but for both of their protection, he reached into a small table and retrieved a foil square.

Before he could open the small packet, Brooke took it, opened it and carefully placed the sheath on his erection.

He reached out and brushed his hand against her cheek. "I want you so much, Brooke," he murmured softly, and then with a primal growl he entered her, throwing his head back as something wild, primitive and obsessive took control inside him.

She was tight, nearly as tight as she'd been the first time they'd made love and she'd been a virgin. It wasn't his imagination, and he met her gaze, ignoring the hunger that propelled him to start moving. She was so tight that it felt like she was squeezing him, locking her feminine muscles securely around him, claiming him, making sure he couldn't pull out even if he wanted to.

She didn't have that to worry about. He wasn't going anywhere other than deeper inside her once he fully understood just what the tightness of her body meant. He met her gaze, and the look she gave him all but said, You figure it out.

So he did.

"This is the first time for you since…?" He couldn't finish the question, since the very thought shocked the hell out of him. Four years was a long time and her devotion to him was the most touching thing he could ever imagine. The very idea that even now he had been her first and only lover tore a soundless howl of possessiveness from his throat. Her body knew him and only him.

At that precise moment he wanted her with a passion he'd never felt before. Grasping her hips he began moving, stroking back and forth inside of her, going deeper. Her muscles clenched with each and every thrust he made, forcing his strokes to become more frantic.

He had to look at her, had to remember this moment for the rest of his life, and he brought his head forward, met her gaze and saw the heat in her eyes and knew neither of them could last much longer although they were fighting to do so. This would be the last time they came together this way, and they intended to make a memory to last a lifetime.

The thought, the very idea of not making love to her ever again, had him leaning forward, nipping at her shoulders, branding her while he felt her fingertips dig into his back as if to brand him, as well.

"Ian, I—"

He kissed the words off her lips. There was nothing to be said and when an explosion sent a million shudders ramming through his body, a loud growl tore from his throat through clenched teeth. He felt her come apart in his arms which caused another orgasm to rip through him. He thought he was going to die and quickly decided if he was about to take his last breath then this was definitely the way to go about it.

And he knew, as he buried himself inside of her to the hilt again as a third orgasm quickly hit him and triggered a similar explosion inside her body and he began rocking back and forth inside of her with a hunger that wouldn't let up, that he had miscalculated his emotions.

He'd erroneously figured he could sleep with her this one last time and be done with it, effectively getting her out of his system. Instead, as he cupped her buttocks tighter in his hands and felt her thighs quake beneath his at the same time his release shot deep into her womb, he knew that she had burrowed deeper into it.

"Stay here and rest. I'll let you know when dinner is ready," Ian's warm breath whispered against Brooke's ear before he slipped out of bed.

He glanced back over his shoulder long enough to see her eyes slowly drift open at the same time an adorable smile touched her lips as she snuggled under the covers. "Um, okay."

His lips twitched into a smile. He'd totally worn the woman out. She needed rest, and the only way to guarantee that she got it was for him to leave for a while. So after putting his pants back on he quietly eased open the door and slipped out of the room.

Talk about him being obsessed with making love to her. They hadn't made it past the foyer. She'd had no idea he'd set the stage for seduction with romantic lit candles. Their pure vanilla fragrance was sending a sweet scent through the rooms. He knew Brooke was partial to Thai food and so he'd had one of the resort restaurants prepare a special meal for them. He hoped the meal he had selected would please her. Making his way across the room, he picked up the phone and within minutes had instructed room service to deliver their dinner to his penthouse.

Knowing there was nothing for him to do but wait, he walked over to the window and looked out. It was dark outside, but the shape of the mountains could be seen across the lake. He would love to share this beautiful view with Brooke.

If he were to go back to his bedroom now and wake her he would do more than just show her the view. It was bad enough that he had to get her up when their meal came. He wouldn't take any chances. Brooke was too much of a temptation, and now that he had made love to her he wanted her more and more.

The memory of their bodies tangled together in his bed was so vivid in his mind that his blood was racing through his veins a little too fast to suit him. Although they had turned the heat up a notch, in fact had kicked it into a full blaze in his bed, a part of him refused to remain anything but cautious where she was concerned. She had hurt him once and could possibly do it again and he wasn't a glutton for punishment.

"Ian?"

At the sound of her soft voice he felt his entire body go tense. Squaring his shoulders and taking a deep breath, he turned around. Immediately he wished he hadn't. She was wearing the shirt he'd worn earlier, but she hadn't bothered to button it up, giving him a good frontal view.

He heard himself groan as his mind savored what he was seeing. There was nothing more beautiful than a naked or half-naked Brooke. A Brooke who'd recently been made love to or a Brooke who was wearing a let's-do-it-again look on her face.

The memories of what they had shared in his bedroom were tossing his mind every which way but loose. He fought for composure. He fought for control. He fought the urge to cross the room and take her again. If she was trying to get him all hot and bothered again, it was a complete waste of time because he was already there. He hadn't cooled down from the last time.

"Yes, Brooke?" he answered in a low, barely audible voice. "What is it that you want?"

He met her gaze. Heaven help him if she even hinted that she wanted him to make love to her again. There was no way he would be able to resist. Even now his arousal was thickening beneath his zipper. "Just tell me what you want, sweetheart. Your every wish is my command."

Brooke's breath caught as Ian's gaze held hers. She tried to remember the last time he had called her sweetheart and couldn't, it had seemed so long ago. But the endearment had flowed off his lips just as easily as it used to. And then there was the way he was looking at her with dark eyes filled with more than just heat and desire. Hope escalated within her at the thought that maybe, possibly...

She quickly pushed the far-fetched thought from her mind. Ian might desire her but he no longer loved her. She tried to think but decided she couldn't think very well with him looking at her like that. He'd said her every wish was his command. Well, she decided to put him to the test.

"How soon will the food arrive?" she asked, sliding into one of the high-back chairs at the casino-style blackjack table in the room.

"How soon do you want it?"

She smiled, wondering if they were still talking about the food. "If the chef decided to cook slowly tonight it won't bother me," she said silkily.

No sooner had the words left her lips than the zing of

the elevator let them know that, unfortunately, the chef hadn't been slow and their food was on the way up. Ian glanced across the room and saw the disappointed pout on her lips. Lips he couldn't wait to devour again.

"There's no law that says we have to eat it as soon as the food gets here. It will keep for a while," he assured her.

Her response was a slow, sensuous smile, and a deliberate shifting of her body in the chair exposed a lot more than a bare leg. He bit back the growl that threatened to roar from deep within his throat.

"Don't you dare move," he said when the elevator arrived on his floor. He quickly left and went to the elevator.

Brooke smiled as a shiver slithered through her, and she found she couldn't sit still as he'd instructed. When she had walked into the room and had seen the flickering candles and inhaled the scent of vanilla, as well as seeing Ian standing at the window shirtless, displaying his muscular shoulders and wearing pants that showed what a great butt he had, she had fought back the need to cross the room and touch him all over, ease down on her knees in front of him and unzip his pants and ultimately savor him the same way he'd done her earlier.

With a long sigh she stood and tried to remain calm. Walking around the blackjack table she concentrated on the huge glass window in front of her and the wonderful view of the mountains.

Moments later when she saw Ian's reflection in the glass, she knew he had come back into the room and was standing not far behind her. Their gazes met, reflected in the glass, and she was tempted to turn around.

Her gaze remained fixed on the windowpane as he walked up behind her and wrapped his arms around her. She leaned back into him, letting her head fall back against the breadth of his chest. She felt the need to share herself with him again, not just her body but her heart, whether he wanted it or not. She loved him and nothing could or would ever change that.

"Brooke."

He said her name in that sexy voice of his while nuzzling a certain spot on her neck that could always turn her on. And then she felt his tongue lick the side of her face, moving to the area just below her ear.

"Feel me," he whispered, and she did when she leaned back against him. She felt the hardness of him pressing deep into her backside at the same time she felt him use his hands to part the front of the shirt she wore. And when one of his hands went to her center to claim the area between her legs, a tantalizing sensation shot all through her.

"Are you sure you aren't ready to eat?" he asked huskily.

"I'm sure," she whispered, barely able to get the words out in a coherent voice. His beard was rubbing sensuously against the side of her neck causing an erotic friction that was sending shivers all through her body.

"Then tell me what you're ready for, Brooke."

He turned her around, evidently needing to look into her eyes when she answered. "You, Ian. I'm ready for you."

Her words made something within him shatter and

he lifted her to sit on the edge of the blackjack table and then stepped back to remove his pants. He kicked them aside before going back to her and tugging his shirt from her shoulders and tossing it to join his pants on the floor.

He reached out and lifted her bottom and wrapped her legs around him. "I'm ready for you, too, Brooke. Let me show you just how much."

And before she could take another breath he swiftly entered her, going deep and locking tight. And then he began moving with a furor that bordered on obsession. At this very moment they were beating the odds. If anyone had told him that she would be here in his private sanctuary, he would not have believed them. There was no logical reason for it. But he didn't want to dwell on logic now. He just wanted to think about making love to her while she teetered on the edge of his private blackjack table.

Tonight he needed this. He needed her.

The only thing he wanted to concentrate on was the sensations that coursed through him with each and every stroke into her body. His hands at her waist tightened even more and he lifted her almost clear off the green felt tabletop, straining to achieve deeper penetration. He leaned forward and kissed her, long and deep, liking the sound of her moan in his mouth. He'd never made love to a woman on a blackjack table before and now in his mind, played the role of a master dealer. But it wasn't his hand he was playing. It was his body over and over into hers, and the last thought on his mind was getting busted. He was on a lucky streak and was determined to come out the winner.

When he broke off the kiss, Brooke looked up at him

with eyes glazed with heated desire. And as if their minds had been running along the same thoughts she whispered, "I got a three and a five." She tightened her hold on his shoulders. "Hit me."

A smile touched Ian's lips. He would hit her all right. He tilted her hips on the table at an angle that gave him greater access and thrust deep inside her, aiming for a spot he knew would drive her wild.

It did.

She screamed his name as an explosion hit. The vibration ricocheted through her directly to him. He threw his head back, loving the feel of her orgasm and knowing it would detonate his body as well. When the climax struck, he shuddered uncontrollably and nothing mattered but the woman he was making love to.

She grabbed hold of his face and brought it back down to her, taking his mouth with a hunger that he still felt. His body was getting hard again. When would they get enough? It was as if they were making up for lost time, but he was okay with that. Tonight they needed each other. Tonight they were both winners.

And they would deal with tomorrow when it came.

Chapter 7

"So what do you think?"

Brooke lifted her head from her meal as a blush tinted her cheeks. If Ian was asking her about the food, her reply could be that it was great. If he was referring to their lovemaking sessions, words couldn't describe how wonderful they had been. No matter what happened after she left the Rolling Cascade to return to D.C., she would always cherish every moment she'd spent with him.

She leaned back in her chair. "You know how much I love Thai food, and your chef did a fantastic job. And if you're asking about something else," she said slowly, provocatively, as she picked up her wineglass to take a sip, looking at him over the rim. "All I can say is that I feel I got treated to dessert before the main course." She then gave him a sultry smile.

Ian chuckled low in his throat. "I'm glad everything was to your satisfaction."

He took a sip of wine and thought about how incredibly sexy she looked sitting across from him wearing only his shirt. At least she had buttoned it up.

The primal male in him wanted to reach out and pull the shirt open. He wanted to once again see how the flickering light from the candles cast a glow against her skin.

"It rated higher than my satisfaction, Ian," she said, reclaiming his attention. "You outdid yourself. I don't think I'll ever be able to look at a blackjack table again without blushing."

He shivered at the memory. Hell, when he saw a blackjack table again he wouldn't blush. He would get aroused. Speaking of aroused, he watched how her fingertips skimmed a trail along her wineglass, remembering how her hands had done that to him. Knowing they were headed for trouble if he didn't get his mind off bedding her again, he asked, "What are your plans for tomorrow?"

She grinned. "I won't be going shopping, that's for sure."

"Would you spend the day with me?"

His question surprised her. She would have thought that after tonight he would avoid her at all cost, if nothing else but to see if she was out of his system. She gazed at him thoughtfully as she leaned forward and rested her chin on her hands. "Um, it depends. What do you have planned?"

He smiled. "After an important meeting with my event planner to make sure all the bases are covered for

Delaney's birthday party, I'll be free to do whatever I want. Do you have any suggestions?"

They fell silent as Brooke contemplated his question. "Blackjack is definitely out."

He chuckled. "If you say so."

"Um, what about a game of golf?"

He lifted a brow. "Can you play?"

"No, but I'd like to learn. Would you teach me the basics?"

"Yeah, I can do that."

"And I'd like to go swimming in your pool again if you don't mind."

He studied her for a long moment, remembering her in his pool. "I don't mind, but this time I'll take a dip with you."

She stared at him, thinking that was exactly what she had hoped he'd do. "All right." She glanced at her watch then back across the table at him before standing. "It's late. I'd better get ready to go."

He stood, his gaze intense. "Stay with me tonight, Brooke."

Her heart jumped at the invitation, spoken in a deep, husky voice. Her mind was suddenly bombarded with all the reasons she shouldn't, the main one being that if he ever discovered the truth as to why she was staying at the Rolling Cascade, he would consider her actions deceitful.

"I don't think that's a good idea, Ian. We were supposed to be doing the closure thing, remember?" she said softly.

"I remember," he said, coming around the table to

stand in front of her. "But at the moment, the only thing I can think about is doing the opening thing with you."

She lifted a brow. "The opening thing?"

A smiled touched the corners of his lips. "Yes, like this," he said, reaching out and working the buttons free on his shirt she was wearing. When the shirt parted he slid his hands over her waist then upward to her chest, tracing his fingertips over the hardened tips of her breasts.

He met her gaze. "Need I say more?"

The gaze that returned his stare shimmered with passion and desire, and when his hand moved lower and touched her between the legs, her breath caught. "No, you don't have to say anything at all," she said after making a soft whimpering sound.

And then she reached out and wrapped her arms around his neck and pulled his mouth down to hers, deciding they would work on that closure thing another time.

Ian blinked. "Excuse me, Margaret. What did you say?"

Margaret Fields smiled. It was obvious something else had her boss's attention. He definitely was not his usual alert self this morning. He seemed preoccupied. She couldn't help wondering if the others present at the meeting had detected it. "I said that I spoke with Mrs. Tara Westmoreland yesterday and she faxed me her preference for the menu. I've given it to the restaurant that will be handling the catering."

Ian nodded. "How many people are we expecting?"

"There are three hundred confirmed reservations."

Ian knew that in addition to family and close friends, because of Jamal's status in international circles, a number of celebrities and dignitaries were included in the mix.

"There's a possibility the secretary of state might make an appearance. We'll know in a few days if her schedule will allow it," Margaret said as if in awe of such an event taking place.

Ian then glanced over at Vance. "I take it security is ready to handle things."

Vance smiled. "Yes, and if the secretary does come, I will work with the Secret Service to make sure her stay here is a pleasant one."

Ian knew that Sheikh Prince Jamal Ari Yasir had also reserved a large portion of the resort to house the guests invited to his wife's surprise birthday bash. Ian glanced at his watch. "Okay, keep me informed of anything that develops. Otherwise, it seems everything is under control."

Ian stood. He was to meet Brooke in half an hour and he clearly had no intention of keeping her waiting. "That will be all, and thanks for all of your hard work. I want for us to do everything in our power to make this a special night for the princess of Tahran."

Brooke sighed as she glanced around. The golf course was a lush green, and the open architecture of the massive clubhouse was breathtaking. The redesigned course had been nominated by *Golf Digest* as one of the best new resort courses, and she could see why. Measuring over eight thousand yards from the back tees, the fairways that wound through large moss-covered hardwoods, oak and pine trees were wide and didn't appear to be squeezed in by the villas.

Ian had told her last night that the first and last holes played along Lake Tahoe and one of the tee-off greens was set on a bluff overlooking the water. Nothing detracted from the ambience of the course. Except for the man she was waiting for.

Ian.

Goose bumps suddenly appeared on her body when she thought of how wonderful it was waking up in his arms that morning. Being the Perfect Beginning that he was, they had made love again and she had fallen asleep, only to awaken an hour or so later to find him dressed and leaning against the bedroom door frame watching her.

They had stared across the room at each other for what seemed like an eternity before he finally moved forward, slowly removing his jacket and tossing it aside. Then he reached for her and pulled her up into his arms and kissed her as if his life depended on it. After a long, deep kiss, he'd left, promising to meet her on the walkway in front of the clubhouse at eleven.

Because Ian had also mentioned that the Rolling Cascade's golf club adhered to a dress code, she had visited one of the golf shops earlier to purchase the proper attire. From what the salesmen told her, golf clothes were often bright and colorful, so she had purchased a black top and a lime-green pair of shorts with belt loops, which the salesman claimed were a must. Shorts with cuffs weren't practical because they had a tendency to trap dirt. The salesman had suggested that she purchase a hat with a visor to keep the sun off her face. And arriving at the clubhouse early, she had gone inside to rent a pair of golf shoes.

Brooke turned and recognized the woman walking down the walkway in her direction. She was the person Brooke had bumped into while out shopping yesterday, knocking the shopping bags out of the woman's hands. Brooke, in one of her rare clumsy moments, hadn't been looking where she was going. She'd been captivated by that black lace dress on a mannequin; the one she'd purchased and worn last night.

"Well, hello again," Brooke greeted, smiling when the woman moved to pass her.

The woman eyed Brooke with surprise and to Brooke's way of thinking acted as if they'd never seen each other before. She decided to jog the woman's memory. "Remember me from yesterday?" Brooke said. "I accidentally bumped into you at one of the shops and knocked your packages out of your hand and—"

"Oh, yeah, that's right. I remember now. Sorry about that. My mind was elsewhere," the attractive thirty-something blonde with a British accent said, striking a friendlier tone. "Hello to you, too. Sorry, I didn't recognize you," she quickly added, and plastered what Brooke perceived as a fake smile on her face.

Brooke shrugged. "No problem." She then noticed her outfit and the golf shoes she was wearing and asked, "You're about to play a game of golf?"

"Yes, I'm supposed to be meeting my husband in the lobby, and as usual I'm late."

Brooke nodded. "Well, don't let me keep you. Enjoy your game."

"Thanks." And the woman rushed inside the building.

Brooke frowned as she watched the woman walk away. It was as if the woman had no recollection of their earlier collision.

"Hey, beautiful. What's the frown for? You been waiting long?"

Brooke turned and smiled when she saw that Ian had driven up beside her in a golf cart. "No, I haven't," she said, sliding into the cart to sit beside him.

"Then why the frown?"

"No reason, I guess, other than a lady who I accidentally bumped into yesterday while shopping didn't remember me today. I'm surprised because I practically knocked all the packages out of her hands and had to help her pick them up. She was pretty chatty then."

"What! You mean there's someone who doesn't remember you? That's not possible," he teased. "You're so unforgettable," he said, and grinned as he pulled the cap over her eyes, just seconds before maneuvering the cart around several trees in their paths.

Brooke turned toward him. "Hey, let's not be a smart-ass," she said chuckling. She couldn't help wondering if he really thought that. Had he had as hard a time forgetting her as she had forgetting him over the years? But then, she'd never tried to forget him. He had remained an integral part of her nightly fantasies.

When Ian continued driving for a while, Brooke asked, "Where are you taking me?"

He smiled over at her as he drove around yet another tree. "To my private golf course. If I'm going to teach you the game, I don't want any distractions. Golf is like blackjack. You have to be focused."

"Oh." Just hearing him say the word *blackjack* was eliciting memories of the night before. And with those memories came heated lust. She wondered if it would always be that way with them and quickly remembered there wouldn't be any reason for things to be that way because in a week they would part ways and there was no telling when they would see each other again.

Not wanting to think about that, she turned her attention to her surroundings and the cart path they were taking, keeping clear of the greens and the fairways.

Finally Ian eased the cart to a stop and she followed his gaze as he took in the area that sat on a bluff overlooking the lake. Brooke glanced at him. "And what am I supposed to do if I hit a ball over into the water?"

He chuckled. "If you're worried that I'd send you to get it, don't be. This is going to be a practice session, and if we lose a ball we play a new one. I brought plenty of them along."

When he climbed out of the cart, Brooke did likewise and waited by his side while he got the golf bag out of the cart. She couldn't help noticing how good he looked in his golf shirt and shorts.

He turned to her after placing the straps of the golf bags on his shoulders and said, "Let's go. Oh, by the way, did I mention that golf involves a lot of walking?"

Over the next half hour he explained golf etiquette, as well as how to fill out the scorecard after each hole and tally it after a round of golf. "Ready to learn how to swing?" he asked, and handed her a club. He then came to stand behind her.

She was about to tell him no, that she wasn't ready and that the nearness of his body pressed against her back would make it impossible to concentrate. But evidently she was the only one with the problem. The close body contact didn't seem to bother him one bit.

Wrapping his arms around her and placing his hands on top of hers, he showed her the proper way to hold the club and swing it. "Just remember," he whispered right close to her ear, "when you're doing a backswing, make sure your body doesn't move slower than the club. And for a downswing," he said, demonstrating, "you don't want your body to move faster than your swing. Your club shouldn't play catch-up with your body."

For the next hour they went through a series of swings, some she decided would work for her and some she knew wouldn't. But her golf swings weren't the only thing she was thinking about with Ian plastered to her back.

"Okay, when do I get to play with the balls?" she asked him, glancing up at him over her shoulder.

"Only you would ask me something with a double meaning at a time like this," he whispered huskily in her ear before pulling her body back to his, letting her feel his aroused state.

She laughed quietly, knowing what balls he was alluding to and moved away from him. "Sorry." She glanced around, trying not to look at him below the belt. "So what's next?"

"Kissing you isn't such a bad idea," he said.

They stood so close that his bare legs brushed lightly against hers. The contact was enough to send heat sizzling through her body, and the fact that he was aroused wasn't helping matters. And when his scent, which had been playing games with her senses for the past couple of hours, finally took hold she parted her lips on a breathless sigh.

That was just the opening Ian needed and he leaned over, and when his mouth touched hers he literally lost it. Never had he needed a kiss more or his common sense less. Now was not a time he wanted to think rationally, since thinking irrationally suited him just fine.

When he'd been teaching her various golf swings, the feel of her butt against his groin had nearly driven him crazy, and overtaken his mind with lust. He'd been hard-pressed not to do something about it. Even now, if he'd thought for one minute that they had complete privacy, he would peel her clothes off this very second. He couldn't take the chance, but he could and would make sure they had some private time together later.

His hands tightened around her waist as he continued to kiss her deeply. He knew he had to slow things down a bit, but still, the taste of her was driving him to get all he could because the getting was definitely good.

The sound of a golf cart coming up along the path grabbed their attention, and Ian broke off the kiss and took a step back. He glanced over at her and watched as she nervously nibbled her lower lip. Feeling a tightening in his gut, he groaned softly.

Lacking the ability to resist doing so, he cupped her face in his hands and kissed her again. Moments later, pulling back, he rubbed the tip of his finger across her top lip. "You still up for swimming?" he asked, knowing he needed to find the nearest pool to cool off.

"Yes, what about you?"

He chuckled from deep within his throat. "Yes, I am definitely up for it."

"Ian," she admonished, watching him take a step back to grab the golf bags and place them over his shoulder. But before she could take him to task, he took her hand in his and pulled her toward the cart.

"What about the rest of my lessons?" she asked.

He smiled as her looked at her. "They're coming." Just like you'll be doing pretty soon, he thought as they continued to walk together.

"Can I ask you something, Ian?"

He glanced over at her as they continued walking. "Sure."

"Am I out of your system yet?"

He stopped walking and stared at her. "No. Now you're so deeply embedded there, it's like you've become an ache."

She smiled as they began walking again. She could imagine how much an admission like that had cost him. "Need an aspirin?" she asked coyly.

He stopped walking again and reached up and lightly brushed the side of her face with the palm of his hand. "Now who's being a smart-ass? No, I don't need an aspirin. I just need you, Brooke. And you know what's so scary about that?"

She held his gaze. "No."

"I swore that if I ever saw you again I would avoid you like the plague. But now I can't seem to bear having you out of my sight."

She smiled slowly. "Sounds like we have a problem."

Ian chuckled, although deep down he really didn't

find the situation very amusing. "Yeah, it seems that way. Come on. Let's grab some lunch."

"So what sport do you want to try next while you're here?" Ian asked after taking a sip of his soda. He and Brooke were sitting outside on the verandah at one of the cafés enjoying hot dogs, French fries and their favorite soft drinks.

She lifted her gaze from dipping a fry into a pool of ketchup and looked at him, smiling. "It doesn't matter as long as it's not a contact sport."

He laughed. "Are you saying that my touch bothers you?"

"No, it doesn't bother me exactly."

"Then what does it do to you?"

She leaned closer so others sitting around them wouldn't hear. "Makes me hormonally crazy."

A smiled touched the corners of Ian's lips. "Define."

She rolled her eyes. He *would* ask that. She was sure that having such an analytical mind he could definitely figure it out. But if he wanted her to break it down for him, then she would. "Whenever you touch me, or brush up against me, the only thoughts that occupy my mind are those of a sexual nature."

"In other words you get horny?" he asked, seemingly intrigued by her explanation.

"No, Ian. Men get horny. Women become hormonally crazy."

"Oh, I see."

Brooke figured as much. She couldn't believe the two of them were sitting here having such a conversation while sharing a meal when just a few days ago there had been more bitterness between them than she cared to think about. And yet just as Ian had admitted on the golf course, they were no closer to resolving what they'd once shared than before.

"So what have you been doing for the past four years?" he asked casually, taking another sip of his drink.

Brooke raised a brow. She wasn't stupid. He was really getting around to asking what she hadn't been doing. A woman's body didn't lie, and Ian knew hers better than any man. He was sure after making love to her the night before he had a good idea what she hadn't been doing. "Mainly working. I've had a couple of tough assignments."

Ian nodded. He'd never liked the fact that she was putting her life on the line with every assignment. But he'd had to accept what she did for a living. After all, she had been a deputy when he'd met her. Besides, he had seen her in action a couple of times. She knew how to kick butt when she had to.

"Do you know how much longer you're going to be an agent?" he asked. When they'd talked about marriage, she'd said she would remain an agent until they decided to start a family.

She shrugged. "I'm not sure. Lately I've been thinking that I'm getting too old for field work. I've made my five-year mark, and the undercover operations are beginning to take their toll. I want to get out before I suffer a case of burnout like Dare did."

Ian was about to open his mouth to say something when his cell phone rang. "Excuse me," he said, standing and pulling it from the snap on his belt. "Yes?"

Moments later, after ending the call, he was looking at her apologetically. "Sorry, that was my casino manager. There's a matter that needs my immediate attention."

"I understand."

"We're still on for a swim later? At my place?"

She smiled. "Yes."

"I'll even feed you again."

She chuckled. "It's hard to resist an invitation like that."

"I was hoping that it would be. Let's say around five. Is that okay?"

She nodded. "That's perfect."

"Good." He then leaned over and whispered in her ear. "And bring an overnight bag so I can help you with that hormonal thing," he said and quickly walked away.

Brooke continued to watch him until he was no longer in sight. It was only then that she released a deep breath. She doubted he would be able to help her with her libido in overdrive. If anything, he would probably make it worse. Ian was and had always been too damn sexually potent for his own good. She smiled at the thought of that, since she of all people should know.

She picked up her glass to take another sip when across the verandah a couple sitting at a table caught her eye. It was the woman she had bumped into yesterday. She frowned. There was something about her, but what it was she couldn't quite put her finger on.

Ian had joked about Brooke being an unforgettable person, which she knew wasn't true. But still, she couldn't understand why the woman had not recognized her. Moments later it dawned on Brooke that today her hair was pinned back and she was wearing a hat. Yesterday her hair had been down. That had to be it, she thought. But still, there was something tugging at her brain, something she should be remembering.

Brooke took another sip of her soda, deciding it must not have been important.

Brooke arrived at Ian's penthouse ten minutes early, wearing a very daring, flesh-tone crocheted dress with a see-through bodice. The scalloped hemline was short and showed off the beauty of her legs. Ian knew he was in trouble the moment the elevator door opened.

He took a step back and eyed her up and down. He then pulled in a deep breath. "Hmm. I'm surprised you made it up here in one piece," he said, imagining how many men's eyes had popped out of their heads when they'd seen her. He figured his housekeeping staff was in the lobby mopping up their saliva as he spoke.

She chuckled as she stepped closer to him and placed her overnight bag down at her feet. "Have you forgotten that I can handle myself?"

No, he hadn't forgotten and had always admired her ability to do so. When she came to stand directly in front of him, the scent of her perfume began playing a number on his libido. He cleared his throat while scanning her outfit again. "I thought we were going swimming."

"We are. This time instead of wearing my bathing suit I decided to bring it with me. But I see you're ready."

In more ways than one, he thought, although he knew she was referring to the fact that the only thing he was wearing was a pair of swimming trunks. "Yes, I thought we'd get our swim out of the way and then enjoy dinner. It will be delivered in a couple of hours. But if you'd rather we eat first, then…"

"No, that's fine. I'll probably be quite hungry by then."

He smiled. He intended to make sure she was totally famished. "I'll take that," he said, leaning down to pick up her overnight bag. He looked surprised because the bag was heavy.

She shrugged and smiled. "When have you known me to travel light?"

"Never."

"Then nothing's changed."

He furrowed his brow. "And what about when you're on assignment and you have to travel light?"

"Then I make an exception."

Ian smiled and nodded quietly. "I'll take this up to the bedroom. You're welcome to change in there if you like or you can use one of the guest rooms," he said.

"I'll change in your bedroom."

He moved aside to let her lead the way, and when they got to the stairs and she began climbing ahead of him, his body became more aroused with every step she took. Every time she lifted her foot to move up a step, her short hemline would inch a little higher and emphasize the sweet curve of her bottom.

He pulled back, deciding to just stand there and watch her, or else he would find himself tumbling backward. When she got to the landing she noticed he wasn't behind her and turned around. She lifted a brow when she saw he was still standing on the fourth stair. "Is something wrong?"

"Nothing other than the fact that we need to do something about that dress."

She leaned against the top banister, and he wondered if she knew that from where she was standing with that particular pose, and with the aim of his vision, he could see under her dress. He might be wrong since her outfit was flesh tone and everything seemed to blend in, but he couldn't help wondering if she was even wearing panties.

"What do you suggest we do with it?"

He blinked and met her gaze. His mind had totally gone blank. "Do with what?"

She chuckled. "My dress. You said we had to do something about it."

"We can burn it."

She grinned. "No we can't. It's an exclusive design."

Ian lifted a brow. "Is it?"

"Yes. Don't you like my outfit?"

"A little too much. I suggest you change into your swimming suit before I decide a swim isn't what we both need."

He then began walking up the stairs toward her. When he reached the landing he handed her the overnight bag. "I think this should be as far as I go considering…"

"Considering what?"

"Considering I wouldn't mind taking you right now on that banister you're leaning against." He'd been fantasizing about her ever since he'd left her in the café.

He'd barely kept his concentration while waiting for her to show up at the penthouse.

She smiled at him as she straightened and gripped the overnight bag. "This should be one interesting afternoon."

He smiled back at her. "Trust me. It will be."

Ian couldn't wait. He had to dive into the pool to cool off. It was either that or change his mind and go upstairs to Brooke. But he knew once he was in that bedroom with her, chances were that's where they would stay until dinner arrived.

He just couldn't get rid of the memory of the two of them on the golf course. Brooke had always been a quick study, and today had been no different. If she practiced there was no doubt in his mind that she would become one hell of a player.

Then there was that point at lunch when he had been tempted to reach out, snatch her up out of her seat and kiss her. Just watching her drink, the way her mouth had fit perfectly around the plastic straw and the way she'd slowly sucked her soda from the cup had made him hard.

He was taking his fourth lap around the pool when he heard her voice. "So you couldn't wait for me."

He glanced over his shoulder and immediately was grateful he was in the shallow end, otherwise he would have clearly sunk to the bottom. Brooke was standing there beside the pool in the skimpiest bathing suit he had ever seen. The one she'd been wearing the other night had been an eye scorcher but this one, this barely there, see-how-far-your-mind-can-stretch piece was definitely an attention getter and erection maker, not that he needed the latter since he was already there.

He pulled himself up and stood in the water and reached out his hand, and in a thick, throaty voice said, "Come here."

Brooke swallowed. When he'd stood, she couldn't ignore how his dripping-wet swimming trunks gave a pretty substantial visual of just how aroused he was. But that didn't keep her from crossing the room, stepping into the pool and taking his outstretched hand.

"You like playing with fire, don't you, Brooke?" he asked when she was standing directly in front of him, so close that their thighs were touching. So close that she could feel his hardness settle against her midsection.

"Not particularly," was the only response she could come up with, since she was so captivated by the dark heat in his eyes.

"Oh, I think you do. And since you like playing with fire I want to see just how hot you can get."

"You already know how hot I can get, Ian," she said, then sucked in a breath when he reached out and wrapped his arms around her waist, bringing her closer to the fit of him.

Ian smiled. Yes he did know. That was one of the things he always loved about Brooke: her ability to let go when they made love and not hold anything back. And speaking of hot…she was like the blast of an inferno, the scorching of volcanic lava, the hottest temperature at the equator. Hell, a summer solstice had nothing on her. And during the four years they'd been apart she hadn't changed.

She'd said she was hormonally in high gear, but that was only because her sex life had stopped after him. It didn't take a rocket scientist to figure that one out. When he'd entered her body and found her so tight, he'd known inactivity was the cause. Whatever the reason she hadn't slept with any other man, he intended to remedy that by helping her make up for lost time.

All the reasons why he should be working her out of his system escaped him, probably because at the moment he couldn't think. All the blood from his brain had suddenly rushed downward to settle in the lower part of his body. The part that desperately wanted her.

"I thought we were going to swim," she whispered as he began lowering his mouth to hers.

"We are. Later." And then his mouth devoured hers with all the want and need he'd been holding inside since he'd last made love to her. Had it been just this morning? The hunger that was driving him made it seem a lot longer than that. She had tempted and teased him since then, bringing out the alpha male inside of him.

As usual, she tasted fiery, seductive and spicy. He hungrily consumed her mouth with wanton lust, but kissing her wasn't enough. He reached out and, without breaking the kiss, with a flick of his wrist he undid the tie of her bikini top at her back. Umm, now all that was left was her bottom.

Moments later he pulled back and, kneeling down, grateful they were still in the shallow end, he began peeling the thong bikini down her hips. His hand ran up the length of her inner thigh and he stroked her slowly, liking the sound of her erratic breathing. He stood back up and lifted her hips.

"Wrap your legs around me, Brooke." And the moment she did he slipped between her thighs to widen them and then he buried himself inside of her to the hilt at the same exact moment he buried his tongue inside her mouth.

She sucked in a breath, and with their bodies connected he moved against the pool wall. Of all the places they had made love, they had never made love in a pool. He'd heard that water was a highly sensual playground and he was about to find out if that was myth or a fact. When her back was braced against the wall, he began moving inside of her, flexing his hips, thrusting in and out.

Brooke closed her eyes, absorbing the intensity of Ian moving between her legs. Her fingers bore down on his shoulders as a scream gathered in her throat. He was amazing and was giving her just what she needed. What she wanted. And just seconds before an orgasm was about to hit, he pulled out of her and spun her around with her back to him.

"Lean over and rest your hands on the ledge, sweetheart," he said, whispering in her ear.

The moment she did so he tilted her hips and parted her slightly and pressed into her, entering her from behind. His body went still and he leaned over and kissed her shoulder and asked in a hoarse tone of voice, "You okay?"

"Yes, but do you know what I want?" she asked, gripping the ledge of the pool, liking the feel of his firm thighs right smack up against her butt.

"No, what do you want?"

"More of you. Now!"

She heard him suck in a deep breath just seconds before he began moving. Each stroke was like an electrical charge that sizzled inside her body. She moaned each and every time his hips rocked against her; each contact was a sexual jolt to her mind and her senses.

A guttural sound tore from her throat the same exact moment he screamed her name and gripped her hips tight, holding her steady for his release. And when it came it shot into her womb like a stream of hot molten lava, stimulating each and every part of her body and bringing her to yet another orgasm.

She moaned in surrender, groaned in pleasure and purred with the satisfaction of a kitten just fed. And she knew that no matter what happened once they parted ways, what they were sharing now, this moment, was hers and hers alone. This memory was one that no one could ever take away from her.

Chapter 8

Instead of cooling down, things were only getting hotter and hotter between her and Ian, Brooke thought, almost a week later as she took an afternoon stroll along the lake's edge. Every morning they woke up in each other's arms and she was spending more time at his penthouse than at her villa.

They did almost everything together. He had taken her sailing again, had played a couple of rounds of golf, had taught her how to play poker, and one night they had even gotten together and whipped up dinner in his kitchen.

And they took long walks and talked about a number of things: the state of the economy, war and the storms that seemed to get worse each hurricane season. But what they didn't talk about was what would happen after she checked out of the casino on Sunday, which was only three days away. And she was smart enough to know that things would never be like they used to be between them. No matter how good things were going now, there was no second chance for them. She felt that he would never fully trust her the way he had before they broke up.

For the past couple of days Ian was busier than usual with Delaney's upcoming party. He had asked her to go as his date, and they pretty much decided they would answer his family questions as honestly as possible by saying, "No, we aren't back together. We've decided to be friends and nothing more."

Friends and nothing more.

That thought felt like a sharp pain through Brooke's heart but there was nothing she could do about it. Things had happened just as she'd predicted. In trying to work her out of his system, Ian had only embedded himself deeper in hers. Although she loved him, he didn't love her.

The shrill sound of her cell phone ringing broke into her thoughts and she quickly pulled it out of the back pocket of her shorts. "Hello."

"So, how are things going, Brooke?"

Brooke drew in a deep breath, surprised that Malcolm had called. Their agreement was that he would hear from her only if she had something to report. Within a few days her two-week stay at the Rolling Cascade would be over, and so far, as she'd known he would, Ian was running a clean operation.

"Things are going fine, Malcolm. Why are you calling?"

"I happened to overhear something today that might interest you."

"What?"

"Prince Jamal Ari Yasir is planning a birthday party for his wife there and he plans to present her with a case of diamonds that's worth over fifteen million dollars."

Brooke folded her arms across her middle. "I'm aware of that."

"And how did you come by that information? Not too many people are supposed to know about the diamonds."

"Ian mentioned it. I'm sure you're aware that the sheikh's wife is his first cousin."

"And Westmoreland trusted you enough to tell you about the diamonds?"

Brooke thought about what Malcolm has just asked her. Yes, he had trusted her enough. "He probably thought it wasn't such a big deal. It's not like I'm going to go out and mention it to anyone. And what do the diamonds have to do with the Bureau?"

"Probably nothing, but one of our informers notified our major theft division of a possible heist at the Rolling Cascade this weekend. And the target is those diamonds."

Brooke shook her head. "That's going to be hard to pull off since Ian's security team is top-notch. I've seen their operation. Besides, the jewels arrived this morning and are in a vault that's being monitored by video cameras twenty-four hours a day."

"That might be the case, but we're dealing with highly trained professionals, Brooke. The informer's claiming it's the Waterloo Gang."

Brooke sucked in deeply. "Are you sure?" The Waterloo Gang was an international ring who specialized in the theft of artwork and jewelry and had a reputation for making successful heists. The group was highly mobile, moving from city to city and country to country, and had been on the FBI's most-wanted list for years. Their last heist, earlier this year, had been a jewelry store in San Francisco where over ten million dollars in jewels were taken. Six months ago they had hit a museum in France where artwork totaling over thirty million was stolen.

"We're not sure if our informer's information is accurate. But the Bureau doesn't want to take any chances because such a theft might have international implications. Although Prince Yasir is married to an American, he's still considered a very important ally to this country and we don't want anything to strain that relationship."

Brooked nodded. "I can see where having his wife's birthday present—especially one of such value—stolen might be a lot to swallow."

"And you're sure you haven't noticed anything unusual?"

"Not really. I'd say strange but not unusual. There are some obsessed gamblers, adulterers and someone with a split personality," she said, thinking about the woman she had bumped into while shopping last week. She'd briefly run into her a few times, and certain days she would be friendlier than others; a regular Dr. Jekyll and Ms. Hyde. "Just the kind of characters you'd expect to find at a casino," she concluded.

"Well, notify me if you notice anything. The reason

the Waterloo Gang's hits are so well orchestrated and planned is that they have their people in place well in advance, mainly to study the lay of the land, so to speak."

"Will Ian be advised of any of this?"

"Not until we determine if our information is accurate."

Brooke frowned. "That's not good enough, Malcolm. By then it might be too late. He should be told so that he can take the necessary precautions. Don't ask me not to tell him."

For a long time there was a pause, and Brooke hoped Malcolm wouldn't pull rank and demand that she not mention anything to Ian. She was determined to warn Ian what was going on regardless of what Malcolm dictated. If she was fired because of it, then that's the risk she would take.

"Something else you should know is that Walter Thurgood has been assigned to the Waterloo Case," Malcolm said when he finally spoke moments later.

"Why?"

"Because if our informer is right and Thurgood can be credited with stopping a major jewel heist, especially one with possible international connections, that feat would be a great-looking feather in his cap. Someone upstairs is trying like hell to make him look good."

"Yeah, like we don't know who that is," Brooke said sarcastically. "Personally I don't give a damn about him getting credit for anything. I just don't want Ian left in the dark about what might be going on."

"Call me if you notice anything, Brooke, and remember that this is hearsay from an informer. Nothing has been verified yet."

"Okay, and I understand."

Ian smiled, hanging up the phone. Talking to his mother always made him chuckle. It wasn't good enough for Sarah Westmoreland that she now had two married sons, she was still determined to marry the rest of them off in grand style sooner or later.

And today she was ecstatic because Durango had called and said there was a possibility that Savannah might be having twins. An ultrasound was being scheduled in a couple of weeks to determine whether there would be multiple births.

Ian shook his head. He hadn't gotten used to Durango being a husband, much less a father, but that just went to show that some things were meant to be.

Like he and Brooke.

He sighed deeply and walked over to the window in his office. It seemed that today Lake Tahoe was more beautiful than ever. Or maybe he thought that way because he was in such a good mood. And all because of Brooke.

Spending time with her had made him realize that what had been missing in his life was the same thing he'd turned his back on four years ago. But now, waking up with her beside him, gazing into the darkness of her eyes, enjoying a warm good-morning smile was what he needed in his life. But only with her. The time they'd spent together over the past week and a half had been wonderful. He couldn't remember the last time he'd smiled or enjoyed himself more. And then the memories of nights they'd shared in each other's arms could still take his breath away.

Over the years he'd tried to shove her into the past and replace her with more desirable women. However, he hadn't found anyone he desired more or who could replace her in his heart. Just the thought that in three days she would be walking out of his life was unacceptable. He wanted what happened in the past to stay in the past, and he wanted to move forward and reclaim her as his and his alone.

His smile widened when he decided that he would tell her how he felt tonight. He loved her. God, he loved her and would go on loving her. He sighed when that admission was wrung from deep inside of him. He hadn't counted on falling in love with her all over again, and if he were completely honest with himself, he would admit that he'd never stopped loving her. And just to think he'd actually assumed he could work her out of his system. More than anything, he wanted to make her a permanent part of his life.

He walked back over to his desk and picked up the phone. He planned on making tonight one that she wouldn't forget.

"Brooke?"

Brooke was on her way up to see Ian in his office when she turned, following the sound of her name being called, and glanced around. Smiling, she crossed the casino's lobby to give Tara Westmoreland a hug.

"Tara, when did you get here?"

"A few hours ago. Since Jamal asked that I coordinate everything for Delaney's party, I thought it was best for me to be in place a couple of days early. Ian's taking Thorn around, showing him some of the new additions, and I thought I'd just wander around in here and play a couple of the slot machines."

Tara gazed at Brooke with a lift of her brow. "But my question is what are *you* doing here? Did you decide to come up early, too?"

Brooke shook her head, chuckling. "No, I've been here for a week and a half now. I'm here on vacation."

"Hmm," Tara said grinning.

"It's not what you think." Brooke then rubbed a frustrated hand down her face before adding, "At least not really."

As if she understood completely, Tara smiled and took her hand. "Come on. Let's go someplace and have some girls' chat time."

"A strawberry, virgin daiquiri, please," Tara told the smiling waitress.

"And the same for me," Brooke tagged on. Not wanting to jump into a conversation about her and Ian just yet, Brooke asked, "And how do you plan on surprising Delaney?"

Tara chuckled. "Jamal is flying her here straight from Tahran. She believes that he's coming here for an investors' meeting with Ian, Thorn, Spencer and Jared, so seeing me and Thorn, Jared and Dana won't give anything away. She also thinks that Jamal is flying her to France to celebrate her birthday once she leaves here."

She paused when the waitress returned with their drinks. "Most of the family and other invitees will begin arriving that day or the day before. It's going to be up to Jamal to keep Delaney occupied while everyone checks in."

Tara smiled. "One good thing is that everyone is being housed in a separate part of the resort than where Jamal and Delaney are staying. That should minimize the risk of her running into anyone."

"And when will Delaney arrive?"

"Tomorrow."

Brooke took a sip of her drink then asked, "You don't think her seeing me here will give anything away, do you?"

Tara's smile widened. "No. She'll assume, like the rest of us, that you and Ian have finally made amends and are back together." Tara then lifted an arched brow. "Well, is that true, Brooke?"

More than anything, Brooke wished she could say yes. But she couldn't. "No. The only thing Ian and I have managed to do while I've been here is to bury any hostility we've felt and become friends. I feel for us that is a good thing. I care a lot for Ian."

Tara chuckled. "Of course you do. You still love him."

Brooke's cheeks tinted in a blush. "Am I that obvious?"

"Only because I'm in love with a Westmoreland man myself. They seem to grow on you, and once you fall in love with one, it's hard to fall out of love…no matter what."

Brooke had to agree. From the first Ian had grown on her and once she fell in love with him that was that. Four years of separation hadn't been able to cure her of

being bitten by the love bug. "So what am I supposed
to do?"

"Wish I could answer that." Tara leaned in closer
and reached for Brooke's arms, squeezing reassuringly.
"We all know how smart Ian is, but unfortunately he
has a tendency to analyze things to death. But I'm sure
once he sits down and considers things rationally, he'll
reach the conclusion that you are the best thing to ever
happen to him."

Brooke just hoped Tara was right. But then, there
was a lot Tara didn't know, like the real reason Brooke
was at the Rolling Cascade. Even if Ian was able to put
behind him what happened four years ago, how would
he feel if he ever found out that she was now here under
false pretenses?

"Don't look now but here come our Westmoreland
men," Tara said, breaking into Brooke's thoughts. "I
swear they are like bloodhounds on our scent. I doubt
there's anywhere we could hide where they wouldn't
find us."

Brooke glanced up, and her gaze collided with Ian's
as he and his cousin Thorn moved toward their table.
Her pulse began beating so wildly that her hand began
shaking and she had to put her drink down.

Surprisingly, it was Thorn who pulled her out of her
chair to give her a huge hug. Thorn, who used to be the
surliest of the Westmorelands, had definitely changed.
It seemed that marriage definitely agreed with him. She
remembered that at Dare's wedding Thorn and Tara
hadn't been getting along any better than she and Ian.
Then a few months later she'd received a call from Delaney saying Thorn and Tara were getting married. She

had been invited to the wedding, but in consideration of Ian's feelings, she had declined the invitation.

"Did Tara tell you our good news?" he asked Brooke once he released her.

Brooke glanced over at Tara and raised a brow. "No, what news is that?"

"We're having a baby," he announced, grinning broadly.

Brooke rushed around the table and gave Tara a huge hug. "Congratulations. I didn't know."

"We just found out a few days ago, so we haven't told anyone yet," Tara said, smiling over at her husband. Brooke could see the love they shared shining in their eyes.

"Well, I think it's wonderful, and this calls for a celebration, don't you agree, Ian?" Brooke asked, glancing over at him.

He smiled. "Yes, but not tonight since we have special dinner plans."

"Oh." Special dinner plans? This was certainly a surprise to her.

"Meet me at six o'clock in the conservatory, all right?" he asked.

She nodded. "Sure."

Ian then checked his watch. "I hate to run but I have a four-o'clock conference call." He turned to leave.

Brooke knew she needed to tell him about her conversation with Malcolm. "Ian, can we talk for a minute?"

He turned back around and smiled. "I'm in a hurry now, sweetheart, but we'll have time to talk later. I promise." And then he was gone.

* * *

Brooke looked down at herself as she stepped into Ian's private elevator. She had decided to wear a pair of chocolate-colored tailored slacks and a short-sleeved beige stretch shirt. Although he'd said it was a special dinner, he had not hinted at how she should dress. Assuming that it would only be the two of them, she figured casual attire would be okay.

It seemed that today the elevator moved a lot faster than it had that first ride up to Ian's special place. Before she could take a deep breath it had stopped at the conservatory.

The door automatically swooshed open, and there he was, waiting for her. Heat suddenly filled her and he took a step back when she took one forward. Over his shoulder she saw a beautiful, candlelit table set for two. "I hope I'm not too early."

"And I'm glad that you are," he said, and then he leaned down and captured her lips, using his mouth, lips and tongue to churn her brain into mush.

At that moment nothing mattered, not even the thought that all he probably intended for tonight was a chance for them to say goodbye before things got too hectic because of Delaney's birthday party. And if that was his intent, she was fine. She had no regrets about the time she had spent with him these few days.

He released her mouth but kept her close to him, in his arms. "I think we did stand beneath a shooting star that night," he said in a low voice, tracing the tip of his thumb over her lips. "There hasn't been anything but nonstop passion between us since then."

She smiled, thinking of all the times they had spent

together since that night, and inwardly she had to agree. "There's always been a lot of passion between us, Ian," she reminded him.

He leaned down and brushed a kiss on her lips. "Yes, things were always that way, weren't they. Do you know that you spoiled me for any other woman?"

"Did I?"

"Yes. I tried to forget you but I couldn't, Brooke."

She sighed. This didn't sound like the goodbye speech she had been expecting. This was a confession. She decided to follow his lead. "I didn't even try forgetting you, Ian. It would have been useless. You were my first lover and a girl never forgets her first."

He grinned. "Sweetheart, the way I see it…or perhaps a better word is the way I *felt* it, I am your one and only. Do you deny it?"

"No. I couldn't stand the thought of another man touching me."

Ian pulled her into his arms. Hearing her admit such a thing touched him deeply.

"Ian?"

He pulled back and looked at her. "Yes?"

"I don't understand why we're talking about these things," she said, confused.

He smiled. "Let's eat and then I'll explain everything."

"Okay, but there's something I need to tell you."

He leaned down and brushed another kiss on her lips. "We'll talk after dinner."

Ian led her over to the beautifully set table and seated her. "Would you like some wine?" he asked, his voice so husky it sent shivers all the way down her spine.

"Yes, please." She watched as he poured the wine in her glass and then in his.

"I had the chef prepare something special for us tonight," he said.

"What?"

He chuckled. "You'll see." And then with the zing sounding on the elevator he said, "Our dinner has arrived."

A half hour later Brooke was convinced there was nothing more romantic than dining beneath the stars, especially when the person you were with was Ian Westmoreland. Dinner was delicious. Melt-in-your-mouth yeast rolls, a steak that had been cooked on an open grill, roasted potatoes, broccoli, the freshest salad to ever touch her lips and her favorite dessert—strawberry cheesecake.

Over dinner he surprised her by sharing with her his dream to open another casino in the Bahamas. He also mentioned the conversation he'd had with his mother earlier and her excitement over the prospect of her first grandchildren being twins.

"I just can't imagine Durango married," Brooke said, shaking her head, thinking about Ian's brother who'd been the biggest flirt she'd ever met. But then, Durango was also a really nice guy and she really liked him.

"Neither could I at first, but after meeting Savannah you'll see why. They may have married because she was pregnant, but now there's no doubt in my mind that Durango really loves her. So it seems another Westmoreland bachelor has bitten the dust."

"Yes, it seems that way," Brooke said, lowering her head to take another sip of her wine to avoid looking into Ian's eyes. Maybe it was her imagination but she had caught him staring at her a number of times during the course of the evening.

When dinner was over he stood and crossed the room to turn on a stereo system. Immediately, music began playing, a slow instrumental performed by Miles Davis. Ian returned to her chair and stretched out his hand. "Will you dance with me, Brooke?"

Brooke sighed, wondering where all this was leading. The thought that he was going through all this just to tell her goodbye was unsettling, and when he wrapped his arms around her, she placed her head on his chest, fighting back the tears. They'd barely made it through the song when she pulled out of his arms, not able to take it anymore, and took a step back, withdrawing from him.

"Brooke? What's wrong?"

"I'm sorry, Ian, but I can't take it anymore. You didn't have to go through all of this. Why don't you just say the words so I can leave."

Ian lifted a brow. He had planned on saying the words, but for some reason he had a feeling that the words he planned on saying weren't what she was expecting to hear. "And what words do you think I'm going to say, Brooke?" he asked, balling his hands into fists by his side to keep from reaching out to her.

"You know, the usual. Goodbye. *Adios. Sayonara. Arrivederci. Au revoir.* Take your pick. They all mean the same thing in whatever language."

He took a step closer to her. "Um, how about *Je t'aime. Te amo. Kimi o ai shiteru. Nakupenda.* And only because I hear Jamal say it often to Delaney in Arabic, how about, *Ana behibek.*"

He took another step closer as his gaze roamed over her. "But I prefer the plain old English version," he said, reaching out and taking her hand and pulling her close to him. "I love you."

The tears Brooke had fought to hold back earlier flowed down her face. Ian had admitted he loved her. Did he really mean it?

As if reading her mind he tipped her chin up to meet his gaze. "And yes, I mean it. I never stopped loving you, Brooke, although God knows I tried. But I couldn't. Spending time with you this week and a half has been wonderful and it made me realize what you mean to me. I've been living and going through the motions these past four years, but that's about all. But the moment you walked into my office that day and I breathed in your scent, a part of me knew what had been missing from my life, and this morning when I admitted in my heart what you meant to me, I decided I don't plan to let you ever go again."

Brooke's heart felt like it was going to burst in her chest because she knew if he ever discovered the real reason she'd been here he would feel differently. She knew then that she had to tell him everything. "Ian, there's something I need to tell you. There're things you need to know."

"Sounds serious, but the only serious thing I want to hear is for you to tell me that you love me, too."

"Oh, Ian," she said, reaching up and smoothing a fingertip over his bearded chin. "I do love you. I never stopped loving you, either."

He smiled and pulled her into his arms. "Then as far as I'm concerned, that says it all."

And then he leaned down and gave her a kiss that made everything and every thought flee from her mind.

Brooke awoke the next morning in Ian's bed to find it empty. They had made love under the stars in the conservatory and then they had caught the elevator to his penthouse and made love again in his bed.

She threw the covers off her knowing she had to find him immediately and tell him what was going on. The sooner he knew the better. Half an hour later she ran into Vance, literally, in the lobby.

"Whoa." He grinned, reaching out his arms to steady her. "Where's the fire?"

"Where's Ian, Vance?"

"He's somewhere on the grounds with Jared and Dare. The two of them arrived with their wives this morning." Vance studied her. Saw her anxious look. "Is something wrong, Brooke?"

She sighed deeply. "I hope not, but I think we should take every precaution."

"Okay. Do you want to tell me what it is?"

"Yes, but we have to find Ian first."

Vance nodded. "That's not going to be a problem," he said, taking his mobile phone out of his jacket. He punched in one number and said, "Ian? You're needed. Brooke and I are on our way to your office. Meet us there."

Vance then clicked off the phone, placed it back in his jacket, smiled and gently took hold of Brooke's arm. "Come on. He's on his way."

* * *

Ian arrived a few minutes after they did. He walked in with Dare. Dare Westmoreland was tall and extremely handsome just like all the Westmoreland men. At any other time Brooke would have been glad to see her mentor, but at the moment she preferred not having an audience when she told Ian everything, including why she'd been there for the past week and a half. She quickly concluded that now would not be the best time to tell him that particular part of it. She would tell him that later. But she needed to tell him about her conversation with Malcolm.

She gladly accepted the huge hug Dare gave her. The Westmorelands were big on hugs, and she always accepted any they gave her with pleasure. As soon as Dare released her, Ian moved in and circled his arms around her. He had a worried look on his face. "Brooke, what's wrong? Are you all right?"

She smiled. "Yes, I'm fine, but I found out something yesterday that you should know. I tried telling you last night but…" She lowered her head, studying the ceramic tile floor, knowing he knew why she'd stopped talking in midsentence and also felt that Dare and Vance had a strong idea, as well.

"Okay, you want to tell me now? Or is it private between the two of us?" he asked in an incredibly low and sexy voice.

She raised her head and met his gaze. "No, in fact Vance needs to hear it and Dare might be able to lend some of his experience and expertise."

Ian frowned. "This sounds serious."

"It might be," she replied.

"Then how about you tell us what's going on."

For the next twenty minutes she repeated her conversation with Malcolm. Most of it, anyway. It would have taken less time if Dare and Vance hadn't interrupted with questions. Both Dare and Vance had heard of the Waterloo Gang.

Ian turned to Vance. "What do you think?"

Vance's face was serious. "I think we should do as Brooke suggested and take additional precautions."

Ian nodded. "I agree." He then turned to Brooke. "According to what you've said, it's this gang's usual mode of operation to set up shop within their targeted site, right?"

"Yes."

"That means they're probably already here then," he said, and she could hear the anger in his voice.

Brooke nodded. "More than likely. But keep in mind nothing has been confirmed yet. The Bureau is still checking out this informer's claim."

"In that case," Dare said, "who gave you the authority to share this information with Ian?"

Brooke met Dare's gaze. She knew what he was asking her and why. "No one gave me the authority, Dare. I felt Ian should know. Even if it's not true at least he should be prepared."

"And if it is true," Vance said, his voice thickening with anger, "then we'll be ready for them."

Ian sighed. "And let's make sure of it. Come on. We need to get up to the surveillance room."

When Vance and Dare turned toward the elevator, Ian called over his shoulder, "You two go ahead. Brooke and I will be there in a minute."

Brenda Jackson 349

Once Vance and Dare had left, Ian crossed the room to sit on the edge of his desk. He drew in a deep breath as he continued to look at her. Then giving her a questioning look, he said, "You're extremely nervous about something. There's more isn't there? There's something you aren't telling me."

Brooke sighed. She knew the time of reckoning had arrived. For a moment she didn't say anything and then, "Yes. I didn't want to say anything in front of Vance and Dare."

He nodded. "Okay, what is it?"

She lifted her chin a notch and met his direct gaze. "There's a reason I've been here at the casino this past week and a half, Ian."

He frowned. "So you weren't here for rest and relaxation like you claimed?"

She shook her head. "No."

Silence surrounded them for a moment and then Ian asked, "You tracked the Waterloo Gang here?"

Her expression became somber. "No, it had nothing to do with the Waterloo Gang," she said, walking over to the window and looking out, trying to hold on to her composure.

He raised a brow. "Then what?"

She turned back to him. "You. I was asked to come here to make sure you were running a clean operation. But at no time did I—"

"What!" he said, coming to his feet. "Are you standing there saying that you were sent here to spy on me and that all those times we spent together—days and nights—meant nothing to you other than you doing your job? That I was nothing but an assignment?"

Brooke quickly crossed the room to him. "No! That's not what I'm saying. How could you think that? It really wasn't an official assignment and—"

"I don't want to hear anything else!" Ian said in a voice that shook with anger.

"Ian, please let me explain things to you," Brooke said, reaching out to grab hold of his hand.

He flinched. "No. I don't think you need to say anything more. You've pretty much said it all."

Chapter 9

Both Vance and Dare glanced up when Brooke walked into the security surveillance room. Vance lifted a brow. "Where's Ian?"

Brooked shrugged as she approached the two men. "Not sure. He left a couple of minutes before I did."

They nodded, too polite to probe any further. "I'm having my men run the tapes of the vault to see if there's any particular person or persons who made frequent trips over in that area," Vance said.

He then turned to the man sitting at a monitor. "Show us what you have, Bob."

Before Bob could pull anything up, Ian walked in. Although everyone glanced his way, no one said anything. It was obvious from his expression that he wasn't in the best of moods. Vance explained to Ian what they were doing.

"Okay, Bob, let her roll," Vance said.

They viewed over thirty minutes of footage, and nothing stuck out to arouse their suspicions. At one point, Brooke glanced over her shoulder and found Ian staring at her. The look in his eyes nearly broke her heart. Whatever progress they had made over the past week had been destroyed. The man who had expressed his love for her last night looked as if he resented her in his sight today.

"Hold it there for a moment," Vance said to Bob, breaking into Brooke's thoughts and claiming her attention. "Give me a close-up."

The monitor zeroed in on the red-haired woman's facial features. Vance shrugged and said, "Okay, move on. I thought for a second she reminded me of someone."

Brooke, who had been sitting in an empty chair beside Dare, stood, her mind alert. She stared at the woman they had just brought up on the screen. "Hey, wait a minute."

Dare glanced up her. "What?"

"I've got a funny feeling."

Dare chuckled and said, "If history serves me correctly, that means she might be on to something."

Brooke glanced over at Vance. "Can we do a scan of the casino for a minute?"

Vance nodded to Bob, and the man switched to another monitor that showed the occupants who were milling around in the casino. Dare laughed. "I see my wife is spending money as usual," he said, when the scanner picked up a pregnant Shelly Westmoreland strolling into a gift shop.

"Can you give us a clue as to what we're looking for?" Ian asked in an agitated tone.

Brooke glanced over her shoulder. "Remember that woman I mentioned last week that I bumped into while shopping and who didn't remember me the next day?"

"What about her?" Ian asked.

"I've always found it strange that every time I ran into her in the casino she acted different. I always got bad vibes from her. It seemed as if she had a split personality."

"Could be she was just a moody person," Vance interjected.

"Or you may have run into her on her bad days," Dare added.

Brooke nodded. "Yes, but there were other things, and something in particular that I just can't put my finger on," she said, tapping her fingers on the desk. Then she remembered.

"That first day I bumped into her and accidentally knocked packages out of her hand, she mentioned she was on her way somewhere but not to worry because she was known to always be an early bird and that she would be on time for her appointment. The next day I saw her at the golf course, she mentioned being habitually late everywhere she went."

Brooke turned her attention back to the monitor and watched as it continued to scan all the occupants in the casino. "Okay, Bob," she said, moments later. "There she is. The blonde standing next to the tall guy with shoulder-length black hair. That's supposed to be her husband."

By this time, everyone's curiosity was piqued and they stood staring at the monitor.

"Do a profile check, Bob, to see who they are," Vance instructed when the screen had zeroed in on the couple's faces. Moments later information appeared on the screen. The woman was Kasha Felder and the man, Jeremy Felder. They lived in London. Both had clean records, no prior arrests or violations. Not even a parking ticket.

"Now go back and run a profile check on the woman with the red hair."

Bob quickly switched screens. "Um, that's strange. I'm not coming up with an ID on her. It's like she doesn't exist."

Brooke nodded and glanced up at Vance. He now knew where she was going with this. "Scan both women's facial structures," Vance instructed.

Moments later, it was evident that even with different color hair, the women had the same facial structure. A more detailed breakdown showed the woman with red hair was a natural blonde and she was wearing a wig.

Ian came to stand beside Brooke. "Same woman?" he asked, frowning.

Brooke shook her head. "No, I don't think so."

He glanced over at her, lifting a brow. "Twins then?"

"More than likely, which would explain my split-personality theory. But I have a gut feeling there's more." She glanced over at Vance. "Can we look at the tapes around the vault from last week?"

Vance smiled. "Certainly."

Brooke chuckled. She could almost imagine the

adrenaline running in the older man's veins. He probably hadn't experienced this much excitement since leaving the nation's capital.

For the next thirty minutes they scanned the footage. Ian, who was still standing beside her, asked, "Just what are we looking for now?"

She glanced up at him and immediately felt her pulse jump at his closeness. "A third woman."

Dare raised a brow. "Triplets?"

"Possibly," she said. "These two are wearing bracelets on their right wrists. One day I happened to notice that she was wearing a bracelet on her left arm." Moments later she told Bob, "Back it up a second and slow it down." Then, "Okay, hold it right there. The lady with the dark brown curly hair. Let's zero in on her for a second."

Bob did, and after they viewed the facial structure, it showed conclusive evidence they were viewing three different women with identical facial structures. All with natural blond hair. Triplets.

"Damn," Vance said. "No wonder they can pull those hits off. We're dealing with triplets, and no telling who else is tied in to their operation."

Ian turned to Vance. "Do you think they have an inside accomplice?"

"That's how it works most of the time." He then turned to Bob. "Okay, let's go through the footage for the past week and a half. I want to concentrate on all three women. What I want to know is whether or not they meet up with any of our employees, no matter how casual it appears."

Three hours later they had their answers. The trip-

let with the brown curly wig had met on two occasions
with Cassie, who worked in the casino's business office.
In one piece of footage, Cassie was even seen handing
the woman an envelope.

"I think we've seen enough, don't you?" Ian said
with anger in his voice.

"Yes," Vance said, shaking his head. "For now. Let's
get Cassie in here and ask her a few questions. She's
only twenty-three and the thought of jail time, especially in a federal prison, should shake her up. I bet
she'll end up spilling her guts to save her skin."

"Then what?" Ian asked, shaking his head as he remembered all the times the young woman had tried to
come on to him.

Vance smiled. It was apparent to everyone that his
mind was already working, going through numerous
possibilities. "And then we set a trap for the Waterloo
Gang. One that will put them out of operation perma-
nently."

Vance had been right. Fearful of jail time, Cassie
had confessed, explaining that she had met a man in the
casino by the name of Mark Saints, a Brit who wanted
to have a good time. She had gone to his room one night
and ended up getting drugged. While she was uncon-
scious, Mark had taped a damaging video which he
used to blackmail her into doing what he needed her to
do—provide the information he needed about the jewels
and the setup of where the vault was located.

Cassie didn't know much about anything else, specifically how the heist would be carried out. However,
she did mention Mark and a woman claiming to be his

sister were particularly interested in the security system and the location of the video cameras.

It was late afternoon by the time Brooke had left the security surveillance room, no longer able to handle Ian's contempt. She was walking across the lobby when she heard her name being called and turned and smiled when she saw Tara, Shelly and another woman she didn't know. Introductions were made and she discovered the other woman was Dana. Dana was married to Ian's brother, Jared. She had a beautiful and friendly smile and Brooke liked her immediately.

"Would you like to join us for dinner?" Shelly asked, smiling. "It seems we've been dumped by our husbands. They plan to hit the poker tables and then go up to Ian's penthouse to see what other trouble they can get into."

Brooke smiled. "Sure, I'd loved to." For the past several days she'd eaten dinner with Ian, but she had a strong feeling that he wouldn't want her company this evening or any other evening. She then glanced around. "Has Delaney arrived yet?"

Tara chuckled. "Yes, they got in around noon today."

"And you still aren't worried about her running into anyone?"

A grin touched the corners of Tara's lips. "No. Jamal has been given strict orders to keep his wife occupied for the next couple of days, and I have a feeling he's more than capable of doing that. Delaney won't be leaving her room anytime soon…if you know what I mean."

Brooke shook her head, grinning. Yes, she had a pretty good idea just what Tara meant. "Isn't she pregnant?"

Tara nodded and said seriously, "Yes, but trust me, that has nothing to do with it. Even after five years of marriage, the attraction between Delaney and her desert sheikh is so strong, keeping her behind close doors for forty-eight hours will be a piece of cake for Jamal."

Brooke enjoyed having dinner with the three women. Afterward, they left the restaurant to check out the various shops, especially the lingerie boutique in the lobby. Deciding to call it an early night she departed their company and was in her room before nine o'clock. She took a leisurely soak in the Jacuzzi and then slipped into a nightgown.

A trap had been set and if everything worked out the way they hoped, they would catch the Waterloo Gang red-handed trying to steal the jewels Jamal was to present to Delaney Saturday night.

Brooke had made a decision that once the gang was apprehended, she would leave and not attend Delaney's birthday bash. She was to go as Ian's date, but she figured she would be the last person he would want to show up with.

As she settled in bed, tears she couldn't hold back rolled down her cheeks. If only Ian would have let her explain. But he hadn't. He had refused to listen to anything she had to say in her defense. Once again he saw her as a very deceitful person. He didn't trust her, and without trust, love was nothing.

"Hey, Ian. You want to play blackjack with us?"

Ian refused to turn around from his stance in front of his penthouse window. Instead he closed his eyes as memories of the night he had made love to Brooke on the same blackjack table at which Jared, Dare and Thorn were seated raced through his mind.

"Ian?"

He recognized the concern in Jared's voice. Being the firstborn, Jared had been bestowed with the dubious responsibility of looking out for his younger siblings. And now, thirty-plus years later, nothing had changed.

Deciding it was best to give him an answer, he turned around and said, "No, you all go ahead and play without me." He couldn't help but smile when he saw the look of relief on their faces. He was a natural ace when it came to blackjack and they all knew it.

"One of you act as dealer while I talk to Ian for a while," Dare said to the others.

Ian raised his eyes to the ceiling. Dare, being the oldest of all the Westmoreland men—although he was only older than Jared by a few months—had always felt responsible for his younger siblings and cousins. He'd always taken being "the oldest" seriously, but at times he could be an outright pain in the rear end. Ian pretty much figured this would be one of those times.

"We need to talk," Dare said when he approached him.

"If it's about Brooke *we* have nothing to say," Ian said before taking a sip of his drink.

"The hell we don't. So let's go somewhere private."

Ian figured he wouldn't be able to get Dare off his case until he complied with his request, and figured the sooner he did so, the better off he'd be. "Fine. We can go into my office."

Dare followed Ian to the room he'd set aside as a small office and closed the door behind them. Ian moved to sit down behind his desk while Dare chose to stand in front of it with his hands on his hips and his expression anything but friendly.

"Say what you have to say, Dare, so we can get this over with," Ian said, setting his glass aside.

Dare leaned over to make sure he could be heard. "For a man who's extremely smart you're not acting very bright."

Ian's lips curled into a smile. Leave it to Dare to speak his mind. "Why? Because I refuse to let the same woman break my heart twice?"

"No, because twice she's looked after your best interest and you're too blind to see it. I know what has you pissed with her, but if you would have given her the chance to explain, she would have told you that if she hadn't agreed to come here to make sure things were running smoothly, they would have sent the federal agent from hell. Although she knew how you felt about her, she came anyway because she trusted you and knew she wouldn't find anything wrong with your operation."

Ian sat back in his chair in a nonchalant posture. "Did she tell you that?"

"No, Vance did."

Ian sat up. "Vance? How the hell does he know anything?"

"Because of his connections within the Bureau. He didn't buy her story of just being here on vacation, so he made a few calls. He approached her while you were out of town and of course she didn't let on to anything. And before you ask, the reason Vance didn't tell you of his suspicions is because he didn't see Brooke as a threat, especially after she told him…and I quote, 'No matter what you or anyone else might think, I trust Ian implicitly.'"

When Ian didn't say anything, Dare continued. "I don't know of too many men who can boast of such loyalty from a woman. But you can, Ian." Without saying anything else, Dare turned and walked out of the room.

Ian remained where he was, sitting in silence while he thought about everything Dare had said. He stood and began pacing the room, replaying in his mind all the times he'd spent with Brooke since she'd arrived at the Rolling Cascade, and he knew Dare was right. She had come here to look out for his best interest.

He rubbed a hand down his face. Why did love have to be so damn complicated? And why was he so prone to letting his emotions rule his common sense where Brooke was concerned? Mainly because he loved her so much. Deep down a part of him was afraid to place his complete heart on the line. But he would. He knew what he had to do. He had to swallow his pride and surrender all.

He moved to the door with an urgent need to see Brooke, wondering if she was downstairs in the casino. His cell phone rang and he stopped to answer it. "Yes?"

"This is Vance. It seems they're going to make their move earlier than planned."

Ian understood. "Is everything in place?"

"Down to the letter. It's like watching a movie and I've saved you a front-row seat."

"I'm on my way."

He quickly walked out of his office and glanced over at Dare. "It seems the triplets are about to put their show on the road. Come on."

Chapter 10

Ian's gaze lit on Brooke the moment he and Dare walked into the security surveillance room. He wanted to go to her, ask her forgiveness and tell her how much he loved her, but knew it was not the time or the place.

Even so, he couldn't help studying her. It wasn't quite eleven o'clock, however it appeared as if she'd been roused out of bed. She had that drowsy look in her eyes, although he knew that with what was going down, she would be alert as a whip.

Knowing that if he continued to stare at her, he would eventually cross the room and kiss her, he fought the temptation and turned to Vance. "Okay, what do we have?"

Vance chuckled. "They did just as we figured they would. They placed the video monitors in a frozen mode so the images my men are seeing are images from three hours earlier. Unknown to our intruders we installed additional video cameras and are able to see everything they're doing. Take a look."

Ian came to stand before the monitor. He saw two figures dressed in black as they silently moved across the room toward the vault. "Where's the third woman? And the guy?"

"They're in the casino," Brooke answered, and Ian could tell she was deliberately not looking at him. She pointed to another monitor that brought the couple into view. "What they're doing is establishing an alibi," she explained. "For the past hour they have been hopping from table to table, playing blackjack, poker, talking with the casino workers, anything they can do to make sure they're seen. Their alibi would be it's impossible to be in two places at the same time."

"It's possible if you're dealing with identical triplets," Dare said, frowning. "But then, no one was supposed to know that."

Ian shook his head. The foursome could have pulled this off as the perfect jewel heist if Brooke hadn't suspected something with that woman. No longer able to fight the urge any longer, he moved to stand beside Brooke and heard the sharp intake of her breath when he did so.

"Did we ever find out why we couldn't pick up a solid ID on the other two triplets?" he asked Vance.

"Yes. It seems they were separated at birth and raised by different families. They hooked up while in college, and nothing is recorded of them getting into any trouble. In fact, all three are from good homes. One of their adoptive fathers is a research scientist in Brussels."

He shook his head and continued. "It's my guess they're doing this for kicks to see if they can get away with it. For four years they have eluded the law, which has made them bolder and bolder and almost unstoppable." A smile lit Vance's eyes when he added, "Until they decided to do business in my territory."

Everyone crowded around the monitor and watched as the two figures tried their hands at getting inside the vault. "They have successfully bypassed the alarm, which makes me think that one of them is a pro at that sort of thing," Brooke said.

Ian knew he didn't have to ask if their security men were in place. What the two intruders didn't know was that once they entered the vault, they would trigger a mechanism that would lock them inside.

He decided to move away from Brooke. Her scent was playing havoc with his mind and had aroused him to a high degree. He walked over to stand beside Dare, who was watching the activity on the monitor intently. Just as Ian knew this was not the time and place to kiss Brooke, he also knew it wasn't the time and place to thank his cousin for taking him to task, making him realize what a jewel he had in Brooke.

"See that wristwatch blondie is wearing," Brooke said, indicating the blonde woman who was standing with her husband and chatting with one of the casino workers. "It's my guess it relays signals to and from the two who are working the vault. If something goes wrong she'll be the first to know."

"And my men will be ready if they try anything,"

Vance said. "All eyes are on them. In fact the woman that blondie is being so chatty with is one of my top people. She's pretending to be a casino worker tonight."

Ian shook his head. "Damn, Vance, you thought of everything."

Vance laughed. "That's why you pay me the big bucks."

They watched as the vault door opened. The kicker to the trap was to make sure both women went inside the vault. To make sure they did, Vance's team had put fake jewels in a big box that would require both of the women to lift it to stuff the jewels into the black felt bags they were carrying.

The plan worked. The moment both women were inside, the door slammed shut behind them. Everyone switched their gazes from that monitor to the one of the casino. And just as Brooke predicted, they read the look of panic on blondie's face when she received a signal from her sisters that something was wrong.

They watched as the woman leaned over and whispered into her husband's ear, not knowing her every word was being picked up. "Something went wrong. I got a distress signal from Jodie and Kay." The couple turned, no doubt to make their great escape, and barged right into several security men who were waiting to arrest them.

Vance grinned and said, "Those two are taken care of, so let's go meet and greet the other two."

Two hours later Ian's office was swarming with the local FBI and the news media. Everyone wanted to know how Ian's security team had been able to pull off what no law officials could—finally end the reign of the Waterloo Gang.

"I have to credit an off-duty FBI agent who just happened to be vacationing at the Rolling Cascade," Ian said into the microphone that was shoved in his face. "This agent was alert enough to notice something about one of the women that raised her suspicions. She brought it to me and my security manager's attention. Had she not, we would have suffered a huge loss here tonight. I'm sure Prince Yasir is most appreciative."

Ian glanced around, but he didn't see Brooke anywhere and figured with all that had gone down, she was probably in one of the lounges getting a much-needed drink. "I also have to thank my cousin, Sheriff Dare Westmoreland, who just happens to be visiting from Atlanta. He helped us figure things out."

Ian then glanced over at Vance and grinned. "And of course I have to credit the Rolling Cascade's security team for making sure we had everything in place to nab the Waterloo Gang and to obtain the evidence we need to make sure they serve time behind bars. The entire thing was captured on film. We have handed the tapes over to the local FBI."

Ian checked his watch. It was almost two in the morning. More than anything he wanted to find Brooke, talk to her, beg her forgiveness, kiss her, make love to her…

"Mr. Westmoreland, were you surprised the Waterloo Gang was triplets?"

"Yes." And that was the last question he was going to answer tonight. He needed to see Brooke. "If you have any more questions, please direct them to Vance

Parker, my security manager. There's a matter I need to attend to."

Ian caught the elevator down to the lobby and quickly looked around. He released a sigh of relief when he saw Tara and Thorn at one of the slot machines. Before he could ask them if they'd seen Brooke, an excited Tara asked, "Is the rumor that we're hearing true? Did your security team actually nab a bunch of jewel thieves?"

"Yes, with Brooke's and Dare's help." Ian glanced around, his gaze anxiously darting around the crowd. "By the way, have either of you seen Brooke lately?"

Tara's smile turned to a frown. "Yes, I saw her a few moments ago. She was leaving."

Ian nodded as he eyed the nearest bank of elevators. "To go up to her room?"

"No, leaving the casino."

He snatched his head back around to Tara and a deep frown creased his forehead. "What do you mean she was leaving the casino?"

Tara narrowed her gaze at him. "Just what I said. She was checking out. She apologized to me for not staying for Delaney's party, but she said that she felt under the circumstances it was best if she left. She then got into her rental car and drove off."

"Damn." Ian rubbed the tension that suddenly appeared at the back of his neck. "Did she say where she was going?"

Tara glared at Ian and placed her hands on her hips. "Maybe. But then why should I tell you anything. You had your chance with her, Ian Westmoreland. Twice."

Ian glared back and then he looked at Thorn for help.

His cousin merely laughed and said, "Hey, don't look at me. That's the same look she gives me before telling me to go sleep on the couch."

Ian held back his retort that, considering Tara's condition, it seemed Thorn hadn't spent too many nights on the couch. He shook his head. He knew how loyal the women in the Westmoreland family were to each other, and there was no doubt in his mind that they had now included Brooke in their little network. That was fine with him since he intended to make a Westmoreland woman out of her—but, he had to find her to do so.

First he had to convince Tara that he was worthy of Brooke's affections. "Okay, Tara, I blew it. I know that now. I owe Brooke a big apology."

She rolled her eyes and cross her arms over her chest. "That's all you think you owe her?"

He drew in a deep breath in desperation. "And what else do you have in mind?"

"A huge diamond would be nice."

Ian thought about strangling her but knew he would have to deal with Thorn. Although Ian would be the first to admit that Thorn had mellowed some since he'd gotten married, nobody in their right mind would intentionally get on Thorn's bad side.

"A huge diamond is no problem. She deserves a lot more than that."

Tara studied him as if she was considering his words. Then she asked, "And do you love her?"

"Yes." He didn't hesitate in answering. "More than life itself, and I just hope she'll forgive me for being such a fool."

Tara shrugged. "I hope she will, too. She looked

pretty sad when she left here tonight and nothing I said could convince her to stay."

Ian nodded and thought he'd try his luck again by asking, "And where did she go?"

Tara looked at him for a long moment before saying, "To Reno. She couldn't get a flight out tonight so she's going to stay at a hotel in Reno and fly out sometime tomorrow."

Panic gripped Ian. He was beginning to come completely unraveled. "Do you happen to know which hotel?"

Tara took her sweet little time in answering. "The Reno Hilton."

With that knowledge in hand, Ian was out of the casino in a flash.

"Yes, Malcolm, I'm fine," Brooke said, biting down on her bottom lip to keep from crying. "No, I'm not at the casino. I'm at a hotel in Reno," she added when he asked her whereabouts. "I'll be flying home tomorrow."

Moments later she said, "It's a long story, Malcolm, and I don't want to go into details tonight. I'll call you when I'm back in town and we'll talk then."

Brooke hung up the phone. According to Malcolm, everyone at national headquarters was blissfully enjoying the news of the capture of the Waterloo Gang. The director wanted to meet with her to express his special thanks. Everyone was celebrating. That is, everyone but Walter Thurgood. From what Malcolm had said, the man was pretty pissed off that he wasn't able to get the credit. In a way, she was glad things had worked out the way they did. Had Thurgood shown up he would have tried to throw his weight around. But she, Dare and Vance had proven to be a rather good team. And then there was Ian.

Ian.

Just thinking his name brought a piercing pain to her heart. During the course of the night, she had felt his eyes on her. And each time she imagined what he thought of her, her heart would break that much more. As she explained to Tara, who'd tried to talk her out of leaving the Rolling Cascade, there was no way she could stay there any longer with Ian thinking the worst of her.

She glanced up when she heard a knock on her hotel room door. She crossed the room wondering who it could be at this hour. It was past three in the morning. "Yes?"

"It's Ian, Brooke."

Her heart began pounding hard in her chest. Ian? What was he doing here? Had he followed her all the way to Reno just to let her know, again, how little he trusted her? Well, she had news for him. Whether he wanted to believe it or not, she hadn't done anything wrong and she refused to put up with his attitude any longer.

After removing the security lock she angrily snatched open the door. "What are you doing—"

Before she could finish getting the words out, a single white rose was placed in her face, followed by a red one. When he lowered the roses she saw him standing there. She had to take a full minute to catch her breath.

"I'm here to ask your forgiveness, Brooke, for a lot of things. May I come in?"

She didn't answer. Instead, after a couple of moments she stepped aside. When he walked past her, her body began humming the moment she caught his masculine scent. Once he stood in the middle of her room, she closed the door and turned to face him. He looked as tired as she felt, but even with exhaustion lining his face, he still looked good to her.

"Is the media still at the casino?" she asked.

"Yes, they're still there. I left them in Vance's capable hands."

She nodded. "I would offer you something to drink but…"

"That's fine. There's a lot I have to say, but I don't know where to start. I guess the first thing I should say is that I'm sorry for being so quick to jump to conclusions. I'm sorry for not trusting you, not believing in you. My only excuse, and it's really not one, is that I love you so much, Brooke, and I was scared to put that much love into your hands again. I was so hurt the last time."

"Don't you think I was hurt as well, Ian?" she asked quietly. "It wasn't all about you. It was about us. I loved you enough to do anything to protect you. And over the years, nothing changed. If I hadn't still loved you as much as I did, I would not have cared if the Bureau sent someone to prove what I already know. You're an honest man who wouldn't do anything illegal."

She breathed in deeply before she continued, "This week has been real. My feelings and my emotions were genuine. I wasn't using you to find out information. The very idea that you thought I had…"

Ian crossed the room and cupped her face in his

hands. "I admit I was wrong, sweetheart. Call me stupid. Call me a fool. Call me overly cautious. But I'm here asking, begging for you to give me, us, another chance. My life is nothing without you in it. I've seen that for four years. I love you, Brooke. I believe in you. I made a huge mistake, one I plan to make up for the rest of my life. Please say you forgive me and that you still love me."

She looked deeply into his eyes. She put the roses on the table, reached up and covered his hands with hers. "I love you, Ian, and I forgive you."

A wave of relief flooded his body just seconds before he lowered his face to hers and captured her lips. He kissed her long, hard and deep, needing the connection, the affection, and the realization that she was giving him, giving them, another chance. Coming here had been his ultimate gamble. But it had paid off.

When she wrapped her arms around his shoulders he picked her up into his arms. He needed to touch her, taste her, make love to her. He needed to forge a new beginning for them that included a life together that would last forever. Knowing there was only one way to get that closeness, that special connection that he craved, he walked over to the bed and placed her on it. Love combined with hunger drove him. He knew he had to show her just how much she meant to him. How much he loved her.

Pulling back slightly, he began trailing kisses along her neck and shoulders as he began removing the clothes from her body. Moments later he dragged in a deep breath when he had completely undressed her. He stood back from the bed and stared at her, absorbing every aspect of her that he loved and cherished.

After removing his clothes he returned to the bed and pulled her closer to him. "I love you, Brooke. I didn't realize how much until I spent time with you these past two weeks. And I knew then that we were meant to be together."

"And I love you, too," she whispered when he cupped her butt and pulled her against the throbbing heat of his erection. And then he was kissing her again, putting into action what he'd said earlier in words. Love was driving him, propelling him to taste every inch of her, feel her moaning and writhing and whimpering under his lips. And when he knew she couldn't take any more, he stretched his body over hers, ran his fingertips down her cheek and whispered, "I love you," just seconds before he drove into her, connecting their bodies as one. And then he began moving, rocking, pushing her toward a climax so powerful he had to fight back the spasms that wanted to overtake him in the process.

Meticulously, methodically and with as much precision and love as any one man could have for any woman, Ian made love to her, igniting urges and cravings to explosive degrees. He took his time, wanting her to feel the love he was expressing. He wanted to show her that she was the only woman he wanted, the only one he could and would ever love.

"Ian!"

And when the explosion hit and skyrocketed them into another world, he held on and groaned when his release shot deep into her body. And when she bucked and tightened her legs around him he knew he was where he would always belong.

When they came back down to earth he pulled her into his arms, needing to hold her. He closed his eyes briefly, knowing this was paradise and heaven all rolled into one. Then he opened his eyes, knowing there was one other thing he had to do to make his life complete.

Rising up over her, he looked into the eyes of the woman he loved. "Will you marry me, Brooke? Will you share your life with me forever?"

He saw the tears that formed in her eyes, saw the trembling of her lips and heard the emotion in her voice when she whispered, "Yes. I'll marry you."

Smiling, he leaned down and rubbed his bearded face against her neck, knowing he was the happiest man in the world. He pulled back and, still smiling deeply, he said, "Come here, sweetheart."

And then he was pulling her into his arms again, intent on making love to his very special lady until daybreak and even beyond that.

Epilogue

Delaney's surprise birthday party was a huge success. Tears rimmed her eyes after she walked into the darkened ballroom and the lights flashed on and she was suddenly surrounded by family and friends. Even the secretary of state made an appearance.

With an expression of pure happiness on her face and love shining in her eyes, Delaney turned to her husband and gave His Highness a thank-you kiss that to Brooke's way of thinking was as passionate as it was priceless.

She had always thought Prince Jamal Ari Yasir was an extremely handsome man and she still thought so, and tonight, dressed in his native Middle Eastern attire, he looked every bit the dashing sheikh. It was evident that he was deeply in love with his wife. But nothing was more touching than the moment the prince presented his princess with that case of diamonds. She quickly became the envy of every woman in the room. Except one....

Brooke smiled, glancing at the tall, dashing, handsome man at her side. Of course, when Ian's family had seen them together they had begun asking questions. Ian and Brooke hadn't given the response they had agreed to earlier. Instead they truthfully and most happily said, "Yes, we're back together and we are planning a June wedding here at the Rolling Cascade."

No one seemed more thrilled with the news than Ian's mom. She had taken Brooke into her arms in a huge hug and whispered into her ear, "I knew he would eventually come to his senses. Welcome to the family, dear."

And speaking of family...

Brooke finally got to meet Uncle Corey's triplets and found that Clint and Cole were two extremely handsome men—typical Westmoreland men. And with her awe-inspiring beauty, Casey Westmoreland was grabbing a lot of male attention.

Brooke also got to meet all the Westmoreland wives. The Claiborne sisters, Jessica and Savannah, married to Chase and Durango. She met Storm's wife, Jayla, and Stone's wife, Madison. Uncle Corey had gripped her in a huge bear hug before introducing her to his new wife, Abby, who was also Madison's mother. Brooke smiled. Talk about keeping things in the family.

After Delaney's party, Ian whisked Brooke off to his conservatory and there on bended knees and under the moon and the stars, he again asked her to be his wife and presented her with a huge diamond engagement ring.

Tears flowed down her face when he slipped the ring

on her finger. When he stood up, she looked at him with complete love shining in her eyes. He pulled her into his arms. "I want to kiss you under a shooting star," he whispered before trailing kisses along her jaw and neck.

"Do you think we can handle any more passion?" she asked, smiling.

"Oh, I think so. I think that together the two of us can handle just about anything."

And when he leaned down and kissed her, she believed him. Considering all they had been through, they *could* handle just about anything.

* * * * *

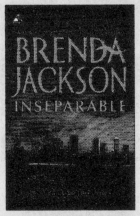

REQUEST YOUR FREE BOOKS!

2 FREE NOVELS
PLUS 2 FREE GIFTS!

KIMANI™
ROMANCE

Love's ultimate destination!